8 Mistakes

of Amy

Maxwell

Heather Balog

The 8 Mistakes of Amy Maxwell
Heather Balog

This book is a work of fiction. Names, places and incidents are either a product of the author's imagination or used fictitiously. Any resemblance to actual persons, living or dead, events or locales is entirely coincidental.

Cover design and Photography by: Anita B. Carroll of Race-Point.com

ISBN 978-1500664770

Published 2014Published in the United States of America

ACKNOWLEDGEMENTS

I'd like to thank everyone who made this book a reality. Thank you to Tyna for reading this book endlessly, tirelessly and putting up with my constant   plot and name changes. Thank you to Anita B. Carroll for my fabulous cover that I LOVE. Thank you to Jessica for all her suggestions and reading every draft of this book; you truly helped me make this better. Thank you to my children for the endless material they have provided me with. And most of all, thank you to my husband who encouraged me when I was ready to throw in the towel. You're only sort of like Roger. I love you.

They say that when you are dying, your life flashes before your eyes. Call me a cynic, but I always thought that was a bunch of malarkey. Now that my life is *actually* flashing before my eyes and I'm looking back, I'm inclined to believe it.

I guess I should have seen it coming. There were signs along the way; indicators that something was amiss. I mean, I had *suspicions*, of course, but I dismissed them. Because sometimes, I live in my own little fantasy world and it's difficult for me to see what's real and what's imagined. But this time, I was right. I was *really* right.

If I think about it, I've made about 8 mistakes. Oh, no…not in my lifetime. *Please*, if I counted up all *those* mistakes, well, we'd be here much longer than 300 some odd pages allows. I'm talking about the 8 mistakes that led me to this point, right here, right now. Hog tied to a chair on a desolate mountaintop in a deserted cabin.

I can just see my sister Beth rolling her eyes, "Oh please, Amy…you are so melodramatic…" No, I am *not* being dramatic. Got news for you Bethie, this is real. And I'm pretty sure I'm going to die. All because of my 8 mistakes.

It all started back in September, the day of my six year old son's birthday party.

~ONE~

"Roger," I call out to my husband in a hushed tone, gently poking him with my left foot. No answer. "Roger!" I repeat, this time with firmness, using my "I'm getting rather annoyed with you" voice that I usually reserve for the children. Still, I get no response from Roger.

At this point, I'm not sure why I'm whispering. Evan is done with his nap and is happily banging away on his xylophone a foot away from where his father's head is lolling off the couch. Roger doesn't even flinch. My heart skips a beat as I examine Roger's chest and realize that I don't see the usual rise and fall. I drop my laundry basket.

"Roger!" I shout as I urgently shake him. But it is to no avail. He doesn't budge. I feel for a pulse, finding none. I let out a bloodcurdling scream and my other three children race into the room.

"Mommy, what's wrong?" asks Lexie, concern crossing her face.

"It's your father!" I manage to squeak out. "He's... **dead!**"

"Did you check his pulse?" inquires 13 year old Allie in a matter of fact tone. She clutches her cell phone in her hand and it is, as usual, attached to her ear.

"Yes! He has no pulse!" I cry out. "Hang up and call 911!"

Rolling her eyes, she mutters resentfully, "Kaitlyn,

I'll have to call you back. My dad is dead." She ends her phone call and dials 911, while the other children sob quietly at their father's feet. We wait for what seems like hours, but in reality, it is only 10 minutes.

The ambulance arrives and the 21 year old, very hot, very muscular paramedic, who looks suspiciously like the neighbor's pool boy, Raul, climbs out of the rig. He is wearing uniform pants that accentuate his sculpted gluteus maximus and a wife beater tee that displays his rippling tanned biceps. I sharply suck in my breath as he edges past me to get through the front door. Once inside the house, he kneels next to the couch and examines Roger. After a moment, he gazes up at me with his pensive chocolate brown eyes and shakes his head grimly. "I'm so sorry ma'am, but he's gone."

"He had a good life," I sob as Raul wraps his muscular forearms around my shoulders and draws me closer to his body. "It was probably all the pork roll, egg and cheese sandwiches he ate! What am I going to do now! I'm all alone!" I wail as I bury my face in Raul's sprawling chest. I inhale deeply and discover that he smells like sun tan oil and coconut. I start to quiver.

"It's ok," he murmurs in my ear. "You can use the life insurance money to hire a nanny for the kids and come live with me. I have a beach house in Bermuda and a ski chalet in Swiss Alps..."

"Oh Raul," I moan. "I can't do that. I must take care of my husband's affairs and funeral..."

"No need, darling," Raul explains. "It's been taken

care of." I blink and see that Roger's body is no longer on the couch. The children are gone and the house is neat and tidy. Raul scoops me into his arms and lifts my face to kiss me....

Roger snorts loudly, interrupting my daydream. His right arm and leg are precariously hanging off the couch.

Why can't he put his whole body on the couch instead of dangling all over the place like a floppy fish? I smile to myself as I imagine Roger as a trout, his flaccid fish body and puckering fish lips.

Sighing heavily and shifting the overflowing basket of laundry to my other hip, I lean over, intending to tap him on the shoulder. Only I don't end up being as gentle as I planned. I trip, lose my footing, and punch my sleeping husband in the face. (In my defense, his leg shouldn't have been blocking my path.)

"Ouch!" Roger yelps as he bolts upright. He rubs his cheek and gawks at me as if I have just shot him in the chest at point blank range. "Jesus Christ, Aim!" Evan begins to wail at his father's *obvious* overreaction, so I drop my laundry basket and scoop up the crying 2 year old child.

I glower at Roger, annoyed that he has startled our son. "I'm sorry! I tripped over your damn foot for God's sake. There's no reason to shout..." I start bouncing Evan up and down on my hip to quiet his screeches. Once this kid gets going, it could be hours before he calms down. I swear he needs Ritalin already.

"Oh, please," Roger retorts while struggling to stand. This proves to be quite difficult as the couch is pretty lumpy from the kids jumping on it and using the cushions to smack each other in the head. Roger falls into the abyss several times in his attempts to get up. I purse my lips together to prevent myself from laughing at him. He scowls at me as he finally gets to his feet. "Was this like when your hand *'just slipped'* and you punched me in the nose the other night?"

I feel my face turn bright red as I recall Friday night at the movie theater. For the first time in ages, we were actually on a *date*. During the previews, I made the unfortunate mistake of glancing lovingly at my husband as *he* adoringly ogled the hot young blonde thing in daisy dukes who was leaning over the seat in search of her wayward cell phone.

I swear I had only meant to swat at him, but I ended up cold cocking him right in the nose, resulting in an immediate gush of blood. The blonde bimbo gasped and sympathetically offered Roger tissues that were tucked in her bra (which he accepted with that annoying goofy grin of his). As she brushed her fake boobs against his body and pinched the bridge of his nose, she pointed out that she was a nurse, but *I* insisted we leave the movie theater *immediately* to get him home. I don't *think* I called her a *slut*, but Roger swears I did. It was one of the many things we fought about on the way home from the first non-animated movie we were going to see in about 8 ½ years.

After Roger handed the shocked babysitter a twenty (I don't think she was expecting us so soon, as she was cozy on the aforementioned lumpy couch with her tongue rammed down her heavily pierced boyfriend's throat), he stomped off to bed and refused to discuss the incident any more.

I admit, I'm extremely jealous at times, not to mention, unfortunately klutzy. But who can blame me, really? I'm incredibly self-conscious of my flabby post baby belly, jiggly arms, dimpled legs and pancake boobs, as most mothers are. I breastfed all four of my kids until they were at least 9 months old, making sure I ate the proper amount of calories during pregnancy and breastfeeding. The ice cream floats and hefty portions of my meals were *necessary* to ensure their healthy futures. They also made up for the lack of coffee and wine. I have sacrificed heavily over the last 14 years in my perpetual state of baby rearing. The *least* my husband could do was not gawk at 21 year olds with asses so tight you could bounce a quarter off of them. But, I digress.

"Once again, it was an *accident* and I apologize for that," I inform Roger as I retrieve my laundry basket. Skillfully tucking both the baby and the basket under my arms, I head up the stairs. "Everyone will be here in less than an hour so if you could *please* make sure that Colton comes inside and at least washes his face..." My voice trails off as I hear Roger groan.

During his nap, he has apparently forgotten about our son's 6th birthday party taking place at our house this afternoon. I have single handedly cleaned the entire house from top to bottom (as best as one possibly can as four kids mess it up in your wake), sent the invitations, hung the decorations, ordered the food, and commissioned the pony, clown and bounce house. I put together goodie bags, assured my neurotic neighbor that there would be no peanut products served and that all the food was gluten free. I *made* a frickin' piñata, for cripes sake. *And Roger has the nerve to groan when I ask him to make sure his son's face is clean?*

Fighting the urge to make a snarky comment as I leave my husband in the living room, I stomp up the stairs and into Evan's room, dump the laundry basket on his bedroom floor and Evan onto his changing table. He fights me as I attempt to pull his drool soaked t-shirt over his head. "No!" His muffled protests fall upon deaf ears.

In true bad mommy fashion, I'm not even listening to him as he babbles away. In my head I am going through my mental to do list. About five minutes ago, I discovered that I lost the post it note on which I had written my *actual* to do list, causing a mini panic attack. Roger is constantly mocking my post it note dependence, threatening to find me a twelve step program, but quite honestly, I think the post its are the only things that keep me sane.

All at once, I realize the most important thing that was on my list and my hand flies to my mouth. *I forgot to bake the cake. Shit.* I will have to run and get a cake from Stop & Shop. I wince as I realize, *Beth will love that.* For my niece Jillian's 5th birthday, my sister Beth not only baked the castle shaped cake from scratch (of course), she painstakingly added the castle details with fondant and cake paint. It was a work of art. I was planning to dump the contents of a Betty Crocker mix in a bowl and hopefully get the damn thing to rise evenly on all sides. Beth would have had a good chuckle.

Beth is perfect. Well, at least, according to my mother and everyone else that knows her, she is perfect. I just *know* she has a fatal flaw hidden somewhere, and I've been fruitlessly searching for it the past 30 something years.

From the first moment I can remember, Beth was always faultless and I was always the mess. Beth was the graceful dancer, the accomplished pianist and the perky cheerleader. I broke my elbow doing the hokey pokey and my violin teacher asked me never to come back because I made her cat run away. Beth got straight As, graduated valedictorian and went to Princeton.

I struggled through school with a C average, came close to flunking out from cuts my senior year of high school, and then dropped out of community college after one semester.

Beth spoke French, travelled abroad and built homes with habitat for humanity, where she met the fabulously wealthy, altruistic and strikingly handsome, pre-med Derek.

Beth married Derek after a socially acceptable engagement of 2 years, had a house built to their specifications and spent the next 5 years as DINKs (dual incomes, no kids) before producing their 2.2 children, who were also beautiful, well mannered, and of course, perfect.

Because of my lack of college education and my parents not "being made of money" as my Dad constantly reminded me, I worked part time at Red Lobster and racked up thousands of dollars in parking fines as I parked downtown in New Brunswick every weekend to party with my friends who had *not* dropped out of college.

I met Roger when I was dating his derelict step-brother and fell in love. Or so I thought. We eloped to Vegas in a hormone, slash, alcohol induced fury. Did I mention that he was 14 years older than me and engaged to someone else at the time? Oh yeah. That didn't go over too well with the folks.

Mom cried for about 3 months straight and Daddy just drank Scotch straight from the bottle while mumbling about pedophiles. Roger was a teacher at the time and made a decent living, but it killed them that he was only 10 years younger than they were.

"Why can't you find a nice boy your own age?" my mother had wailed in between drying her tears. "You're only 20. You can go back to college. Remember those cooking classes you liked so much? Why don't you try them again?"

"Mom, I can still go back to college. I got *married*. I'm not *dying*," I explained while rolling my eyes.

"You don't know anything about him! What if he…" she lowered her voice and her eyes darted suspiciously around the empty room. "What if he has *syphilis*?"

"He doesn't have syphilis, Mom," I retorted with one giant eye roll as I dragged empty boxes up the stairs.

"Are you knocked up?" My father cut right to the chase as his fingers twitched. I could tell he was dying for a cigarette. My mother had insisted he quit when my grandfather died of lung cancer and as far as *Mom* was concerned, he had. We kids knew better. He smoked behind the garage every night when my mother took her hour long bath, and then he doused himself in Old Spice and gargled profusely with Listerine.

"No, I'm *not* knocked up," I had replied defensively. It was just like them to automatically assume I screwed up. They just could not believe I was capable of making an educated decision on my own.

At first, our marriage was of the whirlwind romance variety that I imagine most marriages resemble at first. We spent the better half of the next week in bed, fucking like bunnies until we ran out of condoms. We ordered Chinese food and pizza and had it delivered as we watched movies naked in bed. We talked nonstop about our dreams of living in a quiet suburban community near my parents and having 2 kids, a boy and a girl. We never seemed to run out of conversation and laughed at couples that in restaurants and stores who didn't say a word to each other. Since we had only been together for about 2 months before making the decision to get married, we had our entire lives to fill each other in on.

Roger had a college degree and a real adult job which meant he made real money and didn't have to look through the couch cushions or under the car seats for loose change when he wanted to buy a coffee. Hell, the man actually had a coffee maker in his kitchen! I could have coffee whenever I wanted! This realization on the first day he went back to work after our honeymoon, sent me into a frenzy of tears as I clutched a coffee mug to my chest in his kitchen...*our* kitchen. I, Amy Phillips, er, Maxwell, had actually done something right in my life. I found the right man to marry. At least, I thought so back then. When I was young and naïve.

Now, I can hear that man in the kids' bathroom, gargling with mouthwash. *Oh, how I despise that sound.* Roger can turn the simple task of gargling into a cringe worthy art form. Along with eating soup, chewing and basically, *breathing.*

I scoop Evan back into my arms. Despite his initial protests, I have managed to change him into his adorable little sailor suit. Well, at least *my mother* thought it was adorable. She bought it for him and made a big deal about how much it had cost and how it was handmade by blind nuns and blah, blah, blah, so I have no choice but to pull it out and force him to wear it. Evan is still on the chunky side and in the sailor suit he kind of looks like the Stay Puft Marshmallow Man of *Ghostbusters* fame.

As I change the baby, I can still hear Roger through the walls. He is now arguing with 6 year old Colton, who is a lover of nature. By that I mean, he is constantly covered in dirt, bugs and all things gross. I have to assume he is a typical 6 year old boy, but I would not really have much experience in that subject since I am the middle child of 3 girls. Beth is 2 years older and Joey is 2 years younger. Joey is actually named Josephine, but my father, desperate for a son, gave her a boy's nickname, took her under his wing and handed her a baseball glove. She's been a tomboy ever since, although my father renounced her with a scowl when she had the nerve to grow boobs.

In case you haven't noticed, we are all named after characters in Louisa May Alcott's *Little Women*. Before my mother was swept off her feet by my debonair father (her words not mine), she was an English lit major. Needless to say, she was extremely well read. She had dreamt of having four girls and naming them after the characters of her favorite book. She probably would have gotten her wish, too, if my father hadn't put his foot down and slunk off to get a vasectomy. He muttered about "too much estrogen in this fucking house as it is" while he held a bag of frozen peas to his groin for a week.

Evan and I enter the bathroom just as Colton dashes out like his pants are on fire. He nearly knocks me over in an effort to get out of his father's reach. Roger is staring after him, swinging a washcloth in the direction of the door.

"Colt, get your ass back here, now!" Roger shouts. I can hear Colton giggle as he pounds down the steps and out the back door. Roger tosses the washcloth in the sink and shrugs at me, defeated. "He ran away."

I snatch the washcloth out of the sink and retort with annoyance, "I see that. You didn't try very hard."

Roger wrinkles up his brow. "Listen, I'm getting too old to be fighting a 5 year old about washing his face…"

"He's *six*," I snap. "Remember? He turned *six* last week. This is his birthday party, remember?" I cringe as I try not to dwell on this very sore subject.

For as long as I could remember, I dreamt of the day Colt turned six. The week after Colt turned six, he was going to school full time; first grade. For the first time in almost 14 years, I *was* going to get my life back. I was going to be able to fulfill some of the dreams I had abandoned at the side of the road on my trek through motherhood. I was going to take an uninterrupted shower. I was going to finish a cup of coffee before it got cold. I was going to go grocery shopping…*alone*. I had it planned out from the moment he was born. And then, when he was three and I saw that proverbial light at the end of the tunnel, Roger and I went on a romantic weekend mini vacation to Jamaica. A few weeks later, I found out I was pregnant with Evan. My getaway car crashed into a pole and knocked that damn light out.

My best friend Laura laughed at me. I guess she was getting me back for all the times I had laughed at her pregnancy woes. Laura is Allie's friend Kaitlyn's mom. We met them on Allie's first day of kindergarten when Laura was pregnant with twins and I was towing around a toddler. Allie and Kaitlyn have been inseparable ever since. And being a baby factory myself, I was not often able to get out and make friends, so Laura and I kind of stuck together over the years, through her subsequent pregnancy with triplets two years later, the same time I was pregnant with Colt. Yup. Poor woman had six kids in seven years. And I thought my life was rough? Laura had it worse. But she had the last laugh. This year every one of her kids are going to school full time and I still have Evan attached to my hip. That bitch was going to get to shower alone.

I sigh with melancholy and notice Roger is staring at me. "What?" I challenge, offering no explanation for the far-away look in my eyes.

Roger just shrugs his shoulders, leaving me to stare after him. I stick out my tongue at his back as he retreats down the stairs. I head into my bedroom, wrangling Evan under my arm. Notice Roger did not even offer to take him.

As I dump Evan on the bed and reach for the handle of the closet door, I catch a glimpse of myself in the full length mirror. Whoever had the brilliant idea to place a mirror on the closet door should be shot. My free hand subconsciously grazes my well-padded abdomen. It *used to be* flat once upon a time.

I sigh heavily as I pull on my "fancy" sundress and grimace at how stretched out it is. The material is nearly threadbare and hanging in my chest area from Evan grabbing at it with his hands while I was weaning him off my boobs. I make a mental note to go shopping for some new clothes. *Yeah. Maybe when school starts Laura and I can drop the kids off and have a shopping date...*

Then, I remind myself that I just dropped a cool grand on school clothes for the kids and decide against shopping for myself. *Yeah, yeah, I know. I'm a martyr.*

Not that Roger would even notice if I bought some new things, nor would he likely care. I am in charge of the bills, so I'm sure I could finagle a new dress or two. But it really isn't worth the hassle of dragging Evan out to the store with me. Even if I lock him in the dressing room, he always escapes. For a kid who can barely walk, he's extremely stealthy. Last time I tried to buy a pair of jeans, I was half stuck in them when he crawled underneath the dressing room door. I ran around the store climbing under the racks with jeans around my ankles trying to retrieve him. I'm pretty sure if you google that, there's a You Tube video of it.

I pull the sundress over my head and wriggle into it, avoiding all contact with the vicious mirror next to me. Instead, I spy Evan sucking on the remote control that he found tangled in the sheets.

"No!" I yelp as I reach for it. He has already eaten the 1, 6 and 9 off of our remote in the family room. Thinking I am playing a delightful game with him, he holds the remote out of my reach. I lunge for it as he switches hands. *Damn this kid is fast...and smart.*

After I finally retrieve the remote from the two year old (I'm too embarrassed to say how long this actually took), I reach for the hair brush on my dresser. The goal is to create some resemblance to a hairdo before my guests show up, but the alarming squeal from 10 year old Lexie tells me that I am too late.

"Aunt *Beth*! *Mom*! Aunt Beth is hereeee!" Her screechy voice floats up the steps, causing me to cringe. Lexie screams *all the time*. It sounds as if she is acting in a Slasher film 24/7, every statement she utters has an edge of desperation in it.

"Oh, Mom! Colton jumped off the couch!" "Oh, Mom! Evan has your keys!" "Oh, Mom! The mailman is seven houses away and he will be here soon!" "Oh, Mom! There's a person walking down the street with a dog!"

I constantly have to squelch the urge to scream back, "Oh, *Lexie*, who the fuck *cares*?" Yes, I know. I'm a horrible mother because I don't want to hear my daughter babble constantly in a deafening pitch. I *know* I should be relishing her every word and hanging on to it for dear life. I realize this because Lexie's sister, 13 year old Allie, hardly ever speaks to me unless she's experiencing *pain* of some sort. Ever since she entered middle school a few years ago, she's avoided Roger and me like the plague. I shudder to think what is going to happen next week when she starts high school.

Maybe most mothers are naïve and unaware when their spawn reach high school level, but my husband is actually the principal of the high school. I hear horror stories on a daily basis. Middle school was bad, but damn, I am shaking in my boots thinking about my baby girl entering that zoo on Wednesday.

"Mommmmmmmmm! Come down hereeeeee!" Lexie is causing my ears to reverberate from the unearthly decibels that her voice can reach.

I sigh with what feels like never ending impatience as I collect the baby, swinging him onto my hip as I head down the stairs.

~TWO~

"Why, Amy, your home looks simply divine!" Beth remarks breathlessly as she leans in to kiss my cheek. As she offers me a crooked smile, I notice that she has lipstick on her teeth. "And what is that delicious smell?"

I beam as I reply, "Oh, just my freshly baked apple pie in the oven." A timer dings in the kitchen. "It's done now!"

I stifle a giggle as Beth hands me a gift bag and I notice that one of her nails are chipped. "I didn't have time to wrap it," she apologizes, blushing deeply.

"It's okay," I tell her with a patronizing pat on the shoulder.

"Let me make it up to you. Can I help with anything?"

I glance around the room where everything is in perfect order. "No," I reply while shaking my head. "I've got it all under control."

My mother waltzes in the front door just at that moment. "Of course you do, darling! Your parties are always perfect!" Mom tells me as she pours a glass of wine from the bottle she is holding in her hand.

While my mother hands me the glass, Beth concurs. "Oh yes, Amy! I don't know how you manage to do it all! I mean, I can barely do it with two kids! And you have FOUR! And a husband who never even helps out!"

I smile at them as I shake my head. "It is tough, but

I'm determined to be the best mother ever."

And then, I hear Beth's real voice and it's like nails on a chalkboard.

My sister and her two children are standing in the center of my living room with Lexie. Both children are meticulously dressed as usual; Andrew in a cream colored, button down polo shirt and khakis (who puts *white* on a 7 year old boy?) and Jillian in a flouncy pink sundress, her dark, thick hair piled on top of her head in a neat bun, secured with a flower clip. They look like an ad for JCPenny's. I am willing to bet both kids have sunblock with an SPF of 75 slathered on and insect repellant to boot. Meanwhile, *I'm* not even sure if all my kids have underwear on.

Beth is flawless in her crisp denim capris and green, fitted tee shirt, designed to make her look casual and spontaneous, and probably came with a price tag higher than my living room couch. Her dark, shoulder length hair looks like it was styled at the salon about ten minutes ago. Her face is free of the wrinkles and the worry lines that I wear like a badge of adulthood. Or maybe it's just from her recent trip to the botox center.

I sigh with annoyance as I trudge down the steps because she is early, as usual. I reach the landing just in time to see my sister discreetly running her finger along the top of the TV when she passes it.

Damn it! I forgot to dust the TV! Nothing escaped Beth's eagle eyes. *Must be nice when you have a maid to help keep your home spotless,* I think bitterly. She glances up as I lumber down the stairs, Evan in tow.

"You're early," I practically hiss as I watch Lexie dash from the room in search of someone else to torture.

Beth dismisses me with a wave. "We're *on time,* Amy. When someone says a party starts at 2:00, we are there for 2:00."

"It's 1:45, Beth," I growl as I attempt to stand in between Beth and the coffee table. I forgot to dust that, too.

Beth ignores the comment as Andrew and Jillian file past her into the kitchen. Derek is nowhere in sight, so I assume he has escaped to the man cave with Roger and is clutching a beer already. I can't really blame him, though. If I was married to Beth, I would need an alcohol IV.

"Andrew!" my sister calls out to my 7 year old nephew. "Can you please bring Colton's birthday presents to the gift table? Ask Aunt Amy where it is."

Damn it again! Gift table! Was that on the post it? Shit, I need to find that post it!

"That's ok, Andrew," I tell him as I try to grab the gifts. "I'll take them."

"Nonsense," my sister intercepts me with her free arm. "Andrew will be more than happy to take them." My nephew looks anything *but* delighted, however, I know he would never tell his mother otherwise.

"Besides," Beth lowers her voice to a whisper, "you need to dust the lamp before mom gets here. You know she'll never miss the layer of dust."

Damn it! The lamp, too? Beth pats my arm patronizingly as if she really *believes* she has my best interests at heart.

I seethe as I respond through gritted teeth, "Of course. Andrew, just put the gifts on the kitchen table then."

"Kitchen table?" My sister practically squawks. "But then your guests will have to trek through the house..."

"Yes, I know it's very primitive, but it works for us common folk," I remark with sarcasm, unable to keep my frustration in check any longer.

Beth remains perfectly unflustered as she titters softly, "Oh, *Amy* you're so silly! I only meant it would be a shame for them to come clomping through your house and mess up your *clean* floor." She beams, her Chicklet like teeth sparkling.

That bitch! *She's implying my floor isn't clean!*

My gaze drifts downward and I realize *it isn't.* I *had* vacuumed like a maniac this morning, but our dog Misty had gotten into a tizzy earlier with Furball the cat and now little clumps of cat and dog fur littered my entire living room. Funny, I hadn't even noticed until now.

Who knows how long the little passive aggressive battle with my sister would have lasted had Laura not come crashing through the door with her circus right at that instant.

"Get off of your brother, Zachary! Stop it right now!"

"But *Mooooommmmm*! He's looking at me weird!"

"Don't look at him, Jeffrey! Don't anyone look at anyone else *ever* again!"

I smile to myself. Laura is the only person on earth that makes me look like I've got it together, a fact that doesn't seem to escape my sister's attention. I see her wrinkle up her nose in disgust as the triplets and twins (all boys) stampede into my living room and head straight for the back yard. I actually hear my floor moving even after I can't see them any longer. They are followed by a bored looking Kaitlyn who heads directly up to my daughter's bedroom. And finally, a haggard Laura enters the fray. Her husband is undoubtedly working his second job today, leaving her to battle the kids on her own.

"Hi," she manages to gasp as I lean in to peck her cheek. Evan squeals with delight and reaches for her. She must emit some smell that little boys savor because Evan adores her. He won't go to anyone else willingly other than Laura.

"Hello, Lori," my sister remarks with her haughty attitude.

Laura wrinkles up her nose. "It's *Laura*," my friend stresses; the tension is palpable, "*Elizabeth*," she adds as she scoops my son up.

My sister's mouth is gaping open and before she can retort that her name is *not* Elizabeth, Laura sails out of the room with Evan. "I'll just go keep an eye on my boys," she remarks solely to me, but entirely for Beth's benefit.

"I see you are still friends with that wonderful

influence," Beth drawls in a bored voice. Beth considers anyone who has more than three children, trash or certifiably insane. She has no tolerance for noise and ruckus, which Laura's kids certainly leave in their wake.

I am seething inside at Beth's digs at my only friend and am about to say something I'll probably regret involving Beth's recent visit to the plastic surgeon that she doesn't think I know about, when my mother breezes through the front door.

"Helloooo!" she calls out in her melodious voice.

"Hi, Mom!" Beth chirps back cheerily as she embraces our 60 year old mother who truly doesn't look a day over 45. I swear I don't know how the woman does it. She looks younger than I do. But then again, what stress does she have? She sleeps eight hours (uninterrupted) every single night and she and my father play golf for four hours almost every day. Then she plays Canasta with the women in her "club" and they go out to eat every single evening. She even hasn't used the stove in her house in 6 years. She almost burnt her hand last Christmas because she thought she needed to light the pilot light in the oven. The woman doesn't even have to *drive* anymore. My father chauffeurs her around like the Queen Mum. *And* carries her packages to boot. I would probably look 22 if I had that life. Hell, I wish Roger would just carry the groceries into the house for me.

My thoughts are interrupted by my father clumsily banging into the doorframe, maneuvering a rather bulky package in his arms.

"What the hell is that thing?" I question, skipping the formalities of hellos to either of my parents.

"Now, Amy Francine, there is no need to use foul language," my mother reprimands. "It's a bike. For Colton!" She beams at me as if she was expecting balloons and streamers to fall from the sky and me to collapse at her feet to pay her homage for being the perfect grandmother.

Instead, I groan as I point out, "Colt *has* a bike, Mom. I really wish you would have asked..." I see my mother's face fall and instantly felt guilty. The damn woman can play the guilt card like it's a game of Go Fish.

I quickly scramble to undo the damage to her fragile psyche, because heaven forbid my mother be upset. "But, I'm *sure* his is getting rusty from being left out in the rain. I bet he could use a new one!" I try to perk her up, but my mother's face tells me I am not doing a good job. Of course. I never do a good job at anything as far as my mother is concerned. Sighing, I ask, "Why don't you go outside and find the birthday boy?"

My mother and sister bob their heads in synchrony as they head out to the back via my kitchen. My father has already escaped to man cave after dumping the bike in the middle of the living room.

"Oh, Amy! There's a puddle on your kitchen floor! You really should clean that up before someone slips!" my sister shouts.

Gritting my teeth, I call out, "Yes, thank you!" I

resist the urge to add, *bitch*. I head into the kitchen where I find Beth's gifts on the table, a puddle of milk on the floor and my niece and nephew staring open mouthed at the piñata on the center island.

I should explain. Colt loves bugs. He likes reading about them, catching them, dissecting them, trying to force his sisters to eat them and cleverly disguising them so his sisters *do* accidently eat them. Bugs, bugs and more bugs. He wanted the theme of his birthday party to be bugs. So I searched high and low for piñatas in the shape of a bug. It didn't matter what kind; spider, ant, dragonfly, slug.

They apparently don't make bug shaped piñatas so I cleverly went on Pinterest and found the directions to make your own. I tried to get the kids to help me, but the only one who stuck around longer than 30 seconds was Lexie, and by the time I had started adding the ingredients to the paste, I *wanted* her to leave. *Yeah, yeah, I know...horrible mother again.* But damn it, the kid wouldn't shut up and she was distracting me. A hundred questions a minute; "what are you going to use that for, Mom?", "why are you doing that, Mom?", "what's the next step, Mom?", "how long is this gonna take, Mom?" "how does it harden, Mom?" Finally, I told her to go Google it and let me know what the answer was. Thankfully, she didn't come back until I had succeeded in creating the lopsided spider creature that now terrorized Andrew and Jillian.

"It's a spider piñata," I explain to them. They still

stare at me quizzically. Assuming they know what a *spider* is, I continue, "You know, the things you hit with a bat and all the candy comes out?" Understanding registers with Andrew, but not Jillian. She is only 5, so maybe she never saw a piñata. I can't recall if my sister has ever had piñatas at their birthday parties, but I highly doubt it, considering she is married to a cardiologist and is a neurotic health freak and all that.

I decide to leave it alone. "Why don't you guys go out and see where Colt is?" Andrew gazes at me doubtfully.

When I found out I was having a boy and Andrew had been born the previous year, I was delighted. I envisioned them playing together, having fun and being the best of buds growing up. They could make mud pies and build forts and terrorize the girls.

The only problem with my fantasy was that Andrew did not desire to do any of those things. And for that, Colt hated him. And the more I tried to push them together, the harder they resisted. In fact, Colt enjoyed bullying Andrew almost as much as he loved torturing his sisters. So I can understand where Andrew's doubt is coming from. I realize I must try a different tact.

"Do you guys want to play in the bounce house?"

They glance at each other skeptically and then, broad grins cross both their faces simultaneously. The kids nod their heads and spring towards the back door, still not taking their eyes off my papier-mâché disaster on the counter. I think they believe it is going to spring to life and devour them whole.

When they are gone, I turn my attention to the split milk on the floor, just as Roger trots up the steps.

"Oh good!" I call out to him as he brushes past me to get to the fridge. "Can you grab the mop from the pantry?"

Roger shakes his head as he scoops up four beers from the fridge door. "Sorry, I'm busy right now."

I stare incredulously as he heads back down to the man cave. I can hear the jovial laugher of Derek and my father floating up the steps. Fuming inside, I give Roger the finger, but of course he can't see it.

Groaning with annoyance, I kneel down next to the table and messily clean up the spilt milk with a paper towel. Tears spring to my eyes as I think, *I am so sick and tired of Roger not even being able to help out with anything. He watches me run around like a chicken without a head and doesn't even care.*

I struggle to my feet, dump the wet paper towels into the garbage, and then reach for a napkin to dry my face. "No use crying over spilt milk," I joke out loud to the empty room. Snorting, I laugh at my own pathetic joke.

I find the mop in the pantry and march over to the sink with it. Lifting the old fashioned faucet handle that I had fallen in love with when we bought the house, I listen to the sound of pipes groaning. What I once saw as the cozy and charming appeal of an older home now irks me on a daily basis. Our house was built in the early 1900's and had been meticulously kept by its previous owners.

Not to say that things weren't deteriorating then, but they certainly were now because Roger never seemed to have any time to fix anything that was broken. The once adorable wooden shutters on the front windows hang precariously from their screws. The floors are warped and should have been sanded years ago. The plumbing and heating systems are in dire need of an overhaul. Not to mention the missing slats of our wrap around porch and the shingles peeling off the roof. And heaven forbid he allow me call a professional to do the work. He keeps telling me that he'll "get around to it". Most likely that'll be when the house is 200 years old and needs to be razed to the ground.

Wringing out the mop, I start to step away from the sink until something in the backyard catches my eye. I peer through the spotty window that I need to find time to clean, and see Colt in his fort. With a very large child. I am instantly alarmed. This is not one of Laura's kids, nor is it any of the other friends invited to the party who may have slipped into the backyard unannounced. This is a *stranger*.

I should interrupt here to point out that the events transpiring beyond this point qualify as my Mistake #1. If I had just continued to wring out my mop and clean up my spilled milk, well, maybe things wouldn't have gone down the path that they did. But of course, I did not.

I storm out to the backyard, the French doors slamming behind me. I glance around to see my mother and sister poking nervously at the catering trays while

Andrew and Jillian sit uncomfortably on one of the patio lounge chairs. I wonder why they aren't in the bounce house until I see Laura is trying to pull her kids' shoes off so they can go in the bounce house. Andrew and Jillian look petrified.

Turning my attention to the stranger who is crashing my son's party, I clench my fists and stomp across the backyard towards the fort.

"Where you going, Mommy?" Lexie asks, startling me. "Damn it, Lexie!" I yelp, clutching my chest in shock. "You scared me!"

I can see her head poking out from behind a bush next to the deck and her brand new shoes on her feet, scraping at the ground as she struggles to fit under the dense foliage. In her hand she is holding a notebook and a pen with a fluffy pink ball on the end.

She presses her fingers to her lips. "Shhh! I'm spying on the boys." Normally, I would scold her for putting on the shoes I *just* told her *not* to wear, but I have bigger fish to fry right now.

"That's nice," I murmur as I continue my trek across the expansive backyard. I see Colt and the kid in the window of the treehouse fort. From here, my fears are confirmed. Not only is he older, he is *a lot* older than my Colt. Like, he probably shaves kind of older.

"Colt!" I scream. "You and your friend need to get down here…NOW!"

As he sees me approach, Colt scrambles out of the tree house, his new companion hot on his heels. The kid jumps down from the fort and lands on the ground with a heavy thud. As he stands, I see that he is *definitely* older than Colton and taller than I am, which is actually not that difficult since I'm 5' 3" in heels. Still…

"Who are you?" I ask accusingly, poking at his chest with a freshly chipped fingernail.

The kid balks at my question. Colt answers for him. "This is Sean. He's my new friend."

I glare at Sean as I visually inspect him. His blonde hair is a little scraggly, but that's the style nowadays. His clothes are baggy, but once again, that's probably on purpose. He is *at least* 13 years old judging from his height and appearance. I am instantly on guard. I've never met this kid or seen him around before and our neighborhood is one of those small busybody ones where everyone is up everyone else's ass.

"That's *great*," I lie to Colt in a sickeningly sweet voice. And then I focus in on the teenager hanging out with a kid half his age in a tree house. I narrow my eyes at him suspiciously. "How old are you, *Sean*?"

He sniffs as he answers, "Fourteen." I gasp with horror. I am instantly reminded of a recent news story about a teenager who lured a kindergartener into his house with video games and then used the kid for his own depraved purposes.

Trying to regain my composure I ask, "You do realize that Colt is *six*? And it's extremely *weird* that you're hanging out with a *six year old?*"

Sean sniffs the air again, rubs underneath his nose

like a coke addict and doesn't answer.

"Where do you live?" I continue my grilling.

Sean points towards the house. "Across the street," he replies, slowly and deliberately. By the way he speaks, I wondered if perhaps he really *is* stoned.

"No you don't. The Sanders live across the street," I snap, becoming increasingly agitated by this young derelict's audacity.

Sean nods. "That's Grammy and Grampy. They're the Sanders. I live with them."

"You live with your *Grammy* and *Grampy*?" I ask incredulously. *Was he 14 or 4?*

Sean snorts again and nods as I consider this statement. I've never laid eyes on this kid and he claims to live across the street? Our new neighbor, Mary Sanders, was outside every morning for the last few months, watering her plants. Rain, shine, blizzard. It didn't matter. She was like clockwork. And every morning, she waved when she saw me padding out into the driveway in my robe to retrieve the paper. She always wanted to chat about her husband Walter or how great it was to be retired, while I stood there looking like a moron in my tattered robe and PJs in the middle of Hartford Ave.

Not *once* did she mention a grandson living with her. Now not only am I wary, I am suspicious, too. I don't know what game this kid is playing, but I want him away from my impressionable 6 year old *ASAP*.

"Let's go see *Grammy* and *Grampy* then, shall we?"

I remark with fake cheeriness as I grab his arm. Sean shrugs and allows me to lead him away.

"But I want Sean to come to my party," Colt wails as he runs alongside me.

"Forget it, Colt," I growl as Colt throws himself on the ground at my feet in an attempt to stop me. I step over him and proceed to drag Sean toward the gate, but not before Lexie spots me. She leaps up from her spying position to catch up with me.

"Who's that, Mom?"

"Not now, Lex."

"But who *is* that?"

"Lexie, I said, not *now*."

"But, Mom why can't you just tell me-"

"Go *away*, Lexie. Go play in the bounce house or something." She gives me her pouty lip face and storms off.

I know. I'm a terrible mother. You would think it would be easier to just tell her who the kid is and that would make her happy. But it won't. Make her happy, that is. It will just lead to another never ending series of questions resulting in me screaming and punishing her. My patience for 20 Questions ended two kids ago.

We reach the gate and I push it open with my hip, not releasing my grip on Sean for a moment. I probably should have called Roger to help me, but God knows where *he* was at the moment. Sean whimpers as I drag him across our front yard.

"Oh knock it off. I am *barely* holding your arm," I

snap as I check both ways before crossing our nearly deserted street.

"I don't like it," he whines in a nasally voice. "Let go!"

"Oh yeah, so you can run off? I don't think so," I retort as we march across the road.

We reach Mary's front door, I ring the bell with a purposeful nod, and stand there waiting for the owner of the house to open the door for what feels like an eternity.

Until Sean informs me, "The bell is broken." I see a small smirk curling up in the corners of his mouth.

Shooting him the death stare that I usually reserve for my own children, I rap loudly on the door frame. Almost instantly the heavy red door swings open and the diminutive figure of Mary Sanders graces the doorway. She is dressed in a lavender velour track suit; her short blonde hair with frosted tips closely cropped around her pretty, lightly wrinkled face. I notice she has tears in her eyes and her usual perfect makeup has run down her face.

She sees Sean and her expression changes as she squeals, throws open the screen door, and pulls him in for an embrace. He allows himself to be hugged, but he doesn't put his arms around her.

"Oh, Seany! We've been looking all over for you! Where have you been?" She pulls back to give Sean a stern glare.

"I was playing with my new friend," Sean mumbles as he stares down at his feet.

"Sean, you need to tell Grammy or Grampy where

you are going at all times, ok? We were *so* worried about you."

"Sorry," Sean mumbles again, hanging his head. He looks like an admonished 2 year old that has been put in time out for biting a friend not a rebellious teenager. Something doesn't add up in my mind.

Mary smiles, reaches out and tousles his shaggy blonde hair. "Go tell Grampy you're back, ok? I want to thank Mrs. Maxwell for her help." Sean obediently bounds off into the house. Mary smiles after him and then turns back to me. "Thank you so much for bringing him back."

"I didn't even know he was living here, Mary." I can't help my accusatory tone. "He was in my backyard playing with Colton. Colt's *six*. I thought it was a little…"

Mary cuts me off as she steps onto the front porch and closes the door behind her. "I know, I *know*," she lowers her voice to whisper. "Sean is what we called *challenged*. He was diagnosed as autistic when he was about 5, but he's very high functioning. He does really well in school academically, but socially, he's pretty backwards. He doesn't really know better." Mary pauses for a second as I instantly feel ashamed.

How terrible. I judged this poor kid without knowing the circumstances. And what's more, I yelled at him.

As if she could read my mind, Mary says, "Most people don't realize there's anything wrong when they meet Sean at first. He just seems like a badly behaved 14 year old. That's why we don't take him out in public a lot."

I smile weakly. "I yelled at him, Mary. I'm sorry. I just…well he was with Colt and I…"

Mary pats my arm sympathetically. "It's ok, Amy. You were just being a mama bear protecting her cubs. I feel the same way. When I couldn't find him earlier, I was beside myself. Of course, Walter and Jason told me he would be fine…"

"Jason?" I cut her off without meaning to.

Mary nods. "Yes. Jason is Sean's father. Our, uh, son." Mary fidgets with the zipper on her track suit. "Um, Sean's mother, Stacey, died in a…" Mary pauses once more, searching for the right word, her eyes filling with pain. "*Tragic situation* about three years ago. It makes matters worse for Sean's behavior at times so Walter and I asked Jason to move in with us two months ago so we could help him with Sean. Jason travels a lot for work, so mostly it's just us and Sean."

I'm not sure what to say. I spoke to Mary nearly every morning for the past few months and I never even knew she and Walter had children at all. I've never seen "Jason" or any sign that he and Sean were living there. *Maybe you don't notice your surroundings enough, Amy.* I make a mental note to start paying more attention to what's going on around me.

"I really had no idea he was even living here. You never mentioned him or your daughter in law's death. I'm so sorry." I reach out to hug her awkwardly.

Not to seem insensitive, but out of the corner of my eye, I can see cars lined up in our driveway and at the curb. Colt's birthday party is getting underway and I'm not even there. And Roger is probably parked in front of his 55" LG TV with a beer in hand, oblivious to the fact that there are people in the house. An idea occurs to me.

"Would Sean like to come to Colt's party? Colt wanted him to stay…"

Mary looks shocked. "Oh no, no! That's ok! Go ahead. It looks like your family is all there."

"It's fine, really," I insist.

Mary shakes her head again. "No, no…it's fine. I, um… I'm afraid of how he will act if I'm not there."

"Well, you're welcome to come along." At this point, I don't care if the entire neighborhood is coming along. I need to get home before my family and friends imploded my house. I can just imagine Beth and my mother standing around, admonishing me by making clicking noises with their tongues as they ponder my absence.

Once again Mary shakes her head, so I shrug as I walk away. "Well, give me a call one day next week and he can come over to play if he wants!" I shout over my shoulder, giving a little wave.

"Will do!" I hear Mary say as I cross Hartford Ave. and start toward my backyard with the nagging feeling my neighbor isn't telling me everything.

~THREE~

"This is the FBI! Come out with your hands up!" a booming voice announces.

Startled, I poke my head out of the window to see police cars parked all over the Sanders' front lawn. There is a man with a megaphone standing on top of one of the police cars.

"He really should get down", I gasp. I always tell the kids not to stand on the top of my car.

All of a sudden, members of a swat team swoop in from the trees and others rappel down the sides of the house from the roof, kicking in the windows. The sound of glass shattering reaches my ears and I wince as I cover them. Someone is going to get glass in their leg, I just know it.

"Mommy, mommy!" I hear screams from the doorway. All four of my children are dashing into the room.

"What's that noise, Mom?" asks Allie as she slides protectively under my left arm. This is the most she's said to me in about two years.

"It was so scary!" cries out Lexie as she clutches my leg. Evan grabs the other leg as Colt ducks under my right arm.

I squeeze my children tightly. "It's okay, it's okay." I attempt to reassure them as I continue to peer out the window. The swat team is leading Mary and Walter out *of the house, hands cuffed behind their backs.*

Allie is also peering out the window. "Holy crap, Mom! The Sanders are getting arrested!" I stand corrected. THAT is the most she has said to me in two years.

"Arrested?" Lexie asks, crumpling her adorable little face. "But why? What did they do?"

"Mr. and Mrs. Sanders! You are under arrest for kidnapping a fourteen year old boy and holding him for ransom!" announces the officer with the megaphone. Just then, a limo sweeps down the street stopping in front of the Sanders residence. A man and a woman in expensive attire pop out of the back seat. They wear concerned expressions on their faces.

The officer waves them over to where he is now standing on the ground. Mary and Walter are being placed in the back of a police car. The officer gathers the man and woman around him and then points to the front door.

Sean suddenly appears, rushing at the man and woman, his arms wide open. "Mommy! Daddy!" The man and woman are beaming as they embrace Sean tightly.

"Oh, Sean!" cries the woman. "I will never let you out of my sight again!"

"Yes," chimes in the man. "I can't believe those people! Kidnapping you right off of our front lawn!"

I clutch my babies tighter as the car carrying Mary and Walter speeds away...

"Amy, what on Earth are you staring at?" My mother's melodious voice pulls me from my reverie.

"Um, I thought I saw a police car," I stammer as I back away from the front window.

"Well, that wouldn't be *unusual* for *this* neighborhood," my sister chimes in. I shoot daggers at her with my eyes.

My mother and Beth are perched nearby on the edge of the couch, posteriors barely touching the cushions as if they are afraid of catching the plague from it. They are holding full glasses of wine from which they daintily sip while they peer over their noses at me.

The birthday party is winding down. All the younger guests have been collected by their parents. Laura and her crew have also hastily departed as eight year old Mason was suddenly stricken with a stomach bug. He puked all over the bounce house. Beth was *delighted*. I didn't even get to talk to my friend about the strange kid across the street.

Garbage bag in hand, I plop down amidst a pile of wrapping paper that my child has discarded in efforts to rip through his birthday gifts in less than 2 minutes. Evan is digging through the wrapping paper pile and shoving scraps into his mouth faster than I can get them into a garbage bag. I am attempting to organize the mess by attaching the card to what I *think* is the gift that it matches. Thank you cards are going to suck this year.

Dear so and so, Thank you for the gift. From, Colton, on twenty cards printed from the computer. I'd rather have root canal than hover over Colt as he writes out all the cards. I'm sure Beth will be appalled as usual. The thank you cards from *her* children are all handwritten with a picture in each and a personal note from Beth herself. It makes me want to vomit every time I get one. She even sends them for Christmas presents.

"I'm surprised we haven't heard a cop car go by in the last hour," Beth remarks absently as she flecks the side of the wine glass with her perfectly manicured fingernail. I guess a piece of food has escaped our 22 year old dishwasher's attention.

"And what is *that* supposed to mean, exactly?" I practically growl.

"Now, Amy, that's no way to speak to your sister," my mother admonishes. "How would you like it if your daughters spoke to each other that way?"

I glance down at the ground and roll my eyes. My mother would die if she knew how my daughters spoke to each other.

"Excuse me," I correct. "What do you mean by that, dear sister Beth?"

"No need to be snarky," Beth scoffs. "I am just referring to all the news coverage about the suspected drug ring in this neighborhood."

I sit up, suddenly at attention. *What? Could that be why Mary was all squirrely earlier? Maybe they didn't kidnap Sean, but they are using him as a drug mule!*

I can hear my sister and mother prattle on about how things are so dangerous nowadays and nothing like they used to be but I am too busy considering the idea of Sean as a drug mule.

Don't be ridiculous, Amy, I admonish myself. *Mary and Walter as criminals? Seriously? You couldn't find two less harmless people if you cased out a nursing home. Stop letting your imagination get the best of you.*

I open my mouth to ask my sister what else was in the paper, but she and my mother have moved on to another subject.

"Did you *see* that Donoghue woman's outfit?" My mother is critiquing the ensemble worn by the mother of one of our guests. Cammi (with an I!) Donoghue picked up her son in shortie shorts and a halter top that exposed almost every inch of her surgically enhanced DD breasts. None of the men seemed to mind as they practically fell over each other to help her find her child at the end of the party.

"Oh Gawd, I know!" Beth replies. "So trashy! Didn't she realize this was a kid's birthday party and not a bachelor party?"

I chuckle to myself remembering that my brother in law Derek had made the biggest fool out of himself in front of Cammi by talking directly to her chest until Lexie asked him, *loudly,* "Uncle Derek, why are you looking at that lady's bra?" Derek turned crimson and excused himself to rush inside. Presumably to go take a cold shower. Beth had been mortified. *Good.* My sister was *rarely* mortified.

"If you ever dress like that, Allie, I will personally

drive you to the convent," my mother tells the 13 year old who is not listening to any of this conversation at all. Allie, whose once gorgeous blonde hair has been recently dyed jet black, is sulking on an oversized chair in the corner, clutching her phone as she feverishly sends text messages. I can tell that she is thoroughly disgusted that I had the audacity to insist she be with the family after Kaitlyn reluctantly helped her mother wrangle up her brothers and load them into the minivan. The Princess of Preteen Angst prefers to be locked away in her room where I can only *imagine* what she does.

When this prepubescent funk arose the year she started middle school, I assumed it was her homework, but once we got her report card dotted with Cs and notations like "room for improvement" and "not applying herself", we knew better.

So Daddy and Major Hypocrite Mommy, as Allie so delightfully referred to me, sat our daughter down and explained the rules. Homework was to be a priority. No TV, no phone, no computer or iPod until homework was done and checked by a parent. Preferably Roger, due to my lack of intelligence past fifth grade level.

Allie had rolled her eyes, which were made up to look like a raccoon, asked us if we were "done yet", and promptly went back to ignoring us.

The next marking period, the grades were even more catastrophic. This time, Major Hypocrite Mommy went ballistic and took *away* Allie's phone and iPod. I was rewarded with a scathing look from my daughter. As her grades continued to deviate greatly from her actual potential, I wished desperately that I could get inside her head and figure out how to reach her.

Hopefully, the issue was just a boy or a group of friends that was excluding her, something that would work itself out eventually. I prayed that if something more complex was going on, my baby girl would confide in me.

I'm sure some teenage boy crisis is currently looming on the horizon as Allie's fingers click away at the keys. Her face is neutral, but she hasn't put that phone down yet and every once in a while, she sighs despondently after reading a message.

Knowing conversation with Allie is futile and anxious to connect with my mother and sister, I interject with, "Speaking of outfits, *what* was Joey wearing?"

My sister Joey arrived at the party in some flowing dress thing that screamed *leftover flower child*. She had just left a few minutes prior to go to the airport. She told us that she was picking up her new boyfriend, *Enrique*. Since she was dying for us to meet the flavor of the month, she was bringing him back to the party, which was now over. But Joey wouldn't care. Knowing her, she would show up at 10:00 and not understand why we were all in bed.

My mother instantly jumps to her youngest daughter's defense. "Joey designed that outfit herself, *Amy*. It's part of her new line. *Target* is picking it up next month." She clicks her tongue at me in her admonishing way.

Beth shakes her head, glamourous hair swishing on her shoulders. "Don't you read her *blog*? Seriously, Amy. She is very excited about the whole thing. This is her first big break. You could at *least* be happy for her."

I feel my face turn red as I realize my attempt at bonding has once again gone horribly awry. I should have known that Mom and Beth would defend Joey. Beth considers anything Joey does to be amazing, like she is her pet and Mom is just happy that Joey is not living with her and Dad anymore. She's 33 years old but they act like she's eight and a real living, breathing prodigy.

Truth be told, I *am* very proud that Joey is actually accomplishing things for once, but I am still jealous. I am jealous of the way she reached her goals and accomplishments. She had always marched to the beat of her own drummer, being very artistic, flitting in and out of activities and life in general. She could be found drawing feverishly while lying in the grass one day and then the next, she was holed up in her room writing lyrics to be played on her guitar. My parents indulged their youngest child with art and music classes and ignored her horrific grades, which were even worse than mine. They dismissed my whines of "Why don't you yell at Joey about *her* grades?" with explanations about how Joey was *different* and had different gifts and blah, blah, freaking blah. They believed Joey was going places.

And she did go places. Europe and South America. California and Hawaii. At first, it was on my father's dime, but then once he balked at sending her on any more "getaways" she discovered she could get what she wanted from men by simply batting her eyelashes. Oh did I mention Joey is a drop dead gorgeous brunette bombshell with a Marilyn Monroe figure? Yup. Joey is beautiful and creative, Beth is perky and smart, and I'm the plain Jane without brains wedged in between them. Thank goodness I married Roger or I'd probably still be living with my parents, eating ice cream out of the carton on Friday night while I pet my cat. Yes, that *was* a double entendre.

As if on cue, Joey waltzes through my front door right then, beaming like a sunray. Her perfectly tanned arm reaches out to pull in another perfectly tanned arm. Attached to that arm is perhaps one of the most flawless specimens of manhood I have laid eyes on. He steps into the house and it's like the heavens opened up and we can hear harps playing and angels singing. Every detail of his finely chiseled face is flawless; his dark brown chestnut locks tousled in a sexy hair gel commercial sort of way. He is lean and muscular; his clothes hug his body like they are afraid to leave him, revealing that there is not an ounce of fat on his godlike frame.

Joey flounces to the center of the room, tugging the god of *oh my word* behind her. Out of the corner of my eye, I witness my mother drop her empty wine glass, causing the last few drops of Shiraz to bounce onto the already stained and tattered carpet. Allie's head jerks up so fast I think she might have gotten whiplash.

"Everyone…" Joey announces as we collectively

hold our breath around her. "This is *Enrique!*" She adds a little roll to her R, and Enrique winks, practically causing me to swoon.

Enrique smiles with a sheepish grin. *Oh God. His teeth are white and straight and* he *certainly didn't need braces.* I always notice the teeth of other men. Roger had desperately needed braces as a kid but his mother couldn't afford it and his father wouldn't pay for his son to have "a hunk of metal in his mouth", so instead, my husband looks like a castoff from the Ozarks. On a positive note, maybe he could star in his own reality series.

The room is eerily still as Enrique continues to grin and my sister stands beside him, clutching his hand and beaming like a jackass. Although, I can hardly blame her. If he was holding *my* hand I'd be grinning like a fool, too.

I wonder what his hand feels like. Is it warm and smooth? Or is it rough and calloused by life? Does it feel smooth when he's touching... I blush as I cut off my inappropriate train of thought before I get carried away off to my usual fantasy island.

Finally, my mother rights her wine glass and stands up, brushing fur off of her slacks. She strides confidently over to Enrique and reaches for his hand. From the melting look on her face, I can tell his hand is of the warm and smooth variety. Her eyes nearly roll back in her head orgasmically.

"It's *wonderful* to meet you, *Enrique,*" she gushes, her voice sounding high pitched and girlie. Beth covers her mouth with her hand but not before I catch a smirk appearing on her lips.

Oh, to watch my mother make a fool of herself in front of this hunk of meat would be delicious. It would be ammunition for years to come.

Instead, Mom clears her throat and seems to gain her composure. "Josephine has told us so *much* about you..."

Yeah except she left out the part that you're gorgeous and stunning...oh and she didn't tell us what you do for a living or where you live....nope, Josephine has not told us anything about you.

Joey waves her hand at our mother. "No, no Mom. Enrique doesn't speak English. He only speaks Spanish. He's from Brazil."

Beth furrows her brow which would probably enrage her plastic surgeon. "They don't speak Spanish in Brazil, Joey. They speak Portuguese." Leave it to Beth to know the official language of a foreign country.

Joey is nonplussed. "Oh. Maybe it's Portuguese then. I don't know exactly. Sounds like Spanish."

A red warning flag goes up. "Uh, Jo? Do *you* speak Spanish?" I ask, raising my eyebrow.

My sister shakes her head.

Beth interjects while wrinkling up her pert little button nose, "How do you talk to him then?"

"Um, well, we don't really talk as much as..." Joey stammers, vaguely aware that her 13 year old niece is staring at her with total admiration. I'm sure this guy is Allie's teen dream man. Hell, he's my pre-menopausal, mid-life crisis dream man.

"Oh, for goodness sakes, Joey!" Beth turns bright red, realizing what Joey is implying. Beth is definitely something of a prude.

My mother continues to smile brightly as she stammers, "Donde esta la cucina?" She sweeps her hand toward the couch.

I grimace. My foreign language skills are severely lacking, but I am pretty sure my mother just asked Enrique where the kitchen was. Allie snorts and then covers her mouth, probably embarrassed at erupting into an unladylike noise in front of Enrique. Joey snickers while Beth rolls her eyes. Even Enrique is trying not to laugh at this silly woman.

"What?" My mother glares at us. "I am trying to be polite and offer him a seat on the couch!" She turns back to Enrique and continues to butcher the Spanish language. "Mi llamo es vino?" This statement sends Allie into a fit of giggles, something I have not seen in ages. Enrique is now thoroughly confused and looking to Joey for assistance. She just shrugs.

"Mom, I don't think that means what you think it means..." I start to tell her.

"*Grandma*! You just told him your name was *wine*!" Allie scoffs as she leaps to her feet.

My mother choses *me* to glare at. I guess Allie correcting her gaffe is my fault for giving birth to the child.

"Well if *you're* so smart, *you* talk to him!" She

snatches up her forsaken glass and storms out to the kitchen, presumably for a refill.

I stare at my daughter. "How do you know what she said?"

Allie flops back on the chair. "Uh, duh…just Spanish class." She rolls her eyes for emphasis. The emphasis being on what an idiot her mother is.

A little background here. Allie practically flunked Spanish. Roger and I needed to hire a tutor last year, yet Allie still barely passed. The fact that she could even translate a simple sentence boggles my mind.

"Spanish is a lot like Portuguese. Do you think you could speak to him for us?" I am hoping to buoy her confidence, thinking she will be thrilled that she can do something the adults can't.

Instead, Allie's reaction is that of horror. She leaps to her feet and stares at me as if I have just asked her to lick the toilet bowl. "*Mother*! Are you crazy? No!" She snatches her phone off the chair and storms up the stairs toward her bedroom. Thirty seconds later, her door slams. Beth jumps a little at the sharp noise and stares at me in surprise. *Really, Beth, you didn't know that little slam was coming? I guess your perfect spawn never slam the doors.*

Beth scoffs, "Why do you always have to start drama, Amy? The party was going so nicely."

"What?" My tone is incredulous. "What drama did *I* start?" I cannot *believe* she is somehow making this out to be my fault.

"*Please*! You had to embarrass Mom *and* Allie?"

I continue to stare at my sister in disbelief. Of *course* she would say this was my fault. I can't seem to do anything right today, or any time lately, for that matter. But I hardly think that the fact Joey has no idea how to speak to her boyfriend is in any way, shape or form my fault.

I look to Joey for assistance, but she and Enrique have seemed to forgotten the entire incident and are already sucking face on my couch like they are 15 years old. His hand is inching up her long skirt, exposing her thigh.

"You should go try to smooth things over with her," Beth instructs as she scoops up *my* son like he belongs to *her* and exits the room with a glaring look. "I don't understand why we can't have one family gathering without tears," she mutters to Evan who is fighting her off as she heads back outside, leaving me standing in the middle of the living room, wondering which "her" I need to "smooth things over with" first.

Realizing that my efforts to placate my mother have proven futile for far longer than with Allie, I decide to tackle the problem of Allie's breakdown first. Besides, my mother has Beth and wine to keep her company. Allie only has her cell phone.

I slowly ascend the stairs, my eye trained on the door at the end of the long hallway, Allie's room. The once colorfully decorated door adorned with construction paper flowers and stickers was now painfully bare, devoid of any feeling. I experience a sinking sensation in my gut every time I look at it.

Allie's once pink and lavender bedroom was repainted a beige color at her request last summer. She claimed she wanted something less babyish, so I offered her hundreds of different color samples, every hue imaginable. But no, she wanted brown. She dumped all her old stuff animals and toys into the trash. She removed everything on the walls; framed pictures of flowers, her chalkboard, her cork board with her drawings; all gone. She tossed her American Girl dolls in the hall which Lexie greedily scooped up. I also found bags upon bags of clothing, mostly new, parked in the hallway.

When I confronted her, she mumbled something about them not fitting anymore. With a heavy heart, I packed away the clothing, some still with tags attached, for Lexie. Despite the instance of my friends that this was *normal* teen behavior, I couldn't help feeling like there was something wrong; somehow I had messed up. And for the life of me, I had no idea how to fix it.

Tapping quietly at Allie's door, I call out, "Allie?" I am met by a stony wall of silence. Jiggling the doorknob, I try a different tactic. "*Allie Pallie?*" I call out the nickname that I used for her when she was little. She would curl up in my lap and tell me I was her best pal, so I started calling her "My Allie Pallie". She would take my face in her hands and squeeze it tightly, and then lean in to leave a wet kiss on my lips. Then she would call me her "Mommy Pallie" and tell me we'd be pals forever. I gulp as I recall this piece of nostalgia. I certainly wasn't "Mommy Pallie" to her anymore.

"Go away," is her muffled response. Her face is probably buried under a pillow.

"Come on, Allie. Open the door, please. I just want to talk to you," I plead.

"I have nothing to say to you," she shouts, fury evident in her voice.

"But I have something to say to you," I counter. "Just let me come in."

"Why don't you go *fuck* off?" she screeches, voice raising several octaves.

I suck in my breath, knowing she is just trying to challenge me with her foul language. She's hoping it gets a rise out of me and I end up forgetting why I came upstairs in the first place. *Why* did *I come upstairs in the first place? Oh yeah, to apologize. Don't lose sight of your purpose*, I remind myself. *Don't flip out over the cursing. It's just words.*

"Listen, Al. why don't you come downstairs and we can have some cake? I saved the chocolate pieces. I hid them from your father and sister, but I'll share it with you if you come downstairs," I try to tempt her with her favorite thing ever. Chocolate. I know she can't resist it. She's discovered my hidden chocolate stash more times than I can count. Every time I get a spot that I am certain she will never be able to find, I discover nothing but empty wrappers the next time I need a chocolate fix. I am seriously considering taping the bars to the inside of the toilet bowl tank.

Instead of a joyful teen, thrilled at the mention of chocolate, I am met by the blaring of Allie's stereo. It is some combination of rap and screaming metal. *What the hell happened to Katy Perry and Taylor Swift?* I wonder as I turn and stomp back down the stairs having my own little hissy fit.

~FOUR~

"Mrs. Maxwell?" The FBI agent flashes her badge at me when I open the door. Another female agent in a drab tweed pantsuit stands behind her. They both have FBI agent sunglasses on and look very official.

I clutch my chest, not knowing what the FBI is doing at my house. *"Can I help you?"* I ask timidly, wracking my brain to remember what I might have done that was illegal. I think maybe I ran the red light camera on Route 1 recently, but I highly doubt they would send the FBI to my door for that, would they? Unless, those unpaid parking tickets from my *"college"* days were finally catching up with me. I begin to twirl my hair nervously. Should I run? Where will I go? How will I live? What will I eat? I don't think I'm cut out for life on the lam.

"Can we come in?" the FBI woman asks. *"I assure you, you've done nothing wrong."* She smiles at me with a tight official agent smile. I wonder if that's what she tells everyone so they don't run. I continue to panic anyway while put on a relaxed face.

"Why, of course! Come on in!" I step back, allowing the two women into the house while keeping my eyes peeled for escape routes as I lead them to the kitchen.

"Would you like iced tea?" I inquire politely. *"I also have lemonade if you'd prefer."*

Both women wave their hands to dismiss the suggestion. *"No, thank you,"* says the one who showed *me her badge. Then she sighs heavily as both agents sit at the table. "Mrs. Maxwell, is your husband available?"*

I shake my head. "No, Roger is at work. Is he in trouble?" I immediately begin to sweat.

The first agent shakes her head. "No. He's not in trouble."

"Did...did something happen, then? Is he...dead?" A vision of Roger being crushed by a swarm of angry high school students pops into my head for some reason.

The agents both shake their heads. "No. Roger is fine."

I don't understand. "Well, then, what's wrong?"

The second agent takes my hand. "We are here to give you some distressing news." She pats my hand gently, in a grandmotherly fashion. "Nearly fourteen years ago, your baby was switched at birth. Allie is not your real daughter."

She waves towards the living room and amazingly, a beautiful, smiling teenage girl enters the kitchen. Her dark silky hair hangs at her waist, a stark contrast to her sapphire blue sequined evening gown. She is holding a violin with one hand and a soft calico kitten under the other arm.

"This is Agnes," the agent informs me. "She is your real daughter. She plays for the New York Philharmonic even though she is only thirteen. She is also so bright that she is in college already, studying veterinary medicine because she loves animals."

I leap to my feet and clasp the beautiful child to my

chest. "How wonderful! She must take after my side of the family!"

"Yes," the agent remarks. "And she never gets in trouble. She doesn't curse, smoke or hang out with bad influences. In fact, she's never even talked back in her life! You don't have to worry about her getting into trouble in high school because she finished that years ago! She will be nothing but a help to you. We are very sorry for the confusion this may have caused."

I pull back and beam at my new daughter. The spitting image of me and brilliant to boot! Just what I've always wanted!

"We must go and tell the family!" I exclaim as I take her hand in mine.

"What would you like us to do with the other one?" the first agent asks.

"Oh, I don't know..." I answer with a worried expression. "What will happen to her if I have you take her away?"

"She'll go to reform school," the agent tells me. "And we will find her a suitable family."

"That's probably best," I tell the agent. "After all, she isn't my child. I don't think any of them are my children, to be honest with you..."

Roger's irritating throat clearing brings me back to reality. I am in bed, rubbing lotion on my dry and calloused feet. I begin lamenting to Roger about the day's painful events.

"I don't understand what sets her off, Roger. She was laughing with us one minute and then the next minute she's in tears. I swear to God I'm going to make her wear a mood ring around her forehead." I sigh as I squeeze more lotion out into my palms. "Or at least her neck. Damn it, I'm her mother. I should be able to figure this out. There must be something wrong with her."

I smooth the greasy lotion over my shoulders and rub it in. I must have gotten burnt because my skin is sore to the touch. *Of course you got burnt. You put sunblock on everyone else and forgot yourself as usual, bonehead.*

I stand up and stroll over to the mirror to examine my shoulders, craning my neck to get a view of my back. *Yup, just as I suspected.* My shoulders are a painful shade in between red and purple.

Of course, nobody thought to remind *me* to take care of myself. I watched my mother smooth sunblock on to Joey's exposed shoulders, despite Joey's protests. Did she say, "Amy, come here and let me sunblock *your* shoulders before they get burnt"? No, of course not. She was too busy dividing her time between kissing both of my sisters' asses.

After my blunder in the living room, my mother ignored me for the rest of the evening. She refused to even say goodbye to me as I dragged the garbage to the curb when she was leaving. I kissed my father on the cheek and Mom swept past me like I was some scullery maid and she was frickin' Duchess Kate.

"Ugh, and my mother," I comment as I scoot down

under the covers next to Roger. He is peering at the iPad, trying to kill pigs with flying birds. "She's acting like a spoiled child, too. I mean, I can't even make a little joke? *Seriously*? Everyone in the family makes jokes at *my* expense. I don't give *them* the silent treatment and carry on like a two year old."

"Um, hmm," Roger replies as he pokes at the screen with his index finger.

"I felt like I was in the middle of a hormonal tornado. I thought my mother was done with *the changes*. Apparently there is some five year lag with the hormonal effects…" My voice wanders off as I realize that Roger is paying more attention to his tablet than what I am saying. "Roger? Are you even listening to me?"

"Uh, huh," Roger mutters as he flips the tablet to change the screen orientation.

"What did I say then?" I challenge as I rub lotion on my cheeks.

"Hormones and the weather," Roger mumbles while scratching his head as if he can't quite figure out the iPad. He *is* severely technologically challenged so there is a good chance the tablet is intellectually defeating him. Colt had to program the DVR for him last week.

"You don't even listen!" I wail, knocking the iPad out of his hand and covering my head with the comforter.

"I'm playing a game! I was just about to beat that level!" Roger whines.

I am incensed by his selfishness. Sulking, I remain underneath the covers until Roger realizes I am not speaking to him. Which feels like a decade when you are smothering yourself with heavy fabric.

"Amy?" he finally asks cautiously.

I ignore him, dramatically burrowing my head underneath my pillow.

"Oh come on, Aim! I'm sorry," Roger apologizes as he tugs at the blanket. He manages to uncover my burnt back and leans over, kissing the tops of my shoulders. "I know what will cheer you up."

"Ouch!" I yelp, yanking the pillow off my head and throwing the covers aside. "That *hurts*!" I glower at him.

Roger frowns. "Is it that time of the month again?"

I narrow my eyes at him. "No, it most certainly is *not*," I snap angrily, despite the fact that yes, it actually is. But that has *nothing* to do with why I am angry. *Nothing at all*.

Pulling the covers up to my chin, I offer him a terse, "*Good* night."

"Amy, don't be mad," Roger pleads. "Come on. It's been a long day. You did a great job with the birthday party...the kids had fun." As he edges towards me, he adds, "Maybe it's time the adults had fun, too." He attempts to stroke my cheek but I pull away.

"No, *thank you*. I'm tired. I'm going to sleep." I roll onto my side, hoping to illustrate my unavailability to my tiresome husband.

"It's only 10:00!" Roger exclaims. "How can you be tired already?"

Unable to control myself, I bolt upright. "I *know*

what time it is, Roger. I've been up since the butt crack of dawn getting ready for the party. Not to mention, I've been busting my ass all week to make this party perfect for our child. What did you do? Hand out beers to your buddies?"

"I mowed the lawn," Roger replies indignantly.

"Big frigging whoop," I retort as I flop back down on the pillow. Perhaps a tad bit histrionically.

"Hey, no one told you to have this big party. The kid's 6 years old. Do you think he really cares?"

"Of course he cares!" I bellow. "All kids care!"

"Oh, please," Roger snorts. "I never had a birthday party and I never cared."

"Maybe that's what's wrong with you," I snap at him. "You're a thoughtless boob because you didn't have any birthday parties as a child."

"I highly doubt not having a birthday party as a child screwed me up. And besides, my mother had more to worry about than loot bags and sheet cakes," Roger points out, making me feel guilty.

Roger's parents got divorced when he was only six years old. He and his sister hardly ever saw their dad after he remarried some woman half his age with a baby (the guy I dated way back when). Their mother ended up working several jobs just to support them, so he didn't really see her either. She was a good, hardworking woman, but she never had time or money for those extra "mom" touches like birthday parties. She died at a young age, 47; burnt out and overworked. I never even met her.

"Sorry," I mumble. I couldn't say *anything* right today.

Roger places the iPad on the nightstand and gives me a half-hearted shrug. "Not a big deal."

The earlier events of the day are tugging at the corners of my subconscious and I decide to feel out Roger's thoughts on the matter.

"Hey, Roger, did you know that Mary and Walter had a grandson living with them?"

Roger appears genuinely confused. "Who are Mary and Walter?"

I roll my eyes just like my daughter does. "Our *neighbors*, Roger. Across the street?"

A flicker of recognition crosses my husband's face. "The old people?"

Sighing with annoyance at his insensitivity, I reply, "Yes, our *elderly* neighbors."

Roger shrugs again. "Nah. Never noticed." His fingers walk over my back seductively. "So whatdoya say?" Roger says in his best sultry voice. He almost sounds like the Marlboro Man.

I ignore him. "I just found out that the kid has been living there for two months! *Two months*! Basically all summer and I never saw him before!"

Roger wrinkles his brow. "*Okay...*" I can tell he has no idea where I am going with this.

I let out an exasperated sigh and blow a piece of my bangs out of my face. "Don't you think that's a little *odd*?"

Again with the shrug. "Whatever. Maybe he's shy."

"That's the thing, Roger. Mary claims that he is autistic. I suppose it's possible, but he ended up in our yard somehow today playing with Colt."

"Well that's okay isn't it? Colt needs friends, right?" Roger asked, completely perplexed at my thought process.

"He's *fourteen*, Roger!" I glare at him. *Really, he should understand my concerns here. Why do I have to spell everything out for this man?*

"Oh. Well that's strange. What a weirdo," Roger remarks.

"He's *autistic*. Don't be insensitive," I admonish.

Roger scratches his head at this point. "That's a problem?"

"No! That's not the problem. That's the reason why he's fourteen and he's playing with a six year old."

"Oh. So there is no problem then?" Roger frowns.

"Oh, forget it!" I scoff.

Roger shakes his head. "I'm not sure what I'm supposed to be saying here."

I am sitting up now. "You don't think it's strange that a kid we never met shows up in our backyard and his grandmother claims he's been living with her for months? Where's he been hiding all this time? Better yet, *why* has he been hiding?"

"Maybe he doesn't like the sun?" Roger suggests, eyes growing wide as I hop out of the bed.

"And you don't find it equally odd that Beth

mentioned a neighborhood drug ring today?"

Roger crinkles his eyes. He is thinking really hard. "Um…what does *Beth* have to do with any of this?" He's obviously not following my train of thought.

I shake my head and climb back into bed. "No, forget about Beth. It's not about her. She just mentioned that there's been a lot of news coverage about drugs on the rise-"

Roger rolls his eyes. "Of course there's been coverage about drugs! School starts this week. Every year the news stations roll out their 'exposes' on drug use among teens." He actually uses air quotes.

I fold my knee underneath my body and corner him with my eyes. "So don't you think we should be concerned?"

"You think this kid is doing drugs?" Roger asks incredulously.

I shake my head. "I did at first because he acted strange but Mary explained about his disability. I just…I don't know. I guess I'm just on the lookout for things that don't add up. This drug ring thing just got me nervous."

Roger waves his hand in front of his face and arches his eyebrows. "It's nothing to get all worked up about. There's *always* drugs in the schools no matter how hard we crack down on it-"

"That doesn't make me feel better, Roger! I'm concerned about *our* teenager! I think you should be, too!" I yelp.

He smiles at me in his *I'm older and wiser than you*

patronizing manner. He's going to speak to me like I'm one of the parents at school. "I understand your concerns. I'm just saying that you shouldn't let the news coverage upset you. We've taught Allie well. She knows better than to get involved with drugs. I'm at the school. I *am* the principal, you know. Besides, there's worse things to worry about at the high school level. Like boys." He frowns, knitting his overgrown brows together.

"Oh thanks, Roger. That makes me feel *so* much better."

"I'm just pointing out that there is no reason to suspect Allie of unscrupulous behavior," Roger reasons with me.

"She's been so distant and strange the past few months," I point out.

"Please, that's normal teenage behavior, Amy. Trust me on this one. I work with the little cretins every day."

I slump down under the covers. "It just makes me nervous, that's all."

"Amy…stop," Roger pleads. "I think your imagination is just running overtime right now." In all seriousness he adds, "I think I know what you need."

I glare at him because I'm pretty sure I know what's next. "Oh, really now?"

Sure enough he waggles his eyebrows at me as he inches his fingers up my pajama shorts. "Why don't you just relax and-"

I slap his hand away. "Ha. You're out of your mind if you think I'm going to have sex with you," I tell him as

I glare at him.

"Awww come on, Aim! It's been like two weeks," Roger whines.

"Good night, Roger," I grumble once again as I flip over on my side. I am silent for a moment, wondering if he will try to molest me again or at least say goodnight. But as I hear the soft snores come from the other side of the bed, I realize that Roger is already asleep, leaving me alone to worry about my baby girl, the new kid on the block, and why his grandmother had not mentioned him before.

~FIVE~

"Allie?" The next day, I find myself gently tapping on my daughter's bedroom door. It is almost 10:30 on Sunday morning and she has not yet emerged from her room cocoon. My knocking is met by the sound of Allie's stereo being turned on. I immediately feel the floor shaking under my feet.

Oh good. She's awake.

"Allie?" I call out once more. "Hey, Allie? Do you want to come to the mall with me?" My question is answered by the stereo being cranked higher, if that's even human possibly.

Sipping my coffee this morning, I scoured the paper, looking for an article on Beth's infamous drug ring. I didn't find exactly what I was looking for, but my heart nearly leapt out of my chest when my eyes fell on an article entitled, "Drug Use Amongst High School Students on the Rise".

Despite Roger's assurance that we had nothing to worry about, I couldn't help thinking that something was not right with Allie. And I wanted to ease my fears by getting her to talk.

I devised what I thought was an infallible plan. I would lure Allie out of her room and the house with the prospect of going to the mall. Allie wouldn't be able to resist shopping. It was her favorite pastime, other than ignoring her family, texting and telling her mother off.

Once in the car, I would just continue to drive. She would have nowhere to run and no choice but to talk to me about what was bothering her or what was going on in her life. At least, I *thought* it was an infallible plan. What I had not factored in was my daughter not wanting to spend any time with me at all, even at the mall. I should have realized that after she turned down chocolate.

"I want to go to the mall with you!" sings out a voice behind me. Startled, I nearly jump three feet in the air. Lexie is standing behind me, toothbrush in hand, smiling boldly. "Puleeezeeee, Mommy?"

Oh, just perfect. I'm not going to succeed in my task of breaking down Allie's walls and I'm going have to spend the day listening to Lexie babble tirelessly about everyone and everything we pass in the mall? And I wasn't even planning to really go to the mall to begin with!

"I need new shoes. Mine are all scuffed up," she tells me while pointing her toothbrush towards her feet. A blob of toothpaste falls on the floor.

Well, if you would LISTEN to me and not wear them outside....

"Sure, Lexie," I sigh, rubbing my temples. I should take an Excedrin. Maybe I can ward off the inevitable migraine I was going to get from an afternoon with Lexie the Relentless. I halt my negative thinking to admonish myself.

Stop being a bad mommy! She just wants to spend time with you. You should be grateful any of your children want to be with you. Hopefully, Lexie won't end up shutting you out like Allie has.

Lexie happily bounds off in the direction of her room to finish getting dressed and I head downstairs towards the man cave to inform Roger of my plans. On my way to my husband's sanctuary, I pass Colt and Evan in the living room.

Colt is carefully unpacking each of his new Lego sets while Evan is sitting off to the side, sucking his thumb, staring at his older brother with adoration. Neither child is speaking out loud but Colt seems to be mumbling to himself. For once, he isn't ripping something out of his younger brother's hands or screaming at him. And vice versa.

Colt was the only boy for four years. During those years, his sisters completely doted on him. They dressed him up, put make-up on him and pushed him around in the stroller like he was their own personal baby doll. The kid didn't have to set foot on the ground for years. I would find him in their beds and he would follow them around like a little puppy dog all day long. When Evan was born, Colt was unceremoniously dethroned. Lexie and Allie had a new toy to play with and Colt got the shaft. He's been furious about it ever since and usually takes out his frustration on Evan. He's never nice to his baby brother…*ever*.

Knowing this fact makes me increasingly suspicious of the activity in front of me. It is like watching the calm before the storm. I slide over to the downstairs steps, keeping one eye on the boys and call out to Roger.

"*Honey*! Lexie and I are going to the mall! I need you to come up here and watch Evan and Colt!"

I get absolutely no response. Not an "okay, dear" or even a grunt of acknowledgment. But I guess it's probably difficult to hear me over the TV blasting. I can actually hear the sound of the waves crashing against the side of the boat on the crabbing show that he's watching. Why he enjoys half of what he watches and records, I'll never understand. He isn't a crabber or a fisherman, nor does he cook, have tattoos or drive a motorcycle. Yet, he is dutifully devoted to at least two hours of "reality" TV each and every day, sitting in front of the flat screen with drool pooling at his collar and chips littered across his beer belly. I guess the "reality" TV show called "Mom going nuts with four kids" that aired 24/7 in our house wasn't interesting enough for him to partaking in viewing.

"Roger?" I call out again as I watch Evan stealthily inch towards his brother.

Damn. Should I intercept this now, knowing full well that Evan will have a meltdown if I pick him up? Or do I take my chances that he is not going to touch Colt or anything around him?

There is still no response from the man cave. I drop down one step lower and call out to my husband once more, this time louder and more frantically. "Roger?" Still no sound.

"Good thing the house isn't on fire," I grumble as I

trudge down the stairs, taking comfort in the fact that Evan is now crawling over to his own toys, leaving Colt alone. I am going to have to physically drag my husband out of his chair in order to assure the boys will be looked after properly in my absence.

Entering the darkened den, I can see Roger reclining in his leather armchair, soda in one hand, bag of chips in the other. He is staring wide eyed at the TV, its blue glow illuminating his pale complexion, making him look like some sort of post-apocalyptic zombie.

"Roger. I need you to come upstairs and watch the boys. I am leaving in a minute," I state pointedly while staring at my husband. He registers no comprehension of my declaration. I'm wondering if my daydream of his untimely demise may actually be coming true. My heart races with fear.

"ROGER!" I jump in front of the TV, waving my hands.

"Wah, wah?" Roger snaps out of his trance, attempting to peer around me.

Oh good. He's alive, I think scathingly.

"Go upstairs and watch the boys. Lexie and I are going out," I explain, not able to disguise the annoyance in my voice.

"I can hear them from down here," Roger informs me as he digs his hand deep into the chip bag.

"Ha!" I snort. "I was calling your name for ten minutes and you didn't hear me. They can get into all sorts of trouble alone. Please go upstairs."

As if to illustrate my point, we hear a high pitched screech followed by a thud. I briefly glance at Roger with an *I told you so* look and then without a second thought, I race up the steps two at a time. The screeching continues with sobbing mixed in as I reach the top of the stairs.

Out of the corner of my eye, I can see Colt standing over his little brother, who is lying next to the pile of Legos, holding his head while bawling.

I dash over to my younger son and scoop him up, quickly checking for loose body parts and blood. Satisfied that there are none, I hold the sobbing baby close to my chest and glare at my older son.

"What did you *do*?" I accuse.

Colt throws his hands up in the air. "Why are you blaming *me*? I didn't do *anything*," he answers with the slight whining tone that he uses in all of his less than truthful statements.

"Wego! Wego!" Evan tells me, pointing at his brother. He faces me and bangs himself in the head with his tiny fist. "Colt bop!"

"He touched my Legos," Colt grumbles as he possessively gathers his precious toys into a pile around his body.

"I don't care *what* he touched. I've told you time again and time again, keep your hands *off* of your brother. You call me and I'll handle it. *I'm* the parent, not you." I admonish him as I comfort the crying child. I peek over his head as his tears and boogers soak into my shirt, craning my neck towards the stairs, waiting for Roger to emerge from the den.

Wasn't he behind me when we heard the thud? Doesn't he hear the ruckus up here? Doesn't he care?

Instead of Roger entering the room, a hopping Lexie fills my visual field. In addition to hot pink stretch pants and a lime green tank top, she has a silver sequined purse thrown over her shoulder, a blue beret on her head and purple cowgirl boots on her feet. I guess I should be happy she has on a denim skirt and opted to leave the silver sparkly tutu in the closet.

"Hi, Mom!" she sings out in her customary cheerful oblivion. "I'm ready to go to the MALL!"

"Not now, Lexie," I respond in a distracted manner. "Your brothers are beating each other up."

"Where is Daddy? Why can't Daddy take care of them?" she moans, flouncing onto the couch with her typical melodramatic flair.

"I'd like to know the same thing," I mutter as I sway back and forth with Evan who is now hiccupping from crying so hard.

"I'll go get him!" Lexie volunteers suddenly, popping up from the couch. Before I can protest and tell her it is futile, she dashes down the stairs towards the man cave.

"Daddy!" I can hear her screeching. Somehow, Roger does *not* seem to hear her because she continues to shriek, "Daddy! Mommy needs *you*..."

I finally hear the low murmur of Roger's voice, followed by the high pitched tone of Lexie's. Moments later, as Evan is sighing contentedly in my arms, drifting off to toddler dreamland, Lexie emerges from the den with a cross Roger in tow. *How the hell did she get him out of the chair?*

"Here's Daddy!" Lexie announces proudly.

"What do you need?" Roger asks with irritation. "They're about to find gold in the Yukon."

"I told you. I need you to watch the boys." Apparently, he never actually listens to the words that come out of my mouth.

"Why can't Lexie watch them?" he asks with a frown.

"She's coming with me," I reply, transferring a sleeping Evan into his arms. "I also told you that." Irritation continues to course through my veins.

"Well, what about Allie?" Roger asks as he reluctantly takes his son. He shifts Evan's weight and leans him across his shoulder. Evan doesn't even stir, which does not surprise me. With three older siblings running around and having to take his naps on the go, Evan is so adept at tuning out noise and being jostled, he could probably sleep through an earthquake.

"Oh please," I answer in response to Roger's question about Allie. "She's pissed about something. She's barricaded herself in her room. We'll be lucky if we see her before Halloween."

"Ooo! Can I get a Halloween costume when we go to the mall?" Lexie inquires, bouncing from foot to foot with annoying speed and dexterity.

"No," I answer sharply. "It's September for Christ's sake. Halloween is nine weeks away."

"But all the good costumes will be goooone," Lexie moans as she sticks out a pouty lip. I pity the poor fool who marries her. He better be rich.

I, however, am immune to her charms. "Cut it out, Lexie, or we won't go at all," I tell her as I crouch on the floor, searching for my flip flop under the couch. When I mention not going at all, I catch a glimpse of Roger's hopeful expression out of the corner of my eye.

Damn it. He can't even spend an hour or two with his children? Why is it always on me? Oh, wait. I know the excuse. He works hard all week and it's Sunday and he deserves a break and blah, blah, fucking blah. Like I don't deserve it? What does he think I do all week? Sit around eating ice cream and watching As the World Turns? Is that show even on *any more?*

I find one of my flip flops underneath the couch and I reach over to extract the other one from the dog's slobbery jaw. I lumber to a standing position, sliding my feet into the one dry flip flop and one moist flip flop.

"You think you can handle this?" I sarcastically inquire of my husband.

"Of course I can *handle* this," he grumbles. Nodding towards Evan, he asks, "He's going to sleep for three or four hours, right?"

I snort through my nose. Evan could fall asleep anywhere, anytime, but for twenty minutes, tops. Then he would bounce awake, refueled with energy, raring to go.

Roger would be lucky if Evan was still sleeping when I backed out of the driveway.

"Yeah, sure," I tell him. Maybe that's why he thinks I have all this free time. He is under the impression that our youngest child sleeps for half the day. Hell, the kid barely sleeps through the night. In fact, none of the kids were ever really good sleepers. If I added up the amount of sleep I've gotten in the last fourteen years, it would probably equal a year's worth of Roger's sleep. "Come on, Lexie," I say as I sling my purse over my arm.

Sure enough, as Lexie and I sail out the front door, I can hear Evan stirring. "Hurry up," I hiss to my youngest daughter, practically shoving her on to the porch.

"I *am* hurrying!" Lexie whimpers. Lexie's definition of "hurrying" and mine vary greatly. As she "races" to the car, she skips and brushes her hand across the tops of the tulips that line the front walk, staining her hands yellow from the pistil.

I grumble to myself as I unlock the car door, knowing she is going to get the pollen all over the car, but there is no way I am going back in the house so that she can wash her hands. If Evan sees me leave, he most likely will have a meltdown.

As I am buckling myself in, Roger pokes his head out the door with a screaming Evan in his arms. He is frantically trying to wave me down.

"Mom, Daddy wants you," Lexie remarks in a very matter of fact voice that I think she borrowed from my sister.

"Uh huh," I mumble as I back out of the driveway.

I can hear Roger call out and I ignore him as I put the car into drive and speed away.

"Daddy asked you a question, Mom," Lexie informs me.

"That's nice," I mutter. *Daddy can kiss my ass.* If he can't figure out how to take care of a two year old by now, he might as well move out. There was no use for him then. I mean, was it so wrong to want to escape without a cluster of children in my wake? It's bad enough I have Lexie with me. And Allie doesn't need anyone to look after her other than to occasional check to see that she's breathing and not sending naked pictures of herself to the entire high school student body. So really, all he needs to do this is keep an eye on two boys for an hour or two. I am sure he can handle it. After all, he keeps 1,400 hormonal teenagers in check on a daily basis.

In protest to my reasoning, the Onstar car phone starts ringing. I glance down at the dashboard and let out an audible groan.

"Mom! It's Daddy calling!" Lexie advises me.

"Thank you, Lexie," I reply, checking my rearview mirror as I change lanes.

"Well aren't you going to get it?" she pesters me.

"Nope."

"Well, what if it's an *emergency*?" she asks, dragging out the last word.

"I am certain that it's not," I assure her as I merge into the lane that takes me directly to the mall parking lot.

"But, but, but what if Colt fell out of his tree house?"

"We've been gone four and a half minutes, Lex. Colt couldn't have even gotten outside in that amount of time." I pull into the packed mall parking lot. Tomorrow is Labor Day so of course the stores are celebrating with sales galore. The mall stores have sales for everything from Mother's Day to Peanut Butter and Jelly Day. That's April 2nd, in case you were wondering and wanted to mark it on your calendar.

Snaking around the parked cars, I search for a vacant spot. The phone stops ringing.

"See?" I tell my daughter with an air of triumph. "It must not be important. He stopped calling."

As if to mock my assumption, my cell phone starts to jingle in my purse just as I find a parking spot. I blow out a sigh of annoyance.

"I bet that's Daddy!" Lexie calls out in her sing-song voice.

"I bet it is, too!" I sing-song right along with her. I pull into the parking space, just as Lexie snatches my purse off of the front seat. "Hey! Don't touch my purse!" I admonish, just a bit tad too late. Lexie already has my cell phone out.

"Hi, Daddy!" She answers the phone with her usual cheerfulness. "Uh, huh. Yeah. We did. No." There is a brief pause as I unbuckle and attempt to extract my cell from her hand. I fail miserably. She is too quick for me. She turns her head out of my reach as she tattles on me. "Mommy didn't want to answer it. I told her it could be an *emergency* but *she* said…"

"Give me the damn phone, Lexie," I growl.

"Here's Mommy!" she chirps into the speaker as she hands me the phone, covered with a pink rhinestone case that I had chosen to impress Allie with my "coolness". Allie had not been impressed and I hated the rhinestone case. The rhinestones constantly fell off. I found one in my coffee yesterday.

"Amy! I've been calling you and calling you!" Roger is saying as I press the phone to my ear. "What if it was an emergency?"

"*Is* it an emergency?" I ask curtly, turning the car off.

"Well, sort of…I don't know where Evan's binkies are. He won't stop crying."

I lean my forehead on the wheel, fighting off the urge to bang my head against it. "Roger, Evan hasn't been using a binky since the beginning of the summer," I inform him.

Maybe if you paid attention, you would have noticed that. Or if you listened to me when I was telling you I was getting practically no sleep because I was trying to wean him off of the binky.

"Oh," Roger replies, obviously stumped. "Then why is he crying?"

"I have no idea," I answer as I step out of the minivan. Lexie is bouncing in place next to my door, way too eager. "You're his father. Figure it out," I snap as I practically punch the end call button. Reaching for my daughter's hand while she will still hold it, I grumble, "Come on, Lex. Let's get this over with."

~

"Could you believe the size of that hot dog, Mom? And that guy ate it in two bites? Well, I guess I can believe that he would eat it in two bites because he was so fat. Do fat people eat more food or are they born fat? Can you get fat if you weren't fat before? If Daddy eats too many potato chips will he be fat like the man at the food court?" Lexie pauses for a second and inhales. "Mom? Mom? Why aren't you answering me, Mom? Can't you hear me, Mom?"

We are trudging through the parking lot after an intense three hours of shopping. Well, I am trudging. Lexie is skipping and twirling and prattling on and on like the Energizer Bunny. As I unlock the minivan (*curse you, minivan*), Lexie points towards the exit of Sears. "Hey, isn't that the kid who was at our house yesterday?"

I stare at the door of the department store where she is pointing. Exiting is a teenaged boy. From our vantage point, it does indeed look like Sean. I furrow my brow.

What is he doing at the mall alone? If he can't even be trusted to go across the street, why would Mary and Walter let him go to the mall *by himself?*

"He's coming this way, Mom!" Lexie declares. "Let's go say hi!" She lurches forward but I quickly grab her arm.

"Shhh, Lexie," I hiss and I pull her behind our car.

"But why, Mommy?" She is staring at me with bright green eyes, full of innocence. I don't want to tell her that I want to spy on this kid. See if he's *really* who he says he is.

"Because we're playing a game," I fib.

"Oh, I love games," Lexie announces as she joyfully claps her hands together.

"Oh good," I remark absently as I peek my head around the side of the car. Now Sean is jogging past the front of our minivan.

"Hey, Dad! Wait up!"

Startled, I notice that there is a man walking about 50 yards in front of Sean, cell phone attached to his ear. In my rush to leave the house, I forgot to put my contacts in so, I can't really see him. I *assume* it is a man. It has the shape of a man. Or a woman with a lot of testosterone. But Sean called him *Dad*, so it must be a man.

So this is the famous Jason. He actually does *exist. Hmmm.*

Sean catches up with the guy and together they climb into a silver sedan.

"Come on, Lexie!" I dash to my driver's side door as I unlock Lexie's door with the key fob. It automatically opens, which is just about the only perk of the infernal minivan.

Just for the record, I loved my Altima. I did *not* want to part with it. But after the birth of a fourth child…well, let's just say Roger didn't like my idea of one of the kids riding on the roof rack.

I toss my bag into the back and pull my seat belt over my chest. Of course it sticks. I've been telling Roger he needs to get that fixed for at least a month. I tug harder as Lexie climbs in the car, still chattering away. Once she is buckled, I give up on my own belt and speed off towards the mall exit. *Yes, I'm a bad example for my kids. I should always buckle up. I know. I'm ashamed; I really am.*

"Damn it, I lost them," I mutter, my eyes scanning the parking lot for Sean and his father.

"Who did you lose, Mommy?" Lexie asks.

"Um, nobody, Lex. Nobody," I reply, embarrassed that I am chasing after my neighbor and his son, just to get a glimpse of him.

"If you mean Sean, he probably went home," Lexie pipes up as she blows on the car window and begins to trace her name in it.

Duh, Amy! Of course! He probably went home! All you have to do is get there before he does and you can see him get out of the car!

I am so pleased at Lexie's realization, that I don't even admonish her for writing on the window. I hate that. It's a bitch to clean.

Now, to get home quickly....

I take the short cut down the back roads that Sean's father probably doesn't know, being new to the neighborhood and all. I race down the side streets, blowing stop signs, nearly hitting a bicyclist and rendering Lexie speechless for once. I peek at her in the rearview mirror. She is dry heaving in the plastic bag I keep in the back for puke emergencies.

Finally, I arrive on our street, just to see Jason's car pull into the driveway. Giddy, I punch the gas, then screech to a halt in front of our house. My head nearly hits the dashboard as I realize he has pulled the car all the way up the driveway. He and Sean have their backs to my car as they climb out of their vehicle and head directly into the backyard.

Damn it! They have a back entrance!

"Wow, Mommy! I didn't know you could drive like you were in Nascar!" Lexie says, obviously impressed, despite the fact that she is still trembling from her near death driving experience.

Frowning, I maneuver into the driveway. "Yeah, well sometimes Mommy needs to get somewhere in a hurry." I throw the car into park and sigh. *How am I going to get a look at the damn guy now?*

"I bet Daddy would be impressed," Lexie is still nattering on. "He always says you drive too slow. I can't wait to tell him you can drive faster than him!" She opens the car door and as her feet hit the pavement, I leap from the minivan.

"No, Lex!" I shout. *Roger cannot know I was speeding home! He would instantly be suspicious!*

Lexie, who is skipping up the sidewalk with absolute oblivion, turns and stares at me. "Why not?"

I sigh. "Just let's not tell him, ok? Daddy gets mad if Mommy speeds. That's why I always drive slowly. I just forgot because I…" *Think of a believable lie, Amy.*

"Did you have to poop?" Lexie offers.

"Uh, what? No! Why would you ask that?" I balk at the personal question. Even though I shouldn't. I haven't been alone in the bathroom in thirteen years.

Lexie shrugs and skips ahead of me, turning a cartwheel in the middle of the sidewalk. "Can I have a cookie?" she asks, as I dig into my purse for the front door key.

"No," I mumble distractedly. "We don't even have-" And then, an idea is born. I raise my head, grinning at my daughter. "Actually, yes. Yes, you *may* have a cookie. Come on, Lexie! You're brilliant!" I exclaim as I rush up the front steps.

"I am?" she squeaks with disbelief.

"Absolutely!" I exclaim as I stick the key in the lock. "In fact, I think you may just be my favorite child."

She beams as we step into the house. "I *am*?"

I nod. "Let's go make some cookies."

I know the way to a man's heart is through food, and the way to a neighbor's living room is through cookies. I'm going to meet this Jason and I'm going to do it today.

Yup, you guessed it…Mistake #2.

~SIX~

I'm not sure what I was expecting. *Well, Amy, you shouldn't have believed Colt when he told you he knew how to crack eggs...*

Oh, I'm not even talking about the cookie making debacle. Please. I'm not new. I've made cookies with these kids before. I *do* have this reoccurring daydream that we will all work together and create delicious cookies and warm, fuzzy memories that will make me smile for years to come. It's like one of those bullshit ads you see on TV for Mother's Day. Thus far, that has not happened. In fact, I haven't been able to make a single batch of cookies without throwing out at least half of the product.

I sigh loudly, staring at the pathetic fruits of my labor and the massive mess that resulted from producing it. And by mess, I mean, flour all over the floor, egg dripping from the counter and butter smeared on the door of the fridge.

"Can I have a cookie?" Lexie asks, hopping up and down next to me. She hasn't left my side for a second. *Yah!* Evan is thankfully passed out in his high chair, Colt gave up after he got egg shells in the batter, and Allie refused to even come down to help.

I inspect the cookies on the cooling rack. Approximately half are burnt and the other half are so gooey that they are dripping through the holes of said cooling rack. It appears that approximately seven cookies are salvageable.

"Um…take one of the burnt ones," I instruct.

She wrinkles up her nose. "Ewww! That's gross!"

Grabbing a small Tupperware container I shrug. "Well then take one of the gooey ones."

"That's even grosser!"

I am barely listening as I select the few cookies that I can actually bring over to the neighbor without being mortified. *Hmmm, if I put the good ones on top and then cover the bottom with the burnt ones, they won't notice them…*

"Mommy! You're putting all the good cookies in there!" Lexie wails. "Why can't I have any? I helped you! You said if I helped you-"

"There are Oreos in the pantry behind the-"

I don't even get to finish the sentence before she hops off the counter and darts down the hall to the pantry. My children are addicted to Oreos like a drug addict is addicted to crack. *Ooo, bad analogy, Amy. With that drug ring and all.*

I snap the lid on the container and poke my head down the stairs. "Hey, Roger?"

There is no answer. I hear him snoring.

Clenching my fists at my sides, I refuse to get annoyed. Lexie can watch the boys. I'm only going to be gone a few minutes. Just long enough to get a glimpse of the new neighbor…uh, I mean, to make sure everything is on the up and up across the street.

"Lexie, watch your brothers," I instruct as I sweep through the living room. She is lounging on the sofa, shoving cookies into her mouth as she stares at the TV, eyes glazing over.

"Uh, huh," she mutters as I walk out the front door.

Great. Roger Junior in the making, I think as I cross the street and jog up the neighbors' front walk. Knocking loudly on the door, I am wondering if it was a good idea to leave Lexie with the boys. Roger was home, but you never know.

What if they get hurt? What if they choke on something? What if Evan tries to climb out of his high chair? What if Colt **does** *fall out of his treehouse?*

The door creaks open and I glance up, expecting to see Mary in one of her many velour track suits, or her husband Walter, a jolly, balding older gentleman. Instead, Sean is standing in the doorway, staring at his feet.

"Hi," he says, eyes not meeting mine.

"Hi, Sean!" I call out cheerily, with a voice too high and girlie than necessary. *Cut it out, Amy. He's not a four year old. Treat him like a normal teenager.*

"Sean, is your grandma home?" I ask. He responds with a shrug.

"I brought cookies-"

At the mention of cookies, his head whips up and he lurches forward, snatching the container from my hands. "Cookies!" He dashes off into the house leaving the front door wide open and me staring after him. He turns around the corner and is gone.

Okay, what now?

I step into the foyer of the house while gazing around. I haven't been in this house since the previous owners, Jackie and Bob Hayes, moved out last year after they got divorced. Jackie was bored when her kids went off to college. So she got a hobby. The neighbor's pool boy, Raul. Bob did not approve.

I stand in the foyer, poking my head into the sparsely decorated living room. There is a coffee table in the middle of the room, a TV on a stand in the corner and a couch along the wall opposite the TV. There are no pictures adorning the walls or shelves housing dusty knickknacks like at my house or my parents' house. Of course, *their* knickknacks aren't dusty. Heaven forbid. Only mine.

Very strange, I muse as I step towards what I believe was the kitchen. *They've lived here for three months and they haven't made the place more homey yet? There are no boxes lying around like they're still unpacking. It's not like Mary goes to work or anything...*

I step into the kitchen which seems typical, dishes in the sink and an empty pizza box sitting on top of the recycling container. But just like the living room, there's nothing that screams "we live here!" *Almost as if they're not planning on staying too long.*

A row of prescription drugs lining the counter catches my eye. I step closer to peer at them and see most of them have the pharmacy label ripped off. *Hmmm. Weird.* The only one that is actually labeled says *Sean*

Sanders. It says, *Methylphenidate. What the hell is that?* I wonder as I replace the pill bottle and notice that the others bottles have writing on the tops. *Mary am. Mary pm. Walter am. Walter pm.*

I wonder why they didn't leave the labels on them? Maybe they aren't pharmacy drugs in there, but street drugs instead?

And in my usual fashion, I find that I am arguing with myself. *Oh cut it out, Amy! This is Mary and Walter! Your sweet, elderly neighbors! Don't be crazy!*

"You read too many crime novels," I mumble to myself as I turn away from the counter to examine the rest of the room. On the table is a laptop and a stack of newspapers from neighboring towns. Casually, I peek at the headlines. "Drug Bust in Montclair School", "School Drug Ring Crack Down", and "Feds on the Hunt for School Yard Junkies". *Hmmm. Someone is certainly interested in the drug trade in schools...*

"How did you get in here?" a male voice in the doorway behind me accuses.

I am immediately on the defense as I retort, "Sean let me in." Quickly, I spin on my heel and find myself staring at a middle aged man who can only be described with the cliché phrase *devastatingly handsome.*

My examination of his features starts at his feet. My eyes work their way up his body, probing every inch of the comely stranger. He has a pair of scuffed work boots on; probably Timberlands. They cover his socks if he has any, so I notice how muscular his calves are. He has a tattoo of an eagle wrapped in an American flag that snakes up his left leg and disappears under his cargo shorts. My eyes continue to graze up his body, hastily skipping over the pubic region and settling on his torso. He's wearing a soft faded gray tee shirt that was probably once blue. There are several small pinholes in the fabric and it is tearing at the armpits because it is so form fitting around his taut biceps. Speckles of blue paint are scattered across his lightly hairy arms and the tee shirt.

My roving eyes arrive at his face and they are not disappointed in the view. He sports an angular jaw with a scant amount of dark stubble dispersed on his tanned face. His smiling mouth boasts two rows of very straight, very white teeth that were either an act of a very generous god or the work of a now well off orthodontist. His nose is unremarkable except to say it is underneath the most stunning set of crystal blue eyes I have ever had the pleasure of looking into. His dark hair is slightly shaggy, a curl flopping over his right eyebrow.

I gulp nervously, unable to speak to the man who must certainly be Jason. He is grinning at me in a mischievous way that makes me nervous and giddy at the same time. His teasing eyes seemed to say, 'hey baby, how *you* doing?' like Joey from *Friends*, and 'beware, I'm trouble' at the same time.

Our eyes lock; neither of us seeming to be able to look away. I am nearly catatonic from his stare. *Look away*, his sparkling eyes tease as they bore into mine, but I can't. There is something in his gaze that is holding me captive, almost like hypnosis. It's a sensation that is delighting and scaring the shit out of me at the same time.

Finally, the man holds out his hand and speaks. "I'm Jason, Sean's father. You must be..." he trails off, obviously expecting me to finish the statement.

Shaking his hand slowly, I find that I need to let go before I can finally speak. "Amy Maxwell. I live across the street."

Then appallingly, I start babbling in a Lexie-like fashion. "I live there with my four kids, Allie, Lexie, Colton and Evan." I pronounce their names in one run on sentence. "I'm a stay at home mom. I don't work outside of the house."

Duh, I'm sure he knows what a stay at home mom is, Amy. No need for the explanation. "Oh, and my husband, Roger. He's a principal at the high school. He lives there, too." I add Roger's qualifications as an afterthought. Jason nods appreciatively, but I can see the *get to the point already lady* look crossing his face.

"Um, but anyway, I brought cookies," I finally manage to say, beaming like an idiot.

Jason stares at me. "Really?" He raises one eyebrow, making me feel like the butter I just melted to make the cookies. "Where are they?"

"Uh, Sean took them," I stammer.

Jason shrugs. "Typical. That kid is like a Hoover vacuum." He steps into the kitchen, his body brushing past mine. He touches my arm in the process and the hairs on my arm stand on end.

He saunters over to the cabinet, opens it, and retrieves a bright blue package. Pulling open the top he removes a black and white cookie. "Good thing I prefer Oreos to homemade." He shoves the cookie in his mouth, as he offers me the package. "Oreo?" he asks, crumbs flying everywhere. I hate to admit that I am a little disgusted. The display is actually ruining the godlike image of Jason.

I put my hand up. "Uh, no thank you."

He shrugs and replaces the package in the cabinet after removing three more.

We stare at each other for another second or two before I speak. "I guess I should get going then…if Mary isn't home. I came over to see Mary," I inform him.

"And bring cookies," Jason remarks with a coy smile.

Yes, and bring cookies. Not check you out. I am a happily married woman, thank you very much. Who happens to fantasize about Raul the pool boy and Joe the bagger at Stop & Shop.

"Well, she's not here," Jason tells me as I take a step back towards the living room. "She went out. Walter, uh, my dad, took her to church."

I resist the urge to glance at my watch. But even without knowing the exact time, I am pretty certain it's a little late in the day for church. The hairs on my arm raise slightly. This time it feels more like a warning rather than a turn on.

"Sean and I had things to do, so that's why we didn't

go," he explains.

Is it my imagination or is he looking uncomfortable? Shit! What if he's got Mary and Walter tied up somewhere? Maybe he's part of the drug ring and Mary and Walter found out and threatened to turn him into the police!

My heart is racing as I reply, "Right, right. I'm sure you have a lot to do, just moving in and all. You know, like making yourself at home…" *Shut up, Amy!*

"Oh yes. I was painting," he explains, pointing to the blue splatters on his shirt.

I nod. *Painting, huh? Well, that sounds a little more like something a person would do if they were planning on staying here awhile…*

"I'll tell Mom you stopped by," Jason informs me as I stagger backwards towards the living room, reluctant to take my eyes off of him.

He's not going to kill you, Amy. Just get out of the house and mind your own business.

When we are at the front door and I whirl around, pushing at the screen. "Well, have a nice day!" I call to Jason in a sing song Lexie voice.

"I will," he replies. "I'll have Sean bring over your cookie container. That is, if you really brought cookies over and didn't just come here to snoop."

For a split second, I think he is serious, but then I notice a broad grin cross his face and he adds a wink. My face flushes and I am infuriated at the same time.

"Keep it," I practically growl as I find myself racing

down the sidewalk to get away from this vexatious man. *Why is he so damn good looking, though? It makes it impossible to hate him!* I hear the front door slam as I am considering this conundrum.

Startled, I turn. That's when I notice that all the cars are in the driveway. The nearest church is five miles away and a bit of a hike. Especially in this heat. Walter and Mary definitely did *not* go to church.

Later on, my hand is on the phone. The events of the day are weighing heavily on my mind and I want someone to reassure me there's nothing weird going on. I need to talk to a fellow neurotic and bad mommy, my buddy Laura.

"Yellow?" A small voice pipes into the phone after I dial Laura's cell phone. Anyone else would think they had the wrong number.

"Hi, Frankie. Put Mommy on please," I tell the triplet on the other end of the phone.

"Who's this?" he asks and I can tell he is chewing on something.

"It's Mrs. Maxwell." I hear the phone being tossed aside. Heavy hammering of footsteps follow. I can hear Frankie calling his mother to tell her that I'm on the line and her telling him to bring her the phone. And then...nothing.

"Didn't I tell you to bring me the phone? What's taking so long?" I hear Laura's muffled question.

"I forgot where I put the phone!" The six year old replies.

Oh crap.

"Well where did you leave it?" His mother asks with agitation.

"Here! I'm over here!" I call through the phone, hoping one of them will hear me wherever I've been tossed.

"I don't know!" Frankie wails.

"Jesus, Frankie!" Laura is definitely aggravated now.

"The phone is over here!" I continue to call out.

Evan toddles into the room just then and his eyes grow wide as he sees the phone in my hand.

"Phone!"

Evan absolutely adores babbling on the phone. I had to put all the cordless phones up high once he learned to walk because he was constantly grabbing them and pressing buttons. He called Australia once, much to my dismay. But there *is* one benefit to his phone obsession. I will hand the phone over to him whenever a telemarketer calls. He *loves* telemarketers. And they rarely ever call back after a mind boggling conversation with Evan.

I shake my head. "No phone, Evan. Mommy phone." I realize I am speaking like a moron but that's what happens when the most mental stimulation I get in a day is from *Sesame Street.*

"Hello?" Laura is breathless on the other end of the phone after finally locating it.

"Hi!" I perk up. "I'm glad I caught you…"

"Well probably not for too long because…no! Seriously put him down before you break his other elbow! Matthew! I'm *not* kidding!" I hear Laura drop the phone.

I use the time to offer Evan a soggy cookie so that he doesn't climb on the island in attempts to snatch the phone out of my hand.

"Sorry." Laura is back on the line. "Daryl is traveling for work and I swear the kids are even worse than usual. He's been gone three days and I'm ready to put the triplets on Ebay."

Three days? Geez. I had no idea. I hardly got to speak to her yesterday at Colt's party. And I can't remember the last time we uttered more than a handful of words to each other on the phone.

"Damn, Laura, that sucks. I'm sorry we didn't get to talk at the…*Evan Maxwell*!" I am temporarily distracted as Evan stomps in the dog's water bowl sending a spray of water all over the refrigerator door. It's amazing how a conversation between two moms ends up sounding like a battle between people with Tourette's.

"No big deal. I'm sorry we had to run off like that. Mason strikes again." Mason pretty much puked once a week. Laura's had him checked out numerous times and all the doctor can come up with is "nervous stomach". I don't even think that's a real thing.

"Oh yeah, is he ok?" I ask with concern.

"Of course. He stopped puking the minute he dug into the goodie bag."

Ha. Typical. I had filled goodie bags with the cheap candy that the kids loved. Beth turned her nose up at them, of course, and left them at my house.

"Ooo, and I'm sorry about my sister." This whole conversation thus far had just been one long string of apologies. It was typical of my conversations with Laura lately, each of us apologizing for our kids and their barbarian acts. Beth put a new twist on things, though.

"Oh please," Laura scoffs. "How long have I known you? You think *Beth* is going to get to me?"

"Well she gets to me and I've known her for 35 years," I point out.

"You *let* her bother you. I tell you this all the time. Who *cares* what Beth thinks?"

"It's not that I really care what she thinks. It's just the fact that she makes me feel like a crap mother…"

"Ha! If you're a crap mother than I'm a shit mother."

"You're not a shit mother. But speaking of a shit mother, guess what I did today…" I hear tinkling of glass in the background.

"Oh damn it! Frankie! Now you need to clean that up!"

There is the sound of crying and shouting followed by an abrupt, "Amy, I'll have to call you later when we get back from the emergency room!" A click and a dial tone follow. I am left with the phone in my hand and absolutely no closer to finding out if I am justified in my concerns or just a crazy, neurotic mom.

Staring at the now beeping phone in my hand, I wonder who else can assuage my fears. I can't talk to Roger because I certainly *cannot* mention how Jason's heart made me flutter in my chest even if it *is* most likely because I sense he's dangerous. Plus, Roger has already blown off my concerns.

As much as I love Joey, I won't call her, either. She doesn't have kids and won't understand the menaces I see lurking everywhere. Hell, the woman backpacked across Europe and lived in hostels without knowing a single soul. I need someone who is just as protective as I am about my kids.

Beth? No way. She will blow things even further out of proportion and somehow insult me in the process. *Mom?* I shake my head. No, she's worse than Beth and even more unreasonable if that's humanly possible. As I return the phone to its cradle, I realize I'm going to have ignore my Mommy radar that is currently blipping out of control.

~SEVEN~

The doorbell rings and I rise to answer it, smoothing down my silky, salon styled hair. I throw open the door to find Jason standing on the porch, smiling shyly. My heart flutters.

"Amy, I'm sorry to barge in on you like this, but I couldn't wait."

I glance around at the empty living room and then step out onto the porch, closing the door behind me. "It's okay," I tell him. "The kids are all in the backyard. Except for Allie. But she never comes out of her room anyway."

"And Roger?" he asks with concern.

I wave my hand in front of my face. "Roger is at school. I won't see him again until June."

His grin turns sly as he takes a step closer towards me. My fluttering heart is now racing, my breath coming fast and hard. I can feel the heat radiating from his sizzling body as his hand lightly brushes my arm.

"That's excellent," he murmurs as he leans towards my ear. "They won't even know then..." His lips graze my earlobe, sending chills throughout my body. He scoops me into his arms and I feel as if my body is melting into his like a chocolate bar.

"Oh, Jason," I sigh, as I allow his warm breath on my neck to relax me.

"I knew I had to kiss you the first moment I laid eyes

on you," he tells me, drawing me closer to his muscular body. I close my eyes and…

I race downstairs because whoever is at the door is ringing it urgently. When I reach the living room, I suck in my breath. I was literally upstairs for less than ten minutes putting Evan down for his nap yet the room looks like a small tornado touched down in that time. There are Goldfish crackers dotting the floor in Morse Code, couch cushions thrown everywhere and the dog is licking up juice that is dripping from a Sippy cup. She greets me with a half-hearted head lift in acknowledgement of the mess.

"What the hell happened here, Misty?" I ask, as her eyes say, *I told them and told them to knock it off, but they didn't listen. I just knew you'd be mad, Mom. That's why I'm taking care of this juice spill here…*

I sigh as I turn down the deafening volume on the TV that nobody is watching and I open the front door.

Sean is on the front porch bashfully staring down at his bright orange Nike cross trainers. I glance over his shoulder to see the front door of the Sanders' house close. *Was that Jason?*

Over the course of the last week, I had looked for Jason every day in vain. His car left early in the morning and came back after I went to bed. If I hadn't seen him with my own two eyes, I would wonder if he hadn't been made up.

I did notice Mary outside the last couple days,

watering her plants as usual. The few times I tried to strike up a conversation with her about Jason, she got a little flustered and made some lame excuse to go inside.

"Uh, hi, Sean," I remark casually as he thrusts my Tupperware container into my hands.

"My Grammy says to give you this," he mutters, his eyes darting around. He is craning his neck trying to see inside the house. *He probably wants to play with Colt. Should I let him?* I chew on my bottom lip. *He's harmless, Amy.*

"Do you want to come in?" I ask. "Colt is in the backyard."

His head swivels and he glances back toward his house. "I'm only supposed to drop of the cookie container," he tells me nervously. "I should ask my dad. Or Grammy. They would be worried about me if I don't ask them. They were worried when I didn't ask them last week."

I nod, relieved. "Sure. I understand." I am about to close the door when I notice a maroon colored Buick pull slowly down the street and stop in front of the Sanders' house. There are two men in the front seat wearing dark sunglasses. The man in the passenger seat nervously scans the street and then exits the vehicle when it stops completely. In addition to a briefcase in his hand, he is wearing dark tan khakis, an olive green dress shirt and a tie with colors I can't make out from the front porch. The driver makes a K turn in the middle of the street and speeds off. My interest is instantly peaked.

"I'm sure it's okay," I suddenly say to Sean while watching the man stride rapidly up the sidewalk, glancing from side to side. I pull my body flush with the door and yank Sean inside so the man can't see us. The Sanders' front door swings open without the man even ringing the bell. I can't tell who opened the door. *I really need to update my contact prescription,* I think while squinting. The man steps inside the house and disappears as the door closes behind him. "I'm sure it's okay if you hang out for a little bit," I repeat.

"Hi, Sean!" I hear Colt's perky voice behind me, which causes me to jump. "You wanna come play with me in my fort?"

Sean bobs his head. "Yeah. But I have to ask my dad. Or my Grammy."

"My mom can ask. She always makes my playdates. Right, Mom?" Colt volunteers as he gazes up at me with his big blue eyes. I cringe at the word *playdate.* It's like nails on a chalkboard.

"Sure, Colt," I respond easily without even asking him if he finished his homework. "Why don't you guys go in the backyard and have fun?"

Gee, you didn't have to twist my arm. Now I have an excuse to go across the street and have another look around. There has to be a logical explanation to all this.

Sean looks skeptical. "I don't know. I have to ask Dad…"

No! He might say no and I'll lose this opportunity to snoop, er, I mean uh, say hello and be neighborly.

I pat Sean on the shoulder because I can't reach the top of his head. "I'll go ask for you. I'm sure it's fine. Plus, it's going to be dark soon. You don't want to miss out on playing with Colt, do you?" *Translation: Roger will be home soon and I don't want him to see me snooping around.*

Sean stares at me for a moment as if he is considering my question. I impatiently wave my hand in front of my face. "Sorry, that was just a rhetorical question."

Colt wrinkles up his forehead as if he is thinking really hard. "What's a *retarical* question?"

I open my mouth to respond with "never mind", but I don't get the chance.

"A rhetorical question is a question asked merely for effect with no answer expected because the answer is obvious," Sean remarks with an expressionless affect. Colt now looks even more perplexed.

"Uh, yes, Sean. Thank you. Why don't you guys hurry along now?"

Sean still appears wary, but follows Colt as he bounds through the living room. I glance at the clock on the cable box. Evan has only been down for his nap for about ten minutes. With any luck, I have another ten minutes until he wakes up. Closing the front door quietly, I scurry down the front walk and headed straight towards Mistake #3.

Walk normally, you twit! Don't look suspicious! You're just going across the street to tell them that Sean is playing with Colt. In fact, you would just pick up the phone and call, but you don't have their phone number. This has nothing to do with the strange and suspicious acting man that just went into their house. Nothing at all.

Scampering up the front steps of the Sanders residence, I attempt to peer in the front window before ringing the bell. I stand there like an idiot for a moment before I remember that the bell is broken. I rap quietly on the door and wait for footsteps to indicate that someone is coming to answer, but I hear none.

Hmmm. That's strange. There has to be someone home. I just saw the man go inside.

I consider that maybe I need to knock louder just as I notice Roger's car pull into the driveway. He clamors out of the front seat, looking harried and haggard. His tie is hanging lifelessly from his neck, his collar askew. What's left of his hair is rumpled and his shoulders are slumped forward as he slogs up the sidewalk, briefcase hanging limply from his hand. And the school year just started.

For a second, I almost feel sorry for the guy. Then I recall how my day started and all sympathy flies out the window. Colt tied Misty to a tree and sprayed her with the hose. She thrashed around trying to escape, trampling my rose bushes and getting thorns in her paws. When I finally shut the water off and freed her, she growled at me, furious about the torture she had endured. She wouldn't let me touch her paws and limped off to the edge of the yard to lick her wounds. That was at 8 am before school.

"Roger!" I call out.

He turns to the sound of my voice, surprised to see me across the street.

"What are you doing, Amy?" he asks, perplexed expression on his face.

"I've got to let them know that Sean is playing with Colt!" I shout back. The quizzical look remains unchanged.

"Who?"

"Colt! Our son?" *Seriously Roger...*

He shoots me an exaggerated look. "Not Colt, Amy. Who is *Sean*?"

"The kid that lives across the street!" I shout back. He still looks confused. He has apparently forgotten our conversation from the other night completely.

"Typical," I mutter under my breath before shouting, "Just keep an eye on the kids!" That statement looks like it causes him an angina attack.

"Are you going to be long? I'm really hungry!"

I narrow my eyes at him. Even from across the street I know he sees my annoyance because he shakes his head and I hear him mutter, "I guess I'll get the take out menus."

I ignore him as I turn back to the door and am prepared to knock, except Mary is standing in the open doorway. I let out a little gasp and clutch my chest.

"Oh, Mary! You scared me!" I let out a nervous titter. Mary does not seem too pleased to see me.

"Hello, Amy. Can I help you?" Her clipped tone

clearly indicates that she is not the least bit interested in helping me. In fact, her voice seems to indicate that she wants me to go the hell away.

I smile brightly at her regardless. "Hi, Mary! I just wanted to let you know that Sean stopped over to bring back my container and Colt invited him to play and he wanted me to check to see if that was okay with-"

She cuts me off, nearly closing the door in my face in the process. "Yes that's fine," she snaps. "Just send him home by bedtime." The door slams, shaking the railings on the porch.

I stare at the door, my mouth gaping open. *What the heck just happened here?*

The window to the left of the porch is open and I hear a door slam from inside the house.

"Is she gone?" asks a male voice that I don't recognize. It doesn't sound like Walter and it's definitely not Jason. His voice is husky and throaty...like a country singer. This voice is just plain gruff. And rude. I can only assume the "she" he is referring to is me.

"Yes," Mary says softly. "I hate having to be so evasive all the time. Especially to Amy. She seems so nice."

"Don't start with the whole "seems so nice" bit. You can't trust anyone. You can't let your guard down. You *know* what happens when you let your guard down," the gruff voice remarks. "Need I remind you about Stacey?"

"I know, I know," Mary replies. It sounds as if she is about to cry.

"What are we going to do about this problem?" asks the owner of the deep voice.

"I really think we need to make a move before everyone gets suspicious. Jason said that Amy was snooping around in our kitchen last week," Mary replies. My chest constricts, making it difficult to breathe. I feel light headed and faint. *Why are they talking about me?*

And then, I hear shuffling and scraping, like furniture being moved. *What are they doing in there? What is going on?*

I am certain that the answer to the mystery that plagues me can only be answered by finding out what's going on in that room, I glance down the street and can see that there is nobody around so I swing one leg over the railing in order to get closer to the house and possibly look in the window. I grab onto the shutter and pull myself into a standing position. *Standing on the railing now, Amy? Yeah. I know. Totally unsafe. I would be having a cow if I caught Colt doing this.*

There is a light on in the room. Curtains flutter in the window, obscuring my view, but I can see there is a desk with a computer on it in front of the window. *Probably a home office or something like that*, I am thinking as I hear the sound of throat clearing.

The hairs on my neck prickle as I realize the sound is coming from outside. I slowly turn my head towards the sidewalk. Standing there with a scowl on his face and his muscular arms crossed over his chest, is one pissed off Jason.

"What exactly are you doing, Mrs. Maxwell?" he asks, his piercing blue eyes staring into mine as I try to avert his gaze.

My mind is scrambling to come up with a plausible excuse. *Our cockatoo got out and flew into your shrub? My kids threw a Frisbee and it landed on your roof? I'm spying on your mother and her strange guest?*

"I, uh…" I stammer. Jason's scowl deepens, the worry lines on his forehead furrowing severely.

"Please get down, Mrs. Maxwell," he commands.

Biting my lip, I grab onto the railing and find that I am stuck. Well, I'm not stuck, per se, but I just realized I am about fifteen feet in the air and oh yeah, I'm scared of heights. I am pretty sure I am going to go crashing to the ground which will result in cuts and bruises and maybe even a few broken bones.

One time when I was about twelve years old, we went to a BBQ at a neighbor's house. The boy I had a huge crush on at the time (Anthony Everest) was there and he and a few of his friends were climbing trees. Most of the other girls were on the ground squealing and squeaking like dumb girls seeking male attention do. I was determined to have Anthony notice me, so I scrambled up the tree right behind the boys. They were actually impressed. Until I realized, I was so far off the ground that it paralyzed me with fear. I sat in the tree for a half hour sobbing like a maniac while the boys laughed at me until my father finally took pity on me and got a ladder. The boys never let me live it down, calling me

Amy the Ape for years. One of them even wrote "Dear Amy the Ape, how's it hanging?" in my high school yearbook.

This was exactly like that situation. I had taken a leap before I considered the consequences. And now I was going to look like an ass in front of my, oh so gorgeous, maybe a criminal, maybe just a good guy, neighbor. And I have a feeling he is not going to let me live it down either.

"Come on," Jason sighs as he reaches his hand out to me.

I stare at it, unwilling to accept his help. "Um…"

He rolls his eyes. "I'm not going to hurt you. Just let me help you down from there before you fall and break something."

I glance around and see that Jason is my only hope. Reluctantly, I reach my arm out to him. He grips my elbow with one hand and tucking his other hand underneath my butt, he sweeps me off my feet, climbs down the stairs, and lowers my trembling body to the ground.

Stop shaking! I command myself. But I don't know if I'm shaking from Jason's touch, what I just overheard or the fact that I am completely and utterly mortified right now.

Jason lets out a sigh after he sets me back down on solid ground. "Mrs. Maxwell, you're going to get hurt," he advises me, but I am staring at the ground. Ants are racing towards a crust of bread that has been discarded on the sidewalk.

"Yeah, I don't usually climb railings" I mutter, pushing at the crust with my toe. *Where is an earthquake to swallow up your street when you need one? Or a freak tornado?*

I feel Jason's fingers on my chin as he lifts my face so I can see his eyes. They are serious and foreboding, silently pleading with me. "That's not what I'm talking about and you know it. Please promise me you'll mind your own business? And worry about your *own* family?"

My neck snaps to attention at the mention of my family. *Was that a threat?*

"What do you mean?" I stammer, trying to insert malice in my tone and fail miserably.

Jason shakes his head. "Just stay on your side of the street and everyone will be fine, ok?" His soft look leaves his face and it is replaced by a foreboding expression. He pivots on his heel and heads around the back of the house, leaving me completely undone on the sidewalk.

~

The only thing bruised is my ego as I munch on my slice of pizza later that evening. Jason's "threat" fresh in my mind, I am gazing around the table at my family with trepidation. We are sitting at the kitchen table, having a nice family dinner. Well, *I'm* having dinner. My *family* is all in various stages of participating in dinner.

Roger has been done with his food for a while, but he's sitting at the table with the iPad, scrolling through his work emails. He is guzzling his beer with fervor. Occasionally he slaps his forehead with his palm and mutters stuff about morons and imbeciles. I can tell it's going to be a *long* school year.

Lexie has her doll propped up on the table and she is pretending to feed it little bites of her food while speaking to it in a teensie weensie baby voice.

The real baby is sitting in his high chair smearing pizza sauce in his hair. I sigh as I watch him. I guess another bath is in the near future. That will be his third for the day.

Colt is asleep, face in his pizza. I guess starting off your day aggravating your mother at the butt crack of dawn will do that to a kid.

Allie isn't even eating with us, but is nonetheless giving me new cause for worry. Earlier I rapped on her door to tell her that the pizza was here and she replied with, "Go away!" in a gravelly voice.

Immediately I thought, *did she just wake up or is she smoking? That sounds like a smoker's voice. And what is she smoking? Cigarettes? Pot? Crack?*

I cautiously sniffed the door, hoping none of the other kids walked by and though I had completely lost my marbles. I didn't *smell* smoke.

That doesn't prove anything, Amy. Don't be one of those naïve moms that say "oh, not my kid". Allie's smart. She's probably hanging out the window. Just like you used to do.

"Come on, Allie," I pleaded. "We have company;

you have to eat with us."

I heard a cough, a thud, and the window slamming. *God damn it, she* was *hanging out the window smoking!*

"Allie?" I had my ear pressed up against the door at that point.

"In a minute!" she called out as I heard the distinct sound of air freshener being sprayed. I clenched my right fist at my side, preparing for battle.

No, I am not going to start screaming at her about this. I have lost her enough; I don't need to push her farther away. I will be calm and rational and not...

Then, she poked her head out the bedroom doorway, only opening the door a crack so I could not see inside. "Who?" she asked suspiciously, raising her eyebrow.

I sniffed the air before answering her. I could smell the faint nicotine odor that I had gotten very friendly with in my teen years. *Do not flip out, do not flip out...* my brain is shrieking.

But as I've learned in my 35 years on this planet, my mouth rarely listens to my brain. "Are you smoking in there?" I accused, waggling my finger at her in a very mother-like fashion.

Allie flushed and snapped, "No!"

"Don't lie to me, Allie," I warned as I pushed my way into her room.

"I'm not lying," she stammered as she stumbled backwards, tripping over the edge of her throw rug.

"I smoked when I was 15. I know what's going on here. I'm not stupid."

"You must be, because I'm *not* smoking," Allie growled at me as she kicked her desk chair over in anger.

"Allie," I replied sternly and evenly. "Please tell me the truth. It's worse if you lie about it." *See, Amy, you can be calm. Breathe in through your nose, out through your mouth. Just like yoga...*

Allie rolled her eyes which were heavily lined with black eye liner. "*Please*, you should talk about lying," she scoffed as arranged herself cross legged on her bed.

Bewildered, I asked, "What did *I* lie about?"

"You said we had company..."

"We do. Colt's friend, Sean. He could use some friends his own age..."

Yes. Sean was still with us. I had to assume his father and grandmother wanted him back at some point in time, but when Jason had chased me off the front porch, he had made no mention of his son. Maybe it was just safer for him at our house so I was keeping him until someone came to look for him.

"Oh, *that* weirdo that was hanging around with Colt? What do I care about *him*?" Allie wrinkled up her nose and I craned my neck. *Is that a small hole for a piercing?*

"He's a nice boy..." I started to say when Allie groaned.

"Ugggh, Mother. I don't need to come downstairs and hang out with a *nice boy*."

"Hey!" I barked, suddenly maternal towards Sean. "This isn't just about you, Princess. Sean is going to be new at your school this year. He's in your grade and he could use a few friends…"

"I don't need any more *friends*, Mother. And I certainly don't need a *freshman* boy as a friend." She rolled her eyes as she flopped down on her pillow. I'm starting to wonder how many eye rolls her eyeballs can handle in one conversation before they fall out of her head or she gives herself a migraine.

"Oh well, *excuse me*," I couldn't fight back the sarcasm in my tone. "Freshman boys not mature enough, Miss Big Britches? What's the matter? They can't buy you cigarettes?" *Or drugs*, I wanted to add.

Allie bolted upright and stared me down, anger flashing in her blue robin's egg speckled eyes that I used to think were the most beautiful on the planet. She picked up a notebook and hurled it in my direction, "Fuck you," she said evenly. "Get out of my room. I hate you."

"*Allie…*" my voice warned but I could see it was to no avail as she shoved her earbuds in her ears and cranked her ipod up higher. I toyed with the idea of taking it away, but I am trying not to push her away any more than I already have. Because now I have to find out if she's smoking…or worse.

So an hour later, I now have three awake kids at the table (one of which is not even mine), one asleep child and a husband who has mentally checked out for the evening when the doorbell rings. Misty starts barking like a lunatic, which is odd because Misty hardly ever acknowledges anyone at the door. She is the worst guard dog ever. She never barks when anyone comes to the house, but acts like a maniac whenever someone leaves because she is a herding dog and it upsets her when people leave.

"Roger? Can you get the door?" I ask because I am now wrestling with Evan, trying to get him out of the high chair without wearing the sauce from his grubby little hands. I am wearing my favorite tee shirt; a faded number from my first Bon Jovi concert.

"Mmm hmmm." He doesn't even glance up from the iPad. The doorbell rings again, followed by a knock.

"Roger?" I am getting exasperated. Evan is smearing sauce on my bare arms and giggling. I need to wash him up before setting him down or the "clean" house will have red handprints everywhere.

Ha ha. Clean house. That's a funny joke, Amy.

Roger is not even acknowledging me as I see his eyes quickly scanning an email. He groans audibly. The doorbell is ringing urgently now.

"Hey, Roger," I purr, trying to get him to look up. "I'm naked over here."

I know I've lost him completely because he mutters, "That's nice," as Lexie stares at me wide eyed and Sean giggles. *Shit. I forgot they were there.*

"No you're not, Mom," Lexie points out. "You clearly have clothes on. Naked means no clothes."

"Thank you, Lexie," I mutter. Sighing, I swing the baby onto my hip. *Might as well forget about salvaging this shirt*, I think to myself, as Evan spreads sauce all over my left boob. *Twenty two years. We had a good run.*

The doorbell ringing is now accompanied by frantic knocking and Misty leaping five feet in the air in front of the door, yap, yap, yapping away. Whoever is on the other side of the door clearly does not have the Misty stamp of approval.

I flick on the porch light and peer through the frosted glass. On the other side of the door stands none other than my good friend Jason.

"Damn it," I mutter as I try to smooth my hair down. Evan takes that as a signal to yank on it. Hard.

Why are you even bothering to make yourself presentable, Amy? The man caught you swinging on the side of his house like Spiderman. I'm pretty sure you are done with any chance of him seeing you as anything other than a looney neighbor. And what does it matter? You're married, remember? To the man that is one room away.

I swing the door open and Misty lets out a low guttural growl. Slobber is dripping on my bare feet.

"Hi, Mrs. Maxwell," Jason remarks with a smile. "I've come to pick up Sean." He continues to beam at me, ignoring the rabid nineteen pound attack dog at my heels. I swallow hard, waiting for him to bring up my earlier gaffe.

"Uh, sure." I cock my head towards the kitchen and call out, "Sean! Your dad is here!" I turn back to Jason and explain, "I'd let you in, but Misty wouldn't like that at all." As if to prove my point, Misty lurches forward slightly, teeth bared, but Jason remains stationary.

"That's fine," he says, smile not leaving his face. "So

how was *your* day?"

I stare at him, mouth open. *How was my day? How was* my *day? He's kidding, right? Is he just making small talk or is he screwing with me? Or is he really so crazy that he's forgotten?*

His expression is that of a poker face so I am inclined to believe the latter is the case. Until I see the slight curl of a smirk on his lips and a subtle wink.

Why that maddening man... I want to lean forward and deck him but Sean brushes past me just then.

"Hi, Dad!" he calls out cheerfully.

Jason beams at his son. "Hey, Bud! Did you have fun?"

Sean bobs his head up and down. "Yeah, lots! Colt got this really cool pair of binoculars for his birthday and we took it up to his tree house and..." He is practically stumbling over his words with excitement.

Jason chuckles as he tousles Sean's hair. "Ok, ok, you can tell me all about it but you need to thank Mrs. Maxwell first."

Sean raises his hand but doesn't look at me. "Thank you Mrs. Maxwell." He hops down our front steps, still chattering excitedly to Jason. Jason offers me a wave and maybe it's just the lighting on the porch, but I swear he winks at me again, causing my blood to boil. And then he whispers something that makes that blood run cold.

"Remember what I said earlier about your family, Mrs. Maxwell. Keep an eye on them. Especially that oldest one. You wouldn't want anything to happen to her, would you?"

Then he turns and leaves me standing on my porch, mouth wide open, his menacing words echoing in the night.

~EIGHT~

It's a beautiful fall evening; the breeze is swirling the curtains as I step into my darkened bedroom, ready to change into my pajamas for the night.

I pull my dresser drawer open and select a nightgown, placing it on the bed as the gentle wind ruffles the sheets. It feels delicious on my warm skin as I pull my sweat soaked tee shirt over my head. I toss it in the hamper and tug off my shorts. I am now standing in the bedroom in my bra and underwear, my arms tucked behind my head, enjoying the breeze.

I close my eyes, soaking in the peaceful feeling and when I open them, I notice a shadowy figure moving in the window across the street.

Curious, I step closer to the window, the curtains billowing around my half naked body. I gaze across the street, squinting to make out the figure in the window. I reach for the pair of binoculars that I have confiscated from Colt and peer inside.

Startled, I nearly drop the binoculars as I realize that it is Jason! He is watching me change!

I take a step backwards intending to cover myself up quickly. But then I hesitate.

"Wait a minute, Amy..." I begin to converse with myself. "He wants a show? You should give him a show." This is the first man who has wanted to see me naked in ages. Roger doesn't count...he just wants sex.

I stare straight ahead, knowing Jason can see me and that I am aware he is watching. His binoculars do not move. I feel incredibly powerful as I reach behind my body and unhook my bra with one swift move. I lick my lips seductively as I arch my eyebrows and hook my thumbs into the top of my panties, slowly tugging them down my body. I know that Jason is across the street, fighting the urge to…

My body jerks awake and I gasp audibly. It takes me a moment, but I realize that I am in my bed, tangled in the sheets and a sweaty mess. Glancing around, my face flushes in my darkened bedroom. Roger is snoring softly in the bed next to me, none the wiser of my erotic dream.

*Well, you can hardly blame yourself, Amy. After being sleep deprived for so long, your imagination has to be in overdrive…*I attempt to reason with myself as I squint to read the time on the bedroom clock. The angry red numbers announce that it is 4:41 am.

I sigh as I heave my exhausted body out of bed. The last week has been a nightmare. After Jason's comments, I've been hyper-vigilant about my children, almost to the point of insanity. Allie wanted to sleep over her new friend Victoria's house the other day but I wouldn't let her. I insisted everyone sleep over our house and I regretted it.

As I pull my robe around my body and pad down the hall to peek in on the children, I recall the events of Saturday night and Mistake #4 which may or may not have contributed to the domino effect of subsequent "Mistakes".

"*Please*, Mother, can't you get rid of him?" Allie had whined while peering through the curtains, waiting for the guests of her sleepover party. Colt and Sean were wrestling in the living room. I wasn't sure if she meant Colt or Sean until she continued, "Don't you think it's weird that *boy* hangs around Colt all the time? It's embarrassing," she hissed as the doorbell rang. She tossed her silky hair over her nearly bare shoulder as she dashed off to open the door. I had been begging her for weeks to ditch the shoulder baring shirts, but thus far my requests had gone largely unheeded. "I mean, it's 7:00 on a Saturday night. Why isn't he with his own friends?"

"Probably because he doesn't *have* any of his own friends," Allie's new BFF Victoria had offered with a snort and a giggle. She was perched in the corner on my chair, rocking back and forth. I was seething with fury. That was *my* rocking chair.

That was the first time I had officially met Victoria. She had glided into my living room with her pierced navel clearly visible because her tee shirt was obviously purchased in the toddler section. Her hair was that same black color Allie's had been before I dragged her to the salon to get it lightened and I instantly realized that this girl was most likely responsible for the jet black dye job to begin with.

"That's really not nice, Victoria," I had admonished with annoyance. Sean could have heard her. He *didn't,* but that was beside the point. Someone needed to teach that girl some manners. Obviously her own mother wasn't doing the job.

Just then, another one of Allie's friends waltzed through the doorway, a blonde girl named Nikki or Nitti or something like that. I couldn't really hear what Allie said because all three girls immediately dashed up to Allie's room.

Startled, I called after Allie, "Hey! Don't you want to wait for Kaitlyn?"

The two other girls stared at my daughter who was turning an interesting shade of maroon.

"*Kaitlyn?*" Victoria squeaked, covering her mouth. "Really?"

Allie's eyes widened as she replied, "Um, Kaitlyn's not coming, Mother." Her annoyed/sarcastic voice victoriously cut through the nervous stammer. Then she spun on her heel and joined the other two witches of the coven, er, I mean girls, and headed into her bedroom complete with door slam.

Now, I guess I should have left well enough alone, but as you have realized by now, I try to fix things and sometimes to a fault.

Of course I picked up the phone just then and called Laura.

"Hello?" she answered breathlessly after about seventeen rings.

"Hey, what are you up to?" I asked casually.

"Oh God, I made the mistake of cleaning out the

triplets' toy box while Daryl took them to a birthday party. I have now filled nine garbage bags with crap. And by garbage bags, I mean those giant contractor sized ones. What's up?" I smiled to myself as I could almost see her pushing away that one blonde curl that constantly flops over her eye. Luckily for Laura, her beauty was effortless.

"What's Kaitlyn doing tonight?" I inquired.

I heard Laura snort on the other end. "Besides being holed up in her lair painting her fingernails black and sticking pins in a Mommy voodoo doll?"

I resisted the urge to commiserate simply because I was on a mission. Kaitlyn and Allie had been friends for way too long and I *liked* Kaitlyn. I *liked* her mother. I *liked* her family. I *knew* her family. All qualities I could not attribute to the Witches of Eastwick that were now in Allie's room.

"Allie's having a few friends from school sleep over. She forgot to text Kaitlyn and…" *Insert plausible lie here…* "she couldn't find her phone so I'm calling to invite her over."

Laura perked up. "You don't want a set of twins, too, do you?"

Half an hour later, Kaitlyn was on my doorstep.

"Hi, honey," I remarked warmly as she brushed past me, heading towards Allie's bedroom. She let out a grunt of recognition.

Sighing, I waved to Laura in her sapphire blue minivan, parked at my curb. The passenger window lowered as I stepped onto the sidewalk.

"Hey, you!" I called out, waving enthusiastically to my long lost friend.

"Hey yourself," she replied, leaning towards the window. "What's up?"

I leaned on the car, poking my head in the window. Laura's minivan was completely devoid of children. "Wow," I remarked with a low whistle. "How did you manage to escape?"

Laura gave me a sly grin. "Told Daryl I needed to run to the grocery store and he either had to watch the kids or go himself."

I nodded with understanding. "Ah, the old grocery store trick." Men hate the grocery store and avoid it like the plague.

"Hey, it's the closest I'm getting to a vacation any time soon," Laura pointed out.

"I hear ya." Then I recalled that I've wanted to talk to her for several days. I was still shaken up about Jason's comment. I glanced at his house just as he pulled up to the curb in his sedan.

I cast my eyes downward as he jumped from the front seat and slammed his car door, praying he wouldn't notice me. For the past week he had been cordial whenever he saw me, but there was a weird uncomfortableness lingering in the air. It almost felt like that calm that comes before a summer storm; that electricity that you can almost taste in the atmosphere.

"Dear Lord in heaven, who is *that*?" Laura

practically purred as she lowered her window to get a better look. "He is *scrumptious*."

I felt my face heating up. Jason did look particularly tasty in a pair of track shorts that hugged his rounded bottom and a tee shirt cut off at the sleeves. His hair was messy and tussled and I could make out the faint outline of a sweat stain on his shirt. I bet he had been at the gym. "Um, that's Jason. Our new neighbor."

Laura raised her eyebrows. "The old people moved out?"

I shook my head, realizing I never even got to tell my friend about my run ins with Jason. "No, that's their son. Sean's father."

"Sean?" Laura gave me an odd look.

"Oh, I never told you about Sean? He's the kid who lives across the street."

"Wait a minute," Laura kicked off her flip flop and pulled her leg underneath her butt, getting comfy. "How many people live across the street?"

"Apparently four," I replied with a shrug. "But who the hell knows, people keep showing up all the time."

Laura raised her eyebrows. "Weird."

I bobbed my head enthusiastically. "I know." I glanced around looking for one of my wayward children and then climbed in the car when I saw the coast was clear. Sean had left shortly after the sleepover guests arrived. Evan and Colt were asleep. Hopefully Lexie was zonked out in front of the TV with her doll.

"The whole thing is really suspicious, Laur," I

whispered. "I can't put my finger on it, but that Jason is acting weird. Like really strange behavior."

Laura's face lit up at the prospect of gossip. "Ooo, is he like a neighborhood gigolo?"

"No!" I yelped. "Not like that." And then I considered this possibility for about six seconds before I gulped and continued, "I think it's drug related."

Laura's brown eyes nearly pop out of her head. "Oh my God, I can't believe you said that." She grips my arm, her nails digging into my skin. "Amy, I'm really worried about Kaitlyn! Maybe that's her problem! Drugs! I haven't said anything to Daryl and-"

I could feel a chill course through my body just then. "What makes you think she's into drugs?" I asked cautiously. Kaitlyn and Allie were best friends. If Kaitlyn was into drugs, chances are, so was Allie.

Laura loosens her grip and runs her fingers through her hair. "Not any *one* thing. She's just been so unsociable and moody…"

Sighing with relief, I repeated the mantra that other mothers of teens (and Roger) had drilled into my head. "That's just teenagers, Laura."

My friend shook her head. "No. It's more than that. She doesn't want to *do* anything. Maybe she's depressed or something. I had to practically drag her over here tonight."

"Really?" *Wait a minute…Allie hadn't invited Kaitlyn and Kaitlyn hadn't wanted to come? That was certainly strange. What was going on here?*

The answer to that question was answered about three heartbeats later when my front door slammed and Kaitlyn, complete with overnight bag slung across her chest, came storming out of the house with an audible huff. She marched down my front lawn and pulled open the sliding door to the minivan. Her face was flushed and unreadable as she crossed her arms over her chest.

"Just drive," she mumbled angrily to her mother as she slumped down in her seat.

Laura and I stared at each other for a second.

"What's wrong, honey?" Laura asked in a motherly fashion.

"I don't want to talk about it," she growled, anxiously picking at her fingernails. I knew this was a nervous habit of Kaitlyn's.

"Did something happen between you and Allie?" I inquired with concern.

"I *said*, I don't want to talk about it!" Kaitlyn answered with a screech.

Laura shot me an apologetic look as I climbed out of the car. "I guess I'll go speak with Allie," I whispered.

"I don't want to *ever* talk to her again!" Kaitlyn shouted as her mother turned the key in the ignition. It was my turn to shoot her an apologetic look as she drove off with her pouting teenager. I wondered what my daughter had done to insult her best friend.

With apprehension, I approached Allie's bedroom door. I heard the vulgar music blaring from within and it made me cringe. "Al?" I rapped on her bedroom door timidly. No response. "Allie?" I knocked louder, this time I was met by the sound of the stereo being cranked up, Allie's typical passive aggressive "I'm not answering you" move.

Agitated, I attempted to turn the handle of the door and the knob came off in my hand. *Damn it!*

"Allie!" I thumped loudly on the door with my fist. "Open this *fucking* door!" Mid pound, the door swung open. Allie was standing before me with her eyes even more heavily made up than usual. She seriously looked like she had face planted on a Macy's makeup counter.

"What!" she shouted. It was more like an exclamation rather than a question.

"Why did Kaitlyn leave?" I can see the other two girls huddled over something on the bed. A mirror. *Shit, they better not be snorting coke!* I craned my neck and sighed with relief when I realized they were applying glitter around their eyes.

Victoria's head bobbed up just then. One eyelid looked like the Little Mermaid meets Vegas Showgirl. "That *loser?*" she remarked with a menacing laugh. "*Please!* Allie would never been seen with the likes of *her.*" Her answer was followed up by a giggle from the other girl, whatever the hell her name was.

I stared at my daughter whose facial expression is a mixture of horror and embarrassment. "Allie, what is she talking about?"

Allie rolled her eyes. "*Duh*, Mother. Kaitlyn is a dweeb. We don't hang out with dweebs." The other girls laughed as Allie preceded to slam the door in my perplexed face.

Two days later, I am now staring at that same door at 5:00 in the morning, tempted to creep in and wake her up and demand that she explain why she has tossed off a childhood friend of almost ten years for the likes of Victoria and Nikki. Something is definitely not right with my teen and I recall Jason's chilling words as I wrap my robe tighter around my waist and head down the stairs to make a cup of coffee.

I nearly trip over the dog who manages to tangle herself up under my feet as I enter the kitchen.

"Damn it, Misty," I mutter as I open the French doors, allowing her to head out to the backyard. It's a crisp morning, but not as chilly as I had anticipated. Over the horizon, I see the sun is starting to creep up. I've always wanted to watch the sun rise, so I finish brewing my coffee and then head out to the front porch.

The wicker rocker groans in protest as I lower my body onto it and lean back, closing my eyes to enjoy the early morning breeze. It's supposed to be a scorcher later on, so I am appreciating the pre-dawn relief as I sip my coffee gingerly. Dawn has always been my favorite time of day, when anything seemed possible and problems seemed inconsequential.

As I sigh, I open my eyes and glance across the street noticing there is a light on in the front bedroom. A shadowy figure passes in front of the window and based on size and build, I am guessing that it is Jason.

Suddenly, the curtains part slightly and I can see that it is definitely Jason. *With a pair of binoculars*. He pokes the binoculars against the glass and is focusing on something across the street. My pulse quickens as I remember my dream and consider the possibility that I may be psychic. But then I realize, our blinds are closed and I'm certain he wouldn't be watching Roger in bed anyway. I am wondering what he is looking at until I realize, Allie's bedroom is on that side of the house! *Is he looking inside my daughter's bedroom?*

I cover my mouth with my hand and try not to make any noise as I watch my neighbor adjust the zoom on his binoculars. *Shit! He's trying to look in the window!*

Seething inside, I leap to my feet and dash into the house, not even caring if he has seen me. I take the steps inside two at a time rushing to Allie's room.

Of course, the door is locked as usual. I jiggle the knob and rap lightly on the door. "Al?" I whisper, hoping not to wake up any other family members.

"Whatcha doing, Mommy?"

I nearly leap out of my skin as I discover Lexie standing next to me, hidden in the shadows.

"Jesus, Lex! Stop sneaking up on me like that!" I squeal in shock.

Her lip quivers as I can see she is contemplating whether to cry or not. Her mind is evaluating whether crying or *not* crying would be more beneficial for her in this particular situation.

She opts for the crying. "I'm sorry, Mommy! I just

wanted to say *good morning*!" She is now wailing.

Oh good Lord.

Lexie's cries solicit screeching from across the hall in Evan's bedroom.

"Damn it," I mutter staring at Allie's bedroom door. *I'll check on her in a few minutes.* I shuffle towards the fire engine like noise. Soon the whole house will be up.

Evan is standing in his crib, hair sticking up in adorable blonde tufts around his head. "Good morning Mr. Sleepyhead," I coo, attempting to calm him before he gets too carried away. I scoop him into my arms. He smells like poop. I sigh audibly. I might as well get him ready for the day now.

Allie's door creaks open and I hear her bark, "Get out of my way, brat." I can only assume she is talking to Lexie. I need to hurry up and change this diaper so I can dash into her room and pull the shade down.

As I plop Evan on the changing table, Lexie appears at my elbow.

"I need to go to the bathroom and Allie has been in there for like an hour!" Lexie moans. *Ok, cue the dramatic over-exaggeration. Allie has been up for all of thirty seconds.*

I suck on my teeth. I have been asking Roger to put in another bathroom for two years now. We have the half bath downstairs that the kids refuse to use because it smells like Roger. In the mornings, it's mass chaos around here with the one shower.

"Use the downstairs bathroom, Lexie," I tell her.

"But I need to take a shower!" she whimpers.

"Then you'll have to wait for your sister to come out," I tell her flatly.

"Why is she in there so long?" Lexie whines.

"I don't know, honey. Maybe she's just having girl issues," I manage to mumble.

"Does she have her *period*?" Lexie inquires in her usual sing song manner.

Alarmed, I spin around. "Uh, I don't know," I stutter nervously. Yes, I know she is ten, but Lexie is my dumb naïve child. As far as I knew, she doesn't have any clue about periods, boobs or puberty. I want her to stay a baby for a little longer! I was praying that adolescence would remain at bay for at least another year or two, but someone up there obviously was a comedian. *Ooo, give her two girls going through puberty at the same time! We can pull up our chairs and watch this sitcom unfold!*

"That might be why she's so cranky," Lexie volunteers.

I eye her suspiciously. "Why do you say that?"

"Oh, because Gigi told me that she gets soooo cranky when she has her period," Lexie informs me. That explains it. Gigi is our babysitter and is probably *more* than experienced in the sagas of a worldly woman. Heaven only knows what misinformation and gory details she has filled Lexie in on. I will have to remember to speak with her about that the next time she babysits. But then after our last disastrous date, that might be around the time when Lexie is actually in college.

"Oh, well. That happens sometimes I guess," I shrug indifferently. I am sooooo not in the mood for the puberty discussion as I unleash the toxic scent by undoing the Velcro attached to Evan's diaper.

Lexie doesn't even flinch as she asks, "But why?"

"But why, *what*?" I blindly feel around on the shelf for the wipes as I attempt to keep Evan still. Changing a shitty diaper should be an Olympic sport in my opinion. I'd get a gold medal for sure after having four kids. I think you should get points added to your score if you can manage it without getting crap on any part of your body or clothes. And pee in the face is an automatic deduction of ten points.

Lexie hands me the wipes and clarifies her question, "Why does she get cranky? Is she sad that she's bleeding? I get sad when I bleed, too, but I cry. I don't think I get cranky." *Oh geez. She's still on the period question.*

"I cry, too. But for joy," I mumble, my mind racing to come up with a decent answer for my inquisitive child. Despite the fact Roger had gotten snipped right after Evan's birth at my insistence (I believe I withheld sex for two months before he did it), I still held my breath once a month waiting for blood on the toilet paper and usually thanked the Lord profusely when it happened. Once I was in a stall at Chuck E. Cheese and my period had been late. I believed that time I praised God, Buddha *and* Allah…loudly. I got a round of applause from another mother in the stall next to mine. She was in there with her three kids under the age of four.

"But why? Why do you cry for joy?" Lexie asks, handing me a diaper.

I groan. I really do not have the stamina for the birds and bees conversation with my youngest daughter who would undoubtedly ask "why?" at least three hundred and sixty two times during the lecture. This would be a conversation best had over milk and cookies when I am calm and relaxed. And have a bottle of wine already on board.

"It's hard to explain, Lexie," I tell her as I finish affixing the squirming toddler's diaper to his squishy bottom.

"Can you try?" she probes as I lift Evan from the changing table and set him down on the floor. His diaper falls off and he pees on my foot. Groaning, I reach for a towel to mop up my foot while thinking, *there goes my perfect score.*

"Mom?" Lexie is still standing there waiting for my detailed explanation on why hormones make women want to stab someone or bawl their eyes out. My head is throbbing. Evan squats on the floor and poops on the rug.

"No, Lexie. I can't. Not right now. Later. Go get ready for school," I hiss with aggravation as I reach for some baby wipes and quickly throw a diaper on the baby.

"But I have to shower!" she howls as I pull a onsie over Evan's head. Tears are forming in Lexie's stormy eyes and I can see the dam is ready to burst. Her lip quivers as she indignantly stomps off towards her room. I am met by another slamming door. *Another teenager in the works. Perfect.*

I suck in my breath as I tell myself, *it's just a phase, it's just a phase*. The problem is, all of my kids are going through a *phase*.

I sling Evan on my hip and quickly pad out into the hall. Peeking into Allie's room, I can see that her shade is down and curtains closed.

I breathe a sigh of relief as I realize that Jason was not peering into my teenaged daughter's bedroom after all.

I'm so relieved that I don't even consider what he was actually looking at.

~NINE~

A week later, it is a crisp and clear fall morning. Typical Indian summer days will most likely follow in the next few weeks, but for now, I have to fight the kids to wear jackets on mornings like this. This particular morning, it is 45 degrees and sunny, so the kids are under the impression that sun equals warm. It is on this day that I will be making fateful Mistakes #5, #6 *and* #7. Which are probably the most important ones.

This morning as I sent the kids off to school, Allie was sulking because she claimed she has a headache and wanted to stay home. Roger dragged her to the car, muttering that he was late for a meeting, leaving me with Lexi chattering excitedly about her class trip to the police station and Colt kicking the back of my seat the whole ride to school.

After I pull into the parking lot of the elementary school, Lexie flies out of the car, practically slamming the door in her brother's face while he reluctantly attempts to climb out of the God forsaken minivan. He is *not* a happy camper this morning.

"What's the matter, Colt?" I ask as his hand is poised on the car door handle. I crane around to look at him and notice that Evan is passed out in his car seat. *Typical. The kid manages to fit his cat naps in while I am driving a car and unable to do anything else with my time.*

Colt slumps dramatically against the seat. I wonder if

he has been taking lessons from his sisters. Soon, he'll be swooning.

"I wish Sean was in *my* school," he tells me. "Allie's lucky that Sean is in *her* school. She can see him whenever she wants."

I'm pretty sure Allie did not consider herself lucky. She clearly detested Sean, a fact she made no qualms about. Every time she saw him at our kitchen table doing homework with Colt or prancing around the backyard pretending to be whatever cartoon character Colt wanted him to be, she would roll her eyes and suck her teeth with annoyance. Allie made it perfectly clear that she was not interested in a friendship of any sort with Sean. I thought we had taught her to be understanding of the differences in people, but apparently, impressing *Victoria* with her lack of tolerance was much more important than being a nice person.

At least, I think we did an okay job with Colt as evidenced by his desire to have his friend in school with him. He doesn't care that Sean is a little on the odd side or he is more than twice his age.

I try to reason with my son. "Colt, I'm glad you enjoy playing with Sean and all, but I'm sure there are plenty of children in your class that are just as fun as Sean..."

"No," Colt interrupts. "There's nobody in my school who wants to play with me at recess."

My heart instantly sinks.

"What makes you think nobody wants to play with

you?" I ask, doubt creeping into my voice. Colt had a tendency, as did the rest of my children, to err on the side of exaggeration. I am hoping that this is one of those instances.

"Because Jimmy told all the other kids that I'm a dork because I play with Sean," Colt scoffs, as he resumes kicking the back of my car seat.

My blood begins to boil. Jimmy is the kid next door. The son of Cammi, of fake boob fame. *Damn Jimmy!* I guess he felt slighted when Colton was playing with Sean all the time.

I climb out of the car, open Colt's door and crouch near his feet. "Listen buddy," I crone soothingly as I pat his bruised and battered six year old boy knee. "I will talk to Jimmy's mother about this and see if maybe there is a way you and Jimmy and Sean could all play together at home and then Jimmy would be nicer."

I doubt that this will be the case, though. For a first grader, Jimmy is quite the jerk. He is a spoiled brat of an only child who is used to getting his way and everyone catering to him. And I am not too fond of his bimbo mother, either, but I'm certainly not going to share that with my six year old who desperately needs to get out of the car *now*. I can hear the first bell ringing in the distance. If he doesn't get his butt into school before the late bell, I will have to drag Evan's slumbering body out of the car and sign him in. Which, from past experience I can tell you is a royal pain in the ass.

"Really?" Colt asks, eyes brightening. "That's great,

Mommy!" He unbuckles his seatbelt, snatches up his back pack and bounds out of the car. I watch as he skips over to his class line, happily swinging his back pack; the picture of innocence.

Pleased that I have solved at least one of my children's dilemmas for the mean time, I climb back into my car and notice Laura rushing towards the playground with the triplets and twins in tow. I offer her a friendly wave and call out to her in greeting. Her face colors as she sees me and she tucks her head down towards her chest after offering me a half-hearted wave.

My heart sinks in my chest. This is not the Laura I know. *What have I done to offend my friend?*

After the sleepover incident, I tried several times to contact Laura. My calls went unanswered and my texts went unread. Normally, I would think she was just busy, but her behavior now in the parking lot has caused me to believe that she is flat out avoiding me.

I drum my fingers on the steering wheel as I wait for Laura to pass by again, thankful that Evan is sleeping. It is quite a few minutes before she returns, her head covered by her hoodie.

"Laura!" I call out and I see her glance around anxiously.

"Oh, hey, Amy. Didn't see you there," she chuckles nervously as she steps closer to my vehicle. *Liar, liar pants on fire.*

"Hey," I greet her as she is about three feet away. "I've been trying to get in touch with you."

"Yeah, I know," Laura responds, twisting a curl around her finger. "It's just been crazy, you know?" She glances at me hopefully, as if I'm going to let this whole thing go. I'm not.

"Listen, about Allie and Kaitlyn…I'm sure it'll blow over soon. I'll try to talk to her again and-"

Laura cuts me off. "It's fine, Amy. Actually, I'd rather you not." Her chest puffs out slightly and she twists her curl harder. I know this pose. It's Defensive Laura. It's the same stance she adopts when confronted by her mother in law.

"Uh, what?" I am confused.

Laura releases her curl and it springs back so hard that it nearly hits her in the face. "Maybe it's better the girls go their separate ways."

I am stunned. She could have smacked me across the face with a frying pan just then and I would not have even flinched. She wasn't only saying "the girls should go their separate ways". She was saying "we should go our separate ways".

"What does that mean?" I nearly cry.

Laura inhales sharply. "I'm just thinking, maybe Allie isn't the best influence for Kait right now. She's very impressionable and Allie is a bit domineering."

My jaw nearly hits the car door. "What?" I ask incredulously. "*What?*"

Laura glances at her cell. "Listen, I've got a hair appointment. I'll talk to you later," she remarks abruptly as she dashes away from my car.

Tears trickle down my face on my drive back to the house. I am replaying my conversation with Laura in my head and wondering why she all of a sudden doesn't want Kaitlyn around Allie. It all comes back to my daughter's behavior of late.

I am seriously concerned as I ponder what to do about Allie. She isn't allowing me privy to any of her thoughts and feelings and I feel like I am losing my grip on her. I guess if I think back on it, I probably wasn't too open with my mother when I was that age either. In fact, I am not too open with her right now. But that's different. I was a huge disappointment to her my whole life. Although she would never come out and say that in so many words, I am certain that she would have liked if I were more like Beth. Hell, she probably wouldn't even mind another daughter like Joey. Just anyone but talentless, dumb old Amy.

My car phone begins to ring and I check the radio panel to see who is calling. I groan inwardly as the name and number came up. *Speak of the devil…*

"Hello, Beth," I remark as I pull onto my street. Hopefully this will be a quick and painless conversation. Maybe she just wants to tell me that she is moving to Alaska. Or having a personality transplant. I just can't deal with her today.

"Ameeeeee!" my sister screeches from the other end of the phone. I cringe at the sound of her voice. I know that voice. It is Beth's version of *Amy, you've fucked up again.*

"What, Beth?" I ask as I navigate the minivan of misery into my driveway.

"Do you know what Colt taught Andrew?" My sister's voice continues to shriek from the car speakers.

Maybe how to be a real boy? I am tempted to say, but I bite my tongue to prevent the words from slipping out. "I don't know, Beth. Why don't you enlighten me?"

I glare at Evan, telepathically willing him to wake up so I can have an excuse to get out of the car and end the conversation with Miss Perfect. I have a feeling this was going to be one of those long heart to heart chats with my sister that I detest.

"He taught him a *curse* word, Amy. A very *bad* curse word." I can almost hear Beth's heart palpitating with fury. I cover my mouth with my hand, stifling a laugh. Beth and I have completely different views on kids cursing. Beth feels that it is completely barbaric for anyone to curse and children should be practically whipped to death if they should utter any of the words she deems as foul. Including, but not limited to, moron, idiot or stupid. Yes, *stupid* is on her list of *curse words*.

Now, don't get me wrong. I'm not in favor of potty mouthed children, however, my thinking is that it would be quite hypocritical if I yell at my kids for cursing when both their father and I have mouths like a sailor on shore leave. I don't encourage cursing *per se*, but I think chasing a kid around with a bar of soap because he said *shit* is a huge waste of my time.

"What did he say?" I ask my sister, exasperation

creeping into my voice.

There is a pause on the other end of the line before Beth stammers, "Well, he didn't actually *say* anything…"

What? I am becoming increasingly annoyed; she's wasting my precious car phone minutes. "Then what the hell are you talking about, Beth? Could you get to the point?" I purposely throw *hell* in there, proud that I have refrained from saying *fuck*. After all, I don't want to be responsible for her heart attack.

"He wrote in his diary that Colt had taught him a bad word. And then…he *wrote* the word out!" my sister manages to gasp out. I can almost envision her clutching her chest, smelling salts nearby in case she should get the vapors.

His diary? Really? The words are out of my mouth before I can censor myself. "*Diary?*"

I hear Beth sigh with exasperation. "Yes. His *journal*. His therapist thinks it would help him with his issues of separation anxiety if he writes down his innermost thoughts and feelings," Beth retorts with an air of defensiveness.

"He has a therapist?" I repeat incredulously. *The kid is 7, what the hell does he need a therapist for?* Then I reflect on the fact Beth is his mother and that actually accounted for a lot. In fact, I am pretty sure that his anxiety issues might be solved if she would stop smothering the poor kid to death. She is the epitome of a helicopter parent. I'm almost certain he didn't need her to check after every time he pooped to make sure he had wiped properly.

"Yes, Amy," my sister replies. I could tell it is through clenched teeth.

"So his therapist told you he wrote in his *journal* that Colt taught him a bad word?" I am desperately trying to piece this puzzle together before the Onstar prerecorded lady interrupts to tell me I only have a minute left before they need to charge my credit card again. On the other hand, maybe that won't be so bad…

"No, Amy," Beth scoffs in her *sometimes you are so dense, Amy* voice. "That violates confidentiality."

"Ok, whatever. How do you know then?" I snap back as I hear a noise from the back seat. Evan is starting to stir.

"Well, I read it, *of course*," Beth answers in a matter of fact tone. "How else would I know what's going on in his life if I didn't read the journal?"

"What? I thought the journal was supposed to be for his *innermost thoughts and feelings*?" I accuse. *Now who was the bad mommy? Why I would never…*

And suddenly, a brilliant idea is born in the recesses of my twisted mind.

"I've got to go, Beth!" I remark hastily as I end the call with a press of a button. I turn to a now awake Evan and remark, "Mama's got some spying to do."

~

I am not exactly proud of what happens next because this is where Mistake #5 starts. As I child, my mother had snooped through my diary on a regular basis, causing me to actually use a *decoy* diary at one point in my teenage years. It was embarrassing to think my intimate thoughts were being violated by my mother, a woman whom I felt would never understand the pain and agony of being a teenager. At the time I was pretty sure she was an alien who had been born at age 25. And in all likelihood, my heartfelt emotions and secrets were being shared with all of my mother's bridge playing hens and quite possibly, my father. Imagine the mortification I experienced when Mrs. Young asked me if I was having any luck with that *adorable* Anthony Everest. In front of my friends, including Anthony's younger sister, Stella. Oh yeah, I don't think I'll ever live that down. In fact, when I saw Stella at our 10 year high school reunion, she jabbed me in the ribs to tell me her brother was single again. I just about prayed for the floor to open up and swallow me whole. So needless to say, I swore up and down that if and when I had a daughter I would *never, ever* read her diary.

But that was before my daughter started blowing off her best friend, hanging out with a whole new crowd, and refusing to speak to me. I *have* to know if she is all right. What if she's doing drugs or sleeping around? Wouldn't I be a worse mother if I *didn't* spy on her and left her to her privacy? And *technically*, I wouldn't be reading her diary…just snooping around her bedroom.

All these thoughts swirl through my head as I have my hand on the doorknob of Allie's bedroom. The door is locked of course, but I am one step ahead of her on that. I have already retrieved the screwdriver that we keep in the kitchen drawer for emergencies. Within seconds, I have the door open.

How does she get in here if she locks it before she goes to school? I muse briefly as I step into my once darling baby girl's bedroom. Posters of heavily pierced rock stars making obscene gestures with their crotches and tongues grace the walls that had once been pink with white hearts and purple flower cling-ons. I shake my head in disgust as I catch the unmistakable smell of cigarette smoke lingering on the carpet. That putrid smell permeates so deep that no amount of air freshener will get it out as I know from personal experience. I spent many an hour on my hands and knees scrubbing the surfaces of my bedroom when I was Allie's age.

Well, I was older, I remind myself. *This is ridiculous. Thirteen is too young for the crap she is pulling. If she's smoking what else could she be doing? Selling her body for drugs? Building a meth lab in the garage?*

When my mother snooped in my diary, I was pretty much innocent at the time. The worst thing in the damn diary was my crush on Stella's brother. Heck, my mother had no right snooping for something that benign. It wasn't like I was planning to elope with the kid or anything.

I am mentally justifying my snooping as I run my hand along the edge of the dresser and pick up about a half an inch of dust. *Damn you, Allie! You promised me you were cleaning your room!*

When she was about three years old, Allie had been diagnosed with asthma. One day after running around in the backyard, she started coughing and wheezing and gasping for air. Of course, I rushed her to the emergency room, fearing the worst. They gave her oxygen and the doctor prescribed a whole host of meds to get her asthma under control. As a fairly new mother with a newborn baby at home, I had flipped out. The doctor reassured me that Allie's condition was not terribly serious, but that I needed to keep her sleeping area clean and free of dust and pet dander. I had been busting my butt for the last ten years doing just that, until Allie had forbid me to set foot on her turf any longer. She swore up and down, while rolling her eyes, I might add, that she would clean her room herself. She dutifully dragged the vacuum into her room every Saturday and I definitely would hear it running, but who's to say that she was actually *pushing* it around her bedroom?

Now that I think about it, I realize that her asthma has been acting up over the last few months. It is probably because she wasn't cleaning her room. *And also the smoking. Can't forget about the smoking, Amy.*

I stand in the middle of my daughter's room, typical teenage shrine to pop culture and anti-parenthood, wondering what I should do. I have trapped Evan in his crib at the moment, but he is becoming quite the escape artist lately so I have a limited time frame to work with. I need to get in and out fast and not obsess about the dust.

As I am pondering whether or not my princess of teenaged angst actually *has* a diary, my eyes fall upon her cell phone, conveniently curled up in her pile of sheets and comforter on the bed. My heart does a flip. I can't believe my good fortune. Allie is *never* without her cell phone. She even takes it with her into the bathroom when she showers. Roger had joked that she might need to have it surgically removed from her hand (Allie was not amused by her father's joke at the time).

While my heart is bouncing around uneasily in my chest, my hand begins to shake as I take a tentative step forward and reach out to detangle the phone from the sheets. With my hand touching the black rhinestone case, I hesitate. Part of me is dying to know what is going on in my oldest daughter's world, but the other part of me is petrified that I am going to find out something that a mother wouldn't want to know about her child. She has been so cold and distant lately, I can only assume the worst.

No going back, Amy. If you read her texts, what you find out will be emblazoned on your brain forever. If she is up to no good, you're going to have to act on it. You won't be able to ignore it and she will not only hate you for that, she will know you snooped. Maybe you should just leave it alone and hope that she has learned something from you over the years. In fact, you're going to have to trust her enough to send her out in the world sometime. Why not start that trust today?

My curiosity wins out over my pragmatic side as I

tell my conscience to fuck off. I push the button to retrieve her home screen. Of course, the phone is now asking for a password. I chew on my lip for a second, thinking about what Allie would use as a passcode. The house number? Her locker combination? And then it hits me. She is a self-centered teenager. What's the most important thing to a kid?

I quickly tap in 1013, Allie's birthday, October 13th. The home screen disappears and all of Allie's icons dance in front of me, daring me to open them. *Score one for Mama.*

I scroll down until I see the text message icon and tap it lightly. Several names and message threads pop up in front of me, including one labeled "Victoria". After a quick glance, I see that none of the other names are friends I would suspect of leading my daughter off the path of righteousness. I also note with interest that no boy names were present on this list. I wonder if Allie is purposely deleting any conversations she is having with boys as an added security measure.

She doesn't trust me? What did she think? I was going to snoop? I contemplate defensively. Until I remember, I *am* snooping. *Oops.*

As I tap the message thread with Victoria's name, the conversation spills out on the screen in gray and blue conversation bubbles. Allie has a different phone than I do, so it takes me a minute to figure out which bubble belongs to Allie and which one belongs to Victoria. This is unfortunate because I feel a tugging on my leg at that exact moment.

I glance down to see my darling toddler covered from head to toe in baby powder. Oh, and naked. He is completely naked.

"Ugh! Evan!" I screech. I stare at the naked, powdery baby in front of me and then back at the phone. He looks like Pigpen but instead of dirt following him, he has clouds of white powder drifting off his body. He squeals with delight at my reaction and shoves his fingers into his mouth, drool escaping from both corners. I gaze at the cell phone with dismay.

Damn. Mess trumps snooping. I'm sure that rule is in the Mommy 101 handbook that I have not received a copy of.

I scoop up the squirming child and tuck Allie's phone into the pocket of my oversized hoodie. I can deal with that later, I suppose. It's only...I glance at the clock...10:30. *Holy crap, how did it get so late already?*

~TEN~

Allie's cell phone rings in my pocket as I am changing the baby.

"Mrs. Maxwell?" says the voice on the other end.

"Yes?" I reply, feeling quite cautious.

"This is Mrs. George, the guidance counselor at Allie's school."

I brace myself for terrible news. Allie is in trouble for some reason. I will have to go down to the school or worse, bail her out of jail. Roger will be furious.

"I just wanted to call to congratulate you on having such a wonderful child," the woman on the other end of the phone is telling me.

"What?" I am in shock as I nearly drop the phone.

"Yes, yes," Mrs. George is saying. "She is student of the month. We decided to choose the student who has had the most positive effect on her peers and has done the most volunteer work-"

"Hold on," I interrupt. "Volunteer work? What volunteer work?" I am very confused.

"Oh, you probably haven't heard. That's why she's been so secretive lately. She started a group for kids who are bullied at school and as popular student, she mentors them."

"Why, that's wonderful!" I exclaim.

"It certainly is," Mrs. George agrees. "So you don't have to worry about her any longer.

"Mama!" I am unceremoniously splashed in the face waking me from my daydream. I stare down at my naked toddler in the bath. Evan has a goofy, toothy grin that reminds me all too much of Roger. Except Evan is *much* cuter.

After dunking Evan in his second bath of the day, I clean him up, dress him, tuck him under my arm like a football, and head downstairs. The day is quickly getting away from me as I realize it is already a quarter to twelve and Evan will be squealing for his lunch at any moment.

I force the protesting baby into the high chair as he repeatedly tells me *no, no, no* and bashes me in the head with his tiny fists. I manage to subdue him with a chunky board book that he promptly inserts into his mouth and begins to suck on. Quickly reaching into the cabinet, I withdraw a microwavable container of mac and cheese. After filling it with the required amount of water and placing it in the microwave to cook, I retrieve an apple from the fridge, peel it and cut it into tiny pieces. As soon as the mac and cheese is done, I remove it, spilling the water and scalding my hand. I yelp with pain but ignore the blister starting to bubble on my finger. I place my now cold cup of coffee in the microwave to warm up and stir the mac and cheese before pouring Evan a Sippy cup of milk and snapping the lid on tightly. I taste the mac and cheese, burn my tongue and promptly stick the container in the freezer for a few minutes. All this while keeping an eye on my child to ensure that he does not swallow whole chunks of his book.

Why do I bore you with the minutiae of my day? Oh, it's only in case you are like Roger and are assuming that at noon I'm in the bubble bath with a glass of wine while I watch Lifetime Original Movies on my iPad.

I finally finish feeding the baby with one hand and sipping my coffee with the other. (I burn my tongue on that, too). I offer Evan the plate with apples which he accepts greedily. This allows me a few minutes to scarf down a stick of string cheese and stare at the remaining contents of the fridge. And then I realize with panic, there is nothing defrosting for dinner. *Crap.*

I am debating about whether to order pizza or Chinese when the shrill ring of the phone interrupts my menu planning. Evan, who has been shoveling apples into his mouth at warp speed, pauses mid shovel, his eyes brightening immediately.

"Phone!" he shrieks, opening and closing his tiny little hands with excitement. "Me phone!"

I shake my head as I grab the phone and check the caller ID before answering. It's the elementary school. I sigh.

Damn it. What now? Lexie is notorious for bothering the school nurse with ridiculous made up ailments. Lexie will not only go down to the clinic for every single minor injury that befalls her, she visits the nurse with cuts and scrapes that had happened over the weekend, just so she can get five minutes of Mrs. O'Connor's attention. If Lexie has to fart, she goes to the nurse. If Lexie's zipper is stuck on her pants, she visits the nurse. If Lexie has broccoli stuck in her teeth, she goes to the nurse. She has been known to stalk the nurse as she enters the school. Last week, she met her at her car, starling the poor woman so much that she spilled coffee down the front of her blouse. I'm pretty sure Lexie is the bane of her existence. I make a mental note to get Mrs. O'Connor a nice gift basket for Christmas as I answer the phone.

"Hello, Mrs. O' Connor," I say, smartly preempting her greeting.

There are a few seconds of silence on the other end of the phone before I hear throat clearing and a male voice.

"Um, no, Mrs. Maxwell. It's not Mrs. O'Connor. It's Mr. Rice...the principal of the school?" He poses the statement like it is a question, as if he isn't actually sure if he *is* the principal or not and he's asking me to confirm. Mr. Rice is a very timid man with a stuttering problem; why he is the principal of an elementary school is beyond me. He should have been an accountant. He isn't able to say no to any of the kids and they walk all over him. Not that Roger rules the high school with an iron fist, but he is a lot stricter with discipline than Mr. Rice is.

"Oh, yes," I reply, confused as to why Mr. Rice would be calling me. *Did Lexie annoy the nurse so much that she doesn't even want to call me herself anymore?* I am slight hurt by Mrs. O'Connor's betrayal. Usually we use the daily phone call as a chance to commiserate on

Lexie's obnoxiousness.

"Um, Mrs. Maxwell, I hate to bother you, but I need you to come pick Colton up from school," Mr. Rice says in a very apologetic voice.

Colton?

"I'm sorry, Mr. Rice. Did you say *Colt?*" He must be mistaken. Silly Mr. Rice. He means Lexie. I begin to wonder what he has in his coffee that he can't tell the difference between them.

"Yes, um, Colton," Mr. Rice repeats with a fair amount of throat clearing.

"Is he sick?" I ask with concern as I quickly grab for a paper towel to wipe up the baby.

"Um, not exactly," Mr. Rice tells me. "Actually, I…um, well, I apologize but I had to suspend him. I, um, spoke with Mr. Maxwell first, of course, and he agreed-

Wait! My mind is shouting at me. *Mr. Maxwell? Roger? Suspending Colt?*

Feeling as if I am dangling in an alternate reality, I grab ahold of the nearest kitchen chair and sink into it. Evan is now attempting to escape his highchair with tremendous dexterity. I ignore him as I ask the principal, "Why would you have to suspend him, Mr. Rice?" My tone is not polite. It is more like pissed off Mama Bear.

Mr. Rice clears his throat, obviously uncomfortable with this conversation. I wonder how often he needs to make similar phone calls to parents.

Hi, Mr. or Mrs. So and So. You have to pick up your son/ daughter, he/she has been a bad boy/girl. Oh, yes, I know…not your little darling.

Now granted, I *know* Colt is no angel. At home he can be quite the wild child. But I highly doubt he acts like that in school. Okay, maybe most parents are in denial when they get a phone call from the principal's office (as Roger claims they often are), but this really doesn't sound like my little boy. *And Mr. Rice spoke to Roger already? Why didn't Roger call me? Or text me to give me a heads up?*

"Um, well, the truth is Mrs. Maxwell, Colton got into a fight today on the playground. With Jimmy Donoghue," Mr. Rice explains. I can practically hear him blushing.

Oh crap. I was supposed to take care of that this morning, wasn't I? I was so concerned with spying on Allie that I had forgotten all about the promise I had made to Colt that morning. *Damn, damn, damn. There goes the Mother of the Year award.*

"Oh no. What happened?" I am envisioning the much larger Jimmy Donoghue pummeling my sweet baby boy.

"Apparently he pushed Jimmy off the playground swing without provocation," Mr. Rice stammers.

"What?" I squawk. *Without provocation my ass.* That Jimmy kid was trouble.

"Mrs. Maxwell, I tried to talk to him but he was crying inconsolably. I don't know what happened so I called your husband at the high school and Mrs. Donoghue is on her way in…" Mr. Rice is *definitely* stuttering now. I cringe with the thought of Cammi

Donoghue; he must be besides himself.

"I'll be there in ten minutes," I snap as I promptly ended the phone conversation. I jump to my feet, pull Evan out of the highchair, and set him on the ground as I stick my hand in my hoodie, searching for Allie's phone. It's missing. I must have dropped it upstairs.

I head to the hall closet to retrieve my jacket when I realize that Evan is also nowhere to be found.

"Evan?" I call out, panic creeping into my voice. *Losing the baby would be a perfect cap to your day, wouldn't it, Amy?*

As my eyes are desperately scanning the living room, I hear a giggle coming from the corner. Peeking behind the side of the couch, I find my son, chubby little hands grasping Allie's phone. *How the hell did he get that?*

"Phone!" he squeals with glee as he drools all over the screen. I flinch, knowing that the moisture will ruin the phone and we'll end up shelling out another $300 for a new one. I make a play for the phone as my cunning two year old child continues to hold it out of my reach.

"No, no, Evan!" I gasp. *Please God don't let him delete anything before I get to read it!* After a very short game of "grab it if you can", I manage to pry Evan's grubby fingers from the phone. I wipe it on my shirt and then tap the screen, relieved to see that it is still locked.

Then I remember that I haven't accomplished what I intended to do and read the texts from Victoria. I am very tempted to have a seat, just for a moment and peruse Allie's phone. But damn it, Colt is probably a blubbery mess in the principal's office.

He deserves to sit there and stew for a few minutes, I consider. *Getting into a fight! What kind of Neanderthal is he?* But he is still only six and I didn't know the details of this "fight". That Jimmy twit probably provoked him. The mother inside of me is being pulled in two different directions once again, torn between getting insight into my sulky teenager and dealing with my other child's school yard antics.

Colt wins out over Allie as I toss the phone into my purse, out of the baby's reach. I scoop Evan up into my arms and quickly wipe his face with the sleeve of my hoodie. Yes, it *is* disgusting, but I don't have time to fight with him over soap and water. My poor baby is in the principal's office for heaven's sake!

"Come on, buddy," I crone soothingly as I coax him into the lightweight jacket that he detests. As I attempt to hold him down, he is struggling to pull his arms out of the sleeves while I struggle to force them back in. Sweat is rolling down my back by the time I manage to get the jacket zipped up so I decided to forgo my own jacket.

We dash out of the house, Evan protesting his change of schedule and me attempting to explain to a toddler why we are leaving instead of indulging in his usual afternoon repertoire of crappy children's television programming. Yeah, that's right. I plop him down in front of the TV for an hour every afternoon. Hey, before you judge me, try to entertain a toddler all day while simultaneously doing laundry, cooking dinner and keeping your sanity.

"Your brother has been a bad boy at school and Mommy needs to go pick him up from the principal's office," I explain as I lean on Evan with my elbow in attempts to strap him into the car seat. "You can imagine how embarrassing this must be for Mommy, with Daddy being a principal and all…" Evan does not care about my predicament as he continues to fight me. More sweat and tears ensue from both of us. Finally, I have him strapped in, I have me strapped in, and we are rolling out of the driveway.

As we pull into the street, I notice Jason climbing out of his silver sedan that is parked on the street.

Hmmm, that's bizarre. Wonder what he's doing home in the middle of the day?

I immediately chastise myself, Jason's warning echoing in my head. *Stop it, Amy! No more spying on the neighbors.*

I resist the urge to look back at Jason in the rearview mirror and arrive at the elementary school in record time I carefully tuck my minivan in between two other minivans parked at the curb in front of the school. *How cliché.* The school is like a minivan magnet. The other minivans are poorly parked; one is riding up the curb, the other is almost in the middle of the street.

As I unbuckle myself, I recognize the Mercedes minivan parked haphazardly in front of me. It belongs to our neighbor, Jimmy's mother. I am, of course, silently seething.

You can have a minivan or *a Mercedes, you twit. You can't have both. It's like you can have a clean house* or *kids. Not both. You make the rest of us poor schmucks look...well, like poor schmucks.*

As I am unstrapping Evan, I wonder how Cammi can possibly afford all her extravagances. She is a stay at home mom just like me and her husband is a teacher at the high school. Yet, she always is dressed in the latest fashions, belongs to the country club and always spends plenty of time at the spa. Not to mention her *surgical procedures.* I realize she only has one child, but Roger and I must be doing something wrong because they seem to have a ton of money that we don't. Even more reason to hate her.

I lumber up the school's front walk, Evan wriggling to break free under one arm, his massive diaper bag tucked under the other. The diaper bag strap broke three weeks ago and I left it in the car to remind myself to pick up a new one but so far, um, yeah...I have completely forgotten to do that. *Must make post it note...*

I ring the doorbell of the school's front entrance with my elbow and am promptly buzzed in without the usual interrogation that I am subjected to. No *who are you here to see* or *what can I do for you* in an exasperated tone like I normally get when I'm struggling at the front door with Evan in tow. I think the secretary, Mrs. Morris, gets a perverse thrill in watching me squirm while going through her litany of questions. She obviously has control issues. I guess the secretary is the one watching Colt right now and she is eager to rid herself of him.

I step into the main office and immediately can see my assessment is correct. Mrs. Morris wears her usual Ann Taylor sweater set with matching scowl while tucked in the corner of the room on an orange plastic chair is Colt, simpering and sniveling. Loudly. Boogers are running down his beat red face, tears trickling into his lap. In the other corner of the small office sits a smug Jimmy Donoghue, shooting dirty looks at Colt, ice pack pressed up against a swollen lip but none worse for the wear. He is smirking underneath that ice pack, I just know it.

"Mrs. Maxwell," the secretary remarks in her typical brusque manner. "I will let Mr. Rice know you've arrived. Mrs. Donoghue is *already* here." She picks up the interoffice phone next to her desk. "They've been *waiting* for you," she adds in a venomous tone.

I resist the urge to snap, "Mrs. Donoghue doesn't have a two year old to wrangle and also, obviously does not care if she is correctly parked or not." But I bite my tongue as Mrs. Morris speaks to the principal on the other end of the phone.

"Mrs. Maxwell is *finally* here, Mr. Rice. Mmm hmm. Okay." She covers the receiver with her hand and snarls at me, "He says to go right in."

Ignoring her tone, I nod curtly in her direction as I deposit Evan on the floor so I can stretch my arm which has cramped up. He promptly dashes over to the secretary's desk and grabs at the snow globe sitting on the edge.

"Can you *please* control that child!" Mrs. Morris yelps, one hand still clutching the phone as she attempts to contort her body and snatch the snow globe from Evan's curious fingers.

Startled, he stares at her, his bottom lip beginning to tremble until he realizes that in her hand she holds the holy grail of all toys…a *phone*. His eyes grow as wide as saucers and he claps delightedly. He glances back at me before he starts babbling, "Phone, Mama! Me phone!" He makes a beeline for the other side of the desk and I quickly try to grab him, but I am too slow in my old age. He is behind the desk in an instant, climbing on top of the startled Mrs. Morris, still sitting in her chair, shock written all over her face. Evan climbs onto her desk after using her as a springing board. The secretary teeters on her swivel chair until she lands flat on the floor. Colton manages to stifle a giggle but Jimmy bursts out laughing. This all happens in the length of time that it takes me to blink twice.

I wince as I see my life flash before my eyes. *Roger is going to kill me for allowing Evan to disrupt the office like this. Oh, God I can hear him now, 'Amy, I'm a figurehead in this community. I can't have you embarrassing me in public like that…and blah, blah, blah…' Damn it Roger! I knew you should have gotten a vasectomy sooner! I told you that stocking up on the Sponge was a bad idea! They recalled the damn thing! I am way too old to be chasing after a two year old child!*

I snatch up my youngest child as Mrs. Morris struggles to her feet, ignoring my hand outstretched to help her up. She tugs impatiently at the hem of her salmon colored sweater and tucks her graying hair back into the severe bun on top of her head. Looking at her, I realize that she reminds me of a cupcake. A cranky and sour cupcake. I have to control my own laughter as she shoots me a stern and reproachful glare.

Pursing my lips together, I march past her desk into the principal's office. In the center of the room Mr. Rice sits at his desk. Two uncomfortable looking chairs sit on the opposite side of the desk. On one of those chairs the glamorous looking Mrs. Donoghue is perched, like a Siamese cat ready to pounce. She turns and shoots me a look (raising her botoxed eyebrows and pouting her collagen enhanced lips) to rival Mrs. Morris's evil glare.

Mr. Rice simply looks exhausted and flustered. His collar is undone and flapping against his meaty size 20 neck. Droplets of sweat are beading at his receding hairline as he stammers, "Um, okay, have a seat Mrs. Maxwell." Evan tugs impatiently at my earrings, dying to get down and wreak havoc in the small and cramped room.

I groan inwardly as I step toward the desk, pull out the chair next to Cammi Donoghue and demurely plop myself down. Crossing my arms over Evan's wriggling body, I have him overpowered...for the moment. Mrs. Bimbo, uh, Donoghue continues to glare at me with her permanent expression of distain. I guess she's never heard of controlling her children. *After all, she has never seemed to control Jimmy*, I think smugly.

Rolling her eyes (which can't be easy; I am convinced her eyelashes are going to get stuck together with the ten pounds of mascara on them) she pokes an accusatory finger at my hoodie. "You have a chunk of...*macaroni* on your sweatshirt," she remarks with disgust. I try not to turn bright red.

I don't thank her. Instead, I wordlessly pluck the piece of Mac and Cheese off of my shirt and nearly pop into my mouth before I realize that would actually be pretty disgusting. I toss it in the nearby trash can instead.

"Um, Mrs. Maxwell. Mrs. Donoghue. I'm sorry to, um, interrupt your daily-" Mr. Rice begins to apologize before he is cut off by the deplorable Mrs. Donoghue.

"*You* shouldn't be apologizing, Mr. Rice." She leans forward and lays her hand of perfectly manicured blood red talons over Mr. Rice's beefy paw. Even from my angle I can see her cleavage is precariously dangling in his line of sight. Turning an even deeper shade of red than he already is, he attempts to avert his eyes.

Good Lord, does she know no bounds? Has she no shame? Flirting with the principal now? Seriously, that's not fair! She is 90% plastic and I have a toddler with a possible dirty diaper threatening to escape on my lap. I don't even have make up on and I am not sure when I last washed my hair. I am no match for her skill set.

She turns her head to glare at me. "*Amy* should be apologizing to both of us. For taking up *your* time and for me missing my hot yoga class. I *never* miss my hot yoga class," she purrs as she actually strokes Mr. Rice's hand. *You don't say?* Anger is boiling in my blood, threatening to spill over.

I glower at her as Evan bounces up and down on my lap and hits me in the chin, causing me to bite my tongue. There is now blood dribbling from my mouth. But does the bitch stop? Oh no, she doesn't.

"After all, if her little barbarian didn't hit my innocent little Jimmy..." Cammi pauses to fake a sniffle and I leap to my feet, dumping Evan on the floor in the process.

"You're kidding, right? *Colt* is a *barbarian* now? I'll remember that the next time you dump your little snot nosed Jimmy at our house for eight hours so you can go get your twat waxed!" I spit out as I hold Cammi's eye with my infuriated gaze. She gasps and covers her hand with her mouth as if she has never heard such a word before.

"Mrs. Maxwell!" Mr. Rice sputters, appearing incredibly pained. He actually looks as if he will keel over and die. "This is a school!"

Ok, so maybe I am a tad bit out of line and acted rather juvenile. But I am sick and tired of Cammi Donoghue thinking her precious baby boy is a complete angel. I would like to detail every evil thing that he has ever done while at our house; every nasty trick he has played on Colt (and the dog and the cat) that I held my tongue about over the years. But I take the high road as usual.

"I'm sorry, Mr. Rice," I say, hoping Cammi understood I was not apologizing to *her*. "But I think Mrs. Donoghue is failing to see that there are *two* boys involved here and we don't know the whole story. She needs to not accuse Colt of anything until she knows the whole story." I bend down and seize Evan from underneath the desk where he has managed to scoot in the fifteen seconds since I have released my grip on him.

"We *do* know the story, *Amy*," Cammi tells me in a patronizing tone. She stares at me as if I am an escaped mental patient that she feels sorry for. "Colt *told* us he punched Jimmy."

"Well no shit, Sherlock, Dick Tracey, where'd you park your squad car?" I retort with an insult from my childhood and instantly regret it. Cammi and Mr. Rice are both staring open mouthed at me.

Jesus Christ, Amy, get it together. You're starting to look like a real imbecile here. I stand taller. "Of course he said he punched him. That's obvious. Jimmy is the one with the fat lip, not Colt." I feel strangely triumphant uttering that statement. *Ha ha, my kid knocked out your kid, na na na na poo poo.*

Cammi narrows her winged lined eyelids at me. She knows I am gloating. *Good.*

"What I'm saying is that this may have a whole backstory to it. In fact," I punctuate the air with my pointer finger as I continue to clutch a wriggling Evan in my other arm. "Colt mentioned just this morning that

Jimmy has been making fun of him for playing with his friend Sean." I return Cammi's narrow stare without the benefit of the eye make-up. "Sean is *autistic*. What kind of six year old makes fun of another kid's friends just because they're different? *That* sounds like bullying to me!" Satisfied with my rant, I plop back down in the uncomfortable chair awaiting Cammi's apology.

Instead, of acting contrite, she snorts. Turning to Mr. Rice, she arches her eyebrows. "And that's another thing. What kind of parent lets her six year old play with a fourteen year old boy? A *weird* fourteen year old boy who pretends he's a Tyrannosaurus Rex?"

"That is really unfair, Cammi," I stammer. I can't believe she was going to be mean to Sean. "The boy is-"

She cuts me off. "I don't care *what* he has. He's inappropriate and I am certainly not going to allow *my* child to play with him. My husband, who is a teacher at the high school, as you know, says that Sean has absolutely no social skills at all and may even be a danger to other children. A *good* parent wouldn't let their child play with him."

Now I am fuming as I pull myself to my full height. I grip Evan tightly with one arm as I lean over into Cammi's face and poke my finger into her bony (tanned) shoulder blade. (I'm afraid to poke her chest as my finger may bounce off like a trampoline).

"How *dare* you tell me how to parent my children!" I am having trouble keeping my "inside" voice controlled. "You know, being a parent of four kids is a hell of a lot harder than being a parent of one spoiled brat and I'm pretty sure I'm *still* doing a better job than you are."

I can tell that Cammi is insulted by the slight twitch of her wrinkle free face. But she doesn't grant me the satisfaction of letting me know that I am right.

"Whatever. At least my kid isn't the one suspended," Cammi scoffs, glancing at Mr. Rice with a *can you believe this chick* expression on her face.

Meanwhile, Mr. Rice looks as if he is praying the school would somehow catch fire and he could escape the circus unfolding in front of him. He is probably expecting us to start tearing each other's hair out next. I can see he is mentally evaluating his escape route to the door.

But I decide that despite my fury, I'm not going to waste another breath on Cammi Donoghue or her demon seed. "I will be bringing Colt back to school tomorrow," I announce to Mr. Rice as I snatch my purse from the floor where it landed several minutes ago. A few pennies roll out and stop underneath Cammi's chair but I don't bother to retrieve them.

Mr. Rice opens his mouth to protest, but I ignore him and stomp out of the office. I grasp Colt's hand as I pass him. "Let's go," I mumble, practically yanking him out of the chair and dragging him behind me as I briskly pass Mrs. Morris's desk.

"Did you ask Jimmy's mother if he could play with Sean?" Colt asks eagerly when we are once again out in the hallway.

Seriously? Is this kid really that dense? Doesn't he

realize that Jimmy is a shithead bully that is never going to want to hang out with Sean? And what's more, Colt shouldn't want to hang out with Jimmy? I stare at my tender hearted six year old and sigh. *Poor kid.*

"No, Colt. His mother doesn't want him to play with Sean," I tell him with a sad smile. I watch his face crumble.

"But why not?" he asks, lip quivering.

I resist the urge to tell him that Jimmy's mother is a bullying bitchy bimbo and just shrug my shoulders at my son. "I don't know, Colt."

"So he's going to make fun of me on the playground and not play with me anymore?" he asks, a lone tear streaming down his sweet, chubby cheek. It breaks my heart. It sucks that a first grader already needs to learn that there are mean people in the world and we can't all just get along and color rainbows and eat paste. We battle mean people from the time we are born till the day we die. It's a tough lesson to learn at age six.

I open my mouth to explain, but I don't have a chance to respond because all of a sudden, I hear Lexie cry out, "Mommy!" and then I see her hurling at me full force. And by *hurling*, I mean puking. All over my shoes. And my jeans. And my purse.

I stare at my daughter in disbelief as she covers her mouth and goes dashing across the hall into the nurse's office. I drop to the floor, put my head in my hands and just sob.

~ELEVEN~

A half an hour later we are finally all packed into the car. Colt is sniffling and wiping the snot from his face with his sleeve, Evan reeks of baby poop and Lexie is clutching a plastic bag in which she has been instructed to throw up in if the urge hits. And I am on the verge of a nervous breakdown. I now have exactly thirty three minutes to get home, unload the kids, change Evan, set Lexie up with a puke bucket and find something to occupy Colt so that I can *finally* read Allie's messages before she gets home and makes a bee line right to her phone that she is probably having a major bout of withdrawal from. I lucked out today with her leaving the phone home. And then, I have been nothing but *unlucky* with every turn of events since. I am *not* letting this once in a lifetime opportunity go to waste.

As I pull into the driveway, I notice that Jason's car is still parked where it was over an hour ago when I had departed for school. I check the time because that seems impossible.

Only *an hour ago? Geez, it seems like a week has passed since then.* Something niggles at the back of my mind. Maybe it is the fact I have never seen his car home during the week before. In fact, hardly ever see his car at all. It seems highly suspicious to me for some reason.

Knock it off, Amy! You are not Miss Marple, Nancy Drew or Hercule Poirot!

Realizing that I have no time to brood over Jason's whereabouts, I screech to a halt before I hit the house, throw the car into park, and practically leap from the vehicle. Lexie clutches her bag closer to her face. "Mommy, I feel like I'm gonna puke," she moans as she swings her legs out the car door. And she does. Four times. And gets half of it on herself and the other half into the bag.

When she is finished, I assist the shaking and quivering Lexie out of the car, handing her the already full bag. Sighing, I lift a sleeping Evan, who now smells worse than a toxic waste site, out of his seat. I awkwardly climb up the front steps, one arm around a sniveling Colt, the other propping the baby on my shoulder. Lexie trails behind, dry heaving into the plastic bag. Out of the corner of my eye, I can see a school bus lumbering slowly towards our block.

"Damn it," I curse, shoving the key in the door. I manage to get the door open in record time and launch my body through it along with three kids. Evan stirs as I plop his sleeping body on the couch. The diaper can wait. He probably already has diaper rash. What's another five minutes?

"Mommmmmeeeeee....what do I do with this bag?" Lexie wails. I snatch it from her hands and march into the kitchen. "Go hang out in the bathroom for a few minutes. Take off the pukey clothes," I order over my shoulder. Yeah, yeah, I know. I need to show a little sympathy and I normally would, but the clock is ticking.

As I toss the bag into the garbage, I retrieve Allie's phone from my pocket. Quickly punching in the passcode, I now do not stumble as I am able to find Victoria's messages easily.

"Mommmmeeeeee," I can hear Lexie howling from the hallway upstairs. "Colt locked himself in the bathroom! And he's crying! What if I need to puke?" Even sick she is going to manage give me a headache.

"Lex! Just use the downstairs bathroom!"

"Ewwwww! No! That's gross!"

"Lexie! It's either that or the backyard!" I am praying her screeching isn't waking her brother as I sneak a peek into the living room. *Is Evan stirring?* I hold my breath. *No. Just my imagination. Nope, wait. Yes, he is definitely stirring.*

Crap. I hurry to scan the messages, keeping an eye out for key words like drugs, sex and…*rock and roll*? So far, all Victoria's messages to Allie have been benign and all Allie's to Victoria are equally lame. I'm starting to think she may delete any incriminating messages just to throw me off the scent in the event that I do stumble across her phone…like today. In fact, the idea that this is actually just a decoy crosses my mind. *Damn kid! Is she a chip off the old block?*

Disappointed, I am about to call it quits and shut off her phone when a message from two weeks ago catches my eye. (I have translated from teenager to English).

I got the goods if you want me to bring it to your house (Victoria).

Yeah my mom should be out this afternoon after school (Allie).

I can get more if you like it (Victoria).

The next few messages launch a back and forth discussion which causes my eyes to widen and a sickening feeling to rise in my stomach. *Oh, this is not good.*

I sink into the kitchen chair, phone in hand just as the front door swings open and Allie storms in like a hurricane. She doesn't acknowledge anyone in her wake; instead she just swirls up the stairs, obviously on a very important mission. At the same time, Evan toddles into the room. Naked. With crap stuck to the back of his leg.

"Oh shit," I mutter. *Literally.*

I set the phone on the table, knowing Allie is most likely tearing her room apart looking for it. Sighing, I grab Evan, who of course, tries to escape. I hold him at arm's length carrying him to the kitchen sink where the pot from last night's mashed potatoes is soaking, of course. With one hand, I expertly dump the heavy, water filled pot, cast it aside and shove Evan into the sink.

He wails and protests as I spray his back side with tepid water. "Well, you shouldn't have taken off your diaper," I reason with him as he howls. "If you would have just waited a few minutes…"

"Uh, you know there's baby shit and a diaper on the living room floor, right?" Allie informs me as she enters the kitchen, nose wrinkled up in disgust.

Well, I had *assumed* there was, but I wasn't quite

sure. "Yes, Allie," I reply evenly. I don't even know how to address her. *I need to talk to Roger before I flip out. I must remain calm, act natural...* "Can you dump the diaper in his diaper pail?"

"Ewww, no!" she yelps, wrinkling up her entire face in disgust now. "Have you seen my cell phone?" she asks, with an accusatory tone to her voice. Maybe she's already on to me. I am debating my options when she catches sight of her phone that I tossed aside when the poster child for birth control wandered in.

She snatches up the phone and holds it close to her chest. "What's it doing in *here*?" she inquires in what I would *definitely* categorize as an accusatory tone. She punches her code into the phone, examines the screen for a second and then shrieks, "MOTHER!!!! You were reading my text messages!"

I have no idea how she knows this, so I attempt to feign innocence as I squirt dish liquid on Evan's bare bottom. At the same time, I glance around, wondering what I am going to wash him with. This is one of the problems with having too many children. I can never concentrate on any one task fully and completely since I am constantly being assaulted with one crisis after another. I grab a paper towel and moisten it in a fit of desperation. Needless to say, Evan does not like the rough paper cleaning his tushie.

"Mother," Allie continues to huff as she taps her toe impatiently and Evan howls like a drowning cat directly into my eardrum. "I can't *believe* you violated my privacy. I can't *believe* you disrespected me like that. I can't *believe*-"

I cut her off mid litany since I am done rinsing off the baby. "Can you hand me a clean dish towel?"

She makes a vomitus teen face. "Ewww, gross! We dry dishes with that!"

"No, *I* dry dishes with that," I correct her. "And of course, I'm going to wash it after I dry him."

I'm thinking that her face must be permanently frozen with the smelling shit expression because it doesn't go away as she hands me a blue dishtowel with happy little geese all over it. "I'm pissed off, MOTHER," she reiterates as she crosses her arms over her chest. "You violated my *privacy*. That's like, against my second amendment rights."

"That's the right to bear arms," I mutter as I buff the baby with the towel.

Allie rolls her eyes. "It's October, MOTHER. Nobody runs around with bare arms in October. They don't even sell sleeveless in the stores." She scoffs before she adds, "*Really.*"

My God, your father was a history major, Allie! How did I raise such a moron?

"Democracy starts at the curb, my dear," I remind her of Roger's favorite saying as I head upstairs to re-diaper and clothe Evan. I notice Misty is sniffing at the dirty diaper that is still sitting in the living room. I groan, hoping she won't try to eat it. Right now it will have to wait, though. If I leave Evan diaperless for too long, my house will smell like crap *and* pee.

Allie trails after me. "You're really unfair, you know that?" Her voice is rising several octaves as she follows me into Evan's room. I am clenching my teeth together, trying not to erupt like a volcano. I can only remain calm for so long, you know.

I plop the baby down on the changing table and notice that he has a lump of mashed potatoes sticking to his foot. *Oops.* I pluck it off before I begin the diaper wrestling match. I pull a diaper from the box and shove it under his butt as he rolls over and tries to escape. Leaning on him with one arm, I manage to tuck it between his legs. He yanks out a clump of my hair as I attempted to secure the tabs on the side.

Allie continues to berate me, not even offering assistance. "What do you think? I'm doing drugs or something? Like, don't you trust me?" *Exactly, Allie, I don't trust you. I know you're lying to me! Your texts prove you're doing drugs!*

But I keep my mouth shut as I tug Evan's onsie over his head and attempt to snap it at the bottom.

"*Victoria's* mother doesn't check her cell phone," Allie remarks spitefully. "*She* trusts Victoria."

I've been insulted by my teenaged daughter before. I've been screamed at, spit on, cursed at, stomped at and ignored. But for some inexplicable reason, today, I have reached my breaking point. At the mention of Victoria's name and what Victoria's mother did or didn't do, makes me go absolutely ballistic.

I set the baby on the floor, completely ignoring the fact that his snaps are done wrong and I poke my finger at my daughter's chest. "Oh I guess *Victoria's* mother is perfect, huh? I guess that's why she has a perfect daughter who is participating in criminal activity? And getting my daughter involved?"

Allie gasps and turns bright red. *Didn't think I go back two weeks, did you, Al? Busted.*

I don't even let her speak, not that she looks like she is able to at the moment. "If that's the case then, I'm *glad* I'm nothing like Victoria's mother because I don't want *my* daughter to be anything like Victoria!"

"I can't...I don't..."Allie stammers.

That probably would have been enough, but I had to push the barrel over the edge of the cliff. "So guess what? You won't be seeing your precious Victoria after school anymore!"

"WHAT?" Allie screeches. "You can't do *that*!"

I laugh. *I can't? How amusing. She must be new.* "Oh, yes I can. And I will! And what's more, I'm going to block her number from your phone!" I cross my arms over my chest triumphantly.

"No you can't! I'll run away if you don't let me see Victoria!" Allie screams while she stomps her foot.

Lexie appears in the doorway looking as pale as a ghost, vomit on her shirt, hair matted against her sweaty face. "Mommy?"

"Not now, Lexie," I snap, not moving my glowering eyes from my older daughter's face.

"But I think I'm done throwing up. Can you make me some tea and toast?"

"In a minute, Lexie. I'm busy right now. Allie, give me your phone," I demand as I hold my palm out.

"Over my dead body," Allie replies.

"Ha! Don't tempt me," I laugh.

With her usual streak of defiance, she shoves the phone into her bra.

"Really, Allie? You think I won't go get it?" I remark, raising my eyebrow.

"That's *sick*," she spits out. "You're sick."

I roll my eyes. "I'm your mother. It's my job to be sick."

"I think *I'm* going to be sick," Lexie moans as she dashes back into the bathroom.

"I don't know what your problem is. I don't know why you think that Victoria-"

"I read your texts, Allie! I saw what Victoria said!"

Allie turns bright red. "I didn't do it! Only Victoria!"

I cross my arms over my chest. "I'm supposed to believe you after what I read? Maybe I should reiterate. How's this?" I clear my throat before beginning to speak in Victoria's annoying nasally twang. "I've got the goods if you want me to bring them to your house." Then I switch to Allie's higher pitched voice. "Yeah my mom should be out this afternoon." I raise my eyebrow and narrow my eyes at my daughter. "Would you like me to go on?"

Allie swallows hard. "I don't see what the problem

is! It's not like I did it!"

"You keep saying that, but I'm finding it very difficult to believe."

Allie rolls her eyes as usual. "It's not really a big deal. Everybody does it!"

"Oh really. Name me one adult that 'does it'," I remark while using air quotes.

"The neighbor," Allie smirks. "At the mall. In fact, that's who encouraged Victoria to do it the first time."

My cheeks feel numb. *Jason is doing drugs! And getting teenaged girls hooked on them!*

I am momentarily rendered speechless as I hear a car door slam outside.

At the same time, Colt runs into the room, flings Evan's closet door open and closes himself inside. Evan, who has been happily playing on his floor this whole time, is suddenly intrigued with his brother's whereabouts. He expertly rises to his feet and toddles over to the closet door, banging impatiently on it.

"Go away, Evan!" Colt calls out. "I'm hiding."

"*Who* are you hiding from?" I ask while counting the other children in my head. One, two in here, number three in the bathroom… *He can't possibly be playing hide and go seek with an imaginary friend, can he? Isn't six too old for imaginary friends?*

"Daddy's gonna kill me!" comes his muffled wail. *Oh that's right. The whole suspended from school incident.* In the midst of everything that has transpired with his siblings in the last hour, I completely forgot Colt has been suspended. And Roger is home.

I chew on my lip apprehensively. I don't want to tell Roger about Allie quite yet. (This qualifies as Mistake #6 because *had* I discussed it with Roger and we spoke with Allie about it *together*, we may have been able to put the whole thing to rest before I made subsequent Mistake #7.)

"Helloooooo!" I hear Roger step into the living room. "Why does it smell like a dirty diaper down…oh dear Lord, Misty, no!"

"Can you get that diaper, Roger?" I call back sweetly. "I'm in the middle of reprimanding our daughter."

"I can't hear you!" Roger replies, the sound of his voice fading. *What a liar!*

"Don't you dare go into your man cave, Roger!" I threaten. "I need some help here!"

Silence. *Son of a bitch.*

I point to Allie and growl, "Don't move." I stomp down the steps. "And watch your brothers!" I add as an afterthought. I storm into the man cave just as Roger is kicking off his shoes. "Don't you dare sit down," I roar.

He sighs as he runs his hand over his practically bald head. "Listen, Amy, I had a rough…"

"Don't you *dare* tell me you had a rough day! I had a rough day, too and it involves *your* children so get your ass out of that f'ing chair before I have the garbage men come and take it tomorrow while you're at work!"

Roger stares at me like I have officially lost it.

Maybe I have. Who knows? Thirteen years of stay at home motherhood and a husband who is as useless as tits on a bullfrog can do that to a girl.

"You wouldn't dare," Roger challenges. Of course, all he cares about is his precious chair.

I put my hands on my hips and assume a rebellious attitude. "Try me."

Grumbling, he shoves his smelly feet back into his loafers and follows me out of the room. The diaper is still in the middle of the living room, completely abandoned by the dog. I guess it was even too disgusting for Misty. I bend down and wrap it up and toss it in the garbage. I also notice that Evan's poop filled clothes are next to the couch.

"I'll take care of this. I need you to go upstairs to the bathroom and check on Lexie. She's sick. Oh, and don't talk to Colt about being suspended yet. We need to do that together. He's scared of you."

"Damn right he should be scared of me. You know how embarrassing it is to get a phone call from another principal telling you that your son has been in a fight and he needs to be suspended?" Roger growls. He had obviously forgotten all about Colt's incident at school and my mentioning it reawakened his anger.

"Really, Roger? This isn't about you," I point out as I scoop up Evan's discarded clothing and head down the stairs. *I really need a laundry chute; it would make my life a little easier. Oh well, I guess jogging up and down three flights of stairs helps keep me from blowing up like a Macy's Thanksgiving Day parade balloon,* I muse as I jog down to the laundry room off of the garage. Roger follows me.

"It *is* about me, Amy. I'm a pillar of-"

"The community," I cut him off. "I've heard." *A pillar who can't even keep an eye on his own teenaged daughter when she's within spitting distance the entire school day.* I am seething inside because Roger has managed to make this about himself until I realize that I haven't told him what I've discovered about Allie yet.

"So what's for dinner?" he asks, trailing behind me as I reenter the kitchen.

Ughhhhhhhhhhhhhh! I want to retrieve the dirty diaper from the garbage and shove it in his face. Instead, I shoot him an exasperated glare as I start to climb the stairs.

"Does that mean we're getting take out again?" he calls after me. "Because I've been in the mood for Chinese!"

I ignore him as I stomp back upstairs. Low and behold, Allie has actually done what I told her to do for once. She is still standing in the middle of Evan's room. Evan has abandoned banging the closet door and returned to the floor to build with his blocks. Colt is nowhere to be found, so I can only assume that he is still hiding. As an added bonus, Lexie is also sitting on the floor of Evan's room, playing with the blocks. The very same blocks he is now sucking on. *Fantastic. He's going to be the one puking tomorrow.*

"Hi, Mommy!" Lexie calls out as she waves happily from the floor. "I'm ready for my toast and tea now!" She is wearing pajamas, but her hair is still matted to the side of her face and I'm pretty sure there is puke stuck in it.

"That's great, Lex," I remark and wince as I turn away, only to find Allie feverishly texting on her phone. When she sees me, she shoves the phone back into her bra with a self-satisfied smirk on her face. I don't care. I grip her wrist tightly and yank her from the room.

I am DONE. I have reached my breaking point, the straw that broke the camel's back, yada, yada, yada. Whatever cliché you prefer. And I was about to make a mountain out of a molehill. Oh yeah, here comes Mistake number...what am I up to? Seven? This is it. This is THE BIG ONE. I am going to drag Allie to confront Jason.

"What are you doing? Where are we going?" Allie demands in a whiny, high pitched voice as I drag her protesting body down the stairs. I march her over to the hall closet, grab my jacket and Allie's, tossing hers at her face. All without letting go of her wrist.

Roger is now standing in the living room, hands shoved into his pockets. "Yeah, where *are* we going? Are we going *out* to eat? There's this new Thai place-"

"*Allie* and *I* are going to take a walk and discuss *girl* problems and *you*," I poke Roger in the chest, "are going to make Lexie some tea and toast."

"What?" Both Allie and Roger protest at the same time.

"I am not going anywhere with you," Allie

screeches.

"I don't know how to make tea!" Roger wails. "I don't even know where the tea is!"

"Figure it out," I growl at my husband as I pull on my light jacket. "Put your jacket on," I order my daughter. "It's chilly out there."

"I'm not going anywhere so it doesn't matter," she replies snottily, plopping down on the ground, arms crossed over her chest and legs interlocked.

"Oh yes you are. Because if you *don't*, I will march down to St. Regis Academy tomorrow morning and sign you up faster than you can say *all-girls school*."

Allie blanched. "You won't *dare*."

"Please," I scoffed. "Don't test me on this one. And your father has been dying to sign you up for a nunnery since you were born. I'm pretty sure I have his full support on this one." I glance over at Roger to see him bobbing his head enthusiastically.

"That *is* true," he tells Allie. And he doesn't even *know* about the drugs yet.

Allie leaps to her feet and dashes over to her father. "Daddy, please don't make me go with her!"

Roger looks lost, but he shakes his head. "I don't even know why your mother is mad at you, but I'm sure she has her reasons, crazy as they may be." *Gee thanks, dear.*

Allie glances back and forth between us, like a deer caught in headlights. "This is so unfair!" she wails as she stamps her feet like a two year old.

"Let's go Sarah Bernhardt," I mutter as I hold the door open. More like *Sarah Heartburn...*

"Who?" Allie demands to know as she saunters reluctantly through the door.

"Never mind. Let's just go." As I close the door I tell Roger, "Hold the fort down, okay?" I don't wait for his protests before I slam the door shut. "Come on, let's go," I order Allie as I zip up my jacket.

I squint while glancing across the street. The light is shining in the living room window. I see Jason's car parked on the street and my hand starts to shake. This is going to be one awkward conversation.

Why? My inner voice challenges itself as we stride across the street. *Is it because he's dealing drugs to the neighborhood children or because he's so hot?*

"Shut up!" I mutter, causing Allie to stare at me as we climb the front steps of the Sanders residence.

I shoot a death glare back at her. "Oh please. When you have four kids you'll get to have a nervous breakdown and talk to yourself, too." She doesn't reply, but I can tell she is rolling her eyes behind my back as I step up to the front door and ring the bell.

Several minutes go by and there is no answer. I can see the lights and TV are on and Mary's car in the driveway. In fact, when I peek through the front window, I catch a glimpse of the top of Mary's head. She seems to be relaxing on the sofa.

"Why isn't she answering?" I mumble as I jump to get a better view of her face and maybe catch her attention.

"Maybe she's *sleeping*," Allie replies in her usual snarky tone.

"It's 5:30, Allie."

"So what? She's old. Old people sleep at 5:30. They have dinner at 2:00. What else is there to do after that?"

"She is *not* old," I argue in vain. She did have a point. Mary *was* old.

"Why are we even here?" she whines, pretending to be all innocent. *Oh you know exactly why we are here, Missy. What? Don't want mommy to rip your drug dealer a new one?*

I wave her away. The front window is open a crack. I can clearly hear the evening news. It is cranked to a rather high volume. Maybe Mary just can't hear the bell over the deafening sound of the TV. *Oh wait, didn't Sean say the bell was broken?*

"Mary!" I call through the window. "You hoo! Mary!"

"Oh *God*," Allie drawls as she covers her face with her hands. "Did you really just say *you hoo*?" she shakes her head in her hands. "You're so *mortifying*, Mother."

Annoyed, I reply as I continued to rap loudly on the front door, "To whom, Allie? There's nobody on the steps but us."

"One of my friends could walk by," she scoffs, removing her hands from her face. "It's a free country, you know."

Yes, I know. One with plenty of second amendment

rights being violated by bad moms like me. I ignore her as I continue pounding on the door.

Why doesn't Mary hear me? Even if she is sleeping...and really, how could she sleep with the TV that loud? Allie is right, she *was* old and maybe she had a heart attack or a stroke and couldn't move or answer the door. *So where is Jason?*

Pursing my lips, I head down the front steps.

"Oh thank *God*," Allie huffs as she follows me.

I cut across the lawn and swing open the gate to the backyard. "What are you doing?" she hisses as she chases me. "Mother!" she screeches to a halt and dramatically pounds her foot into the grass.

"Come on," I order. "I need to get in to see if Mary needs help!"

"Why would she need help? She's probably just ignoring you because she doesn't want to talk to you! I can totally relate!" Allie scoffs as she reluctantly follows me into the backyard.

"Zip it," I snap. I stop when I reach the back of the house and notice that the kitchen window is open and the screen has fallen to the ground.

"You never told me why we're here. Why are we here?" Allie demands as she chases after me.

"So I can confront Jason about the *drugs*," I hiss.

Allie shakes her head, "What *drugs*? *Who?*"

I narrow my eyes at her. "Let's not play games, Allie."

"Hoist me up to that window." By the way, at no

point in time does it strike me as odd that the screen is lying on the ground in the backyard.

Allie recoils like I have slapped her across the face. "Are you *insane*? That's like breaking and entering!" *Oh, now she decides to be a law abiding citizen.*

"I'm trying to help the neighbor, Allie. I'm not planning on *stealing* anything. I'm pretty sure that is okay in the eyes of the law."

She parks her hands on her hips and resumes her defiant stance. "No way. I'm not going to jail."

"Listen, you're headed there if you continue your friendship with Victoria. I'll turn you both in myself."

Allie honestly looks frightened. "I told you I didn't-"

"Just save it, Allie." I curse under my breath at her as the garbage cans near the edge of the driveway catch my eye. Grumbling, I drag one over to the window. Lumbering ever so gracefully onto it, I stand underneath the window. Peeking inside, I can see that it is over the kitchen counter, so all I need to do is pull myself up and climb right on to the counter.

I shove the window open and try to hoist my body over the ledge, but it certainly isn't as easy as TV shows lead you to believe. Apparently, to accomplish this feat, you need something called *upper body strength* which I am severely lacking. I end up flailing in midair for a few minutes, legs floundering, body half in the window, half out. Allie is just staring at me, humiliation evident on her face.

"Oh. My. *God*, I *cannot* believe you are doing this,"

she groans as I manage to wiggle my entire body through the window. I slide in and promptly slip right off the counter which has recently been wiped down.

"Shit," I yelp, falling to the floor with a thud. I quickly jump to my feet and examine my body parts for injuries. The only thing that seems to be bruised is my ego. *Of all embarrassing things to do in front of your teenager*, I think as I headed over to the back door to let Allie in.

But I find that she is already inside the house, standing by the back door, tapping her ballet flat encased foot impatiently. "Maybe next time you'll use the open door," she remarks with sarcasm as she demonstrates that the door was open the whole time. She offers me a smirk while I turn crimson.

Okay, so *maybe* I should have checked to see if the back door was open before I climbed in but the point is, I am in now and I need to check on Mary.

"Stay here," I order Allie, warding off further discussion regarding my foolish daredevil stunt. She rolls her eyes and follows me into the living room anyway. The TV is still blasting as we round the corner. Allie and I can see Mary is still on the couch.

And then, we both begin to scream.

~TWELVE~

Allie and I are frozen in place, screaming for what seems to be an eternity as we both stare at our friendly, elderly neighbor sitting on the couch in an emerald green velour track suit. She looks like she is just chilling, propped up on an oversized couch cushion, crossword puzzle book on her lap, glasses folded neatly on top of that. Only problem is, there is a large gaping hole where her chest should be and blood splattered all over the back of the couch, the wall and the front of Mary's body. It appears that she has been shot.

I have never seen a dead body before, other than at a funeral parlor, of course, but I am fairly certain there is no need to check Mary's pulse. She is dead as a doornail.

"Oh my God, oh my God, oh my *God...*" Allie is muttering over and over and over. I can't even console my traumatized teenager because I am shaking, shocked, and not sure what to do. *Should I call the police? And ambulance? Roger? Mary's husband? Son?*

Just then, an even more sickening thought punches me in the gut. *Where is Jason? What has he been doing all day? Where did he rush off to? Did he kill Mary because she found out he was dealing drugs? And where the hell is Sean? Was Sean home when it happened? Oh my God, did he kill Sean, too?*

"Jesus Christ, Sean," I yelp. "Allie, check Sean's room, I'll call the police!"

She stares at me as if I just told her to go give the dead woman mouth to mouth. "Are you *crazy*, Mother? We have to get out of here! Someone could still be in the house! And waiting to chop us up and put our bodies in little baggies and toss us in the river!" Her voice raises an octave with every high pitched word.

I shake my head. "I don't think so. She looks like she's been dead awhile. And besides we didn't hear any gunshots and we've been outside the house for almost twenty minutes," I point out. *Oh really, Amy? Remember we discussed this earlier? You are **not** in an Agatha Christie novel!*

"It would be hard to hear over the TV blasting," Allie snaps back sarcastically, but I can tell she is petrified as she clutches my arm tightly.

Ok, Amy. You need to reassure her. Tell her she is safe. But the problem is, I'm not so sure I believe it myself. I open my mouth to speak but Allie is squeezing me tighter.

"What if he's gone now, but he comes back?" my paranoid daughter shrieks while shaking me frantically. I am a wreck but she is becoming physically undone. "Oh my God, what if he kills *us*! Why did you bring me over here? This is scary, Mother!"

"Well if *you* hadn't been doing drugs we wouldn't even be over here to begin with!" I snap at her.

It is at this point that Allie gives me a look I can only describe as *perplexgitated*. Both perplexed and agitated at the same time.

"*Drugs*, Mother? Seriously? What gave you *that* idea?" Insert eye roll here.

Now it is my turn to be *perplexgitated*. "Well isn't that what you and Victoria were talking about?"

"When?" She wrinkles up her pert little nose.

"Your text messages, Allie! About the *goods?*" I am just plain agitated now.

"I don't know what you're talking about, Mother!" Allie is just plain perplexed at this point.

"Victoria's text message said that she had the goods and you said ok, my mom's not home or something along those lines," I explain, poking my finger into her shoulder. She is almost as tall as I am, so I turn my back so neither Allie nor I can see Mary's body.

Here I must pause. At this point in my story you may be wondering why the hell we didn't get out of the house. Or pick up the phone and call the police. Woman dead from an obvious gunshot wound to the chest on the couch and I am grilling my teen about her texting. *What the hell is wrong with you? What kind of mother are you? Get your kid out of the house and call the police!* Isn't that what you're screaming at me right now? Possibly tossing this book across the room because you just can't believe my stupidity?

Well, as we've established, I'm not the best mother in the world and I certainly make mistakes. This definitely qualifies as one of them. This is part of Mistake #7 for those of you following along at home. Walking in on your neighbor shot at point blank range in her own living room kind of messes with your brain a little bit. I am not thinking too clearly. I assume you've probably never experienced this, so you're going to have to take my word for it.

Allie's face turns bright red as she gasps and covers her mouth with her hand. At first, I think she is crying, but then I realize she is laughing. She must be delirious from the shock. *Should I slap her like they do in movies?* "Oh. My. God. Mother. You thought she meant *drugs*?"

Hands on my hips I retort, "Well...*yeah*!"

Allie offers me a complimentary eye roll. "Duh. She was talking about *make-up*!"

Huh? Now I am really confused. *First of all, why would Allie be so secretive about make-up? It's not like I don't let her wear it. And also, why would she say saw Jason 'doing it' at the mall? Is he secretly a cross dressing, make-up wearer?*

I am about to ask my daughter to clarify, when I hear a thunking noise from somewhere within the house. Allie grips my arm so tightly I can feel her fingers imprinting on my skin.

"Allie," I whisper. "Do you have your cell phone?"

Of course she has her cell phone! What teenager goes anywhere without their cell phone? As a matter of fact, didn't she just shove it into her bra before we came over here?

"Yes," she replies in a hushed voice and my chest does a happy little flip. "But the battery is dead. You didn't close out my apps when you were snooping today and it drained the battery," she continues in an accusatory tone.

Oops. My bad. I grimace. "Sorry."

"What is that noise?" she asks, lip trembling.

I have no clue and I don't want to find out. "We need to get out of here and call the police. *Now*." I tug her towards the back door.

At this point in time, I am looking at Allie, not really paying attention to where I am going, but I can see her eyes grow wide with fright as I speak.

"What?" I ask as I proceed to turn my head and smack right into a bulky male form. As I gaze downward, I see that it is a bulky male form with size 12 sneakers. With blood on them. *Oh shit.*

My heart is sprinting as I cautiously raise my head, taking in the man's sweaty, blood stained tee shirt, rippling biceps crossed over his formidable chest, thick neck muscles, and finally, Jason's quite pissed off expression on his face. Allie grips my arm so forcefully I can feel the bruises forming on my skin underneath her fingertips.

Oh shit, I repeat in my head. *We're gonna die. And Allie is going to torture me in the afterlife about this bonehead move of mine.*

"Uh, hi," I wave to my neighbor timidly. "Um…"

"What in *God's* name are you doing here?" he snaps. "What are you…" his voice trails off. He is obviously as surprised to see us as we are to see him.

I have no answer to offer him as I stand there, mouth

gaping open, knees knocking together, hands twitching like a junkie looking for a fix. In my head, I frantically try to assess the situation.

Okay, I don't see a gun. I can probably grab Allie and rush him, get out the back door and get the hell out of here, dash across the street and call the cops without him catching us. I took kickboxing classes at the Y and that self-defense course with Joey once. I can take him, I assure myself.

Then I take another gander at the ropelike forearms he has crossed over his tee shirt which is, by the way, screaming from the strain of the well-defined pectoral muscles underneath. *Yeah, we're dead.* I gather Allie underneath my wimpy arm, trying futilely to protect her.

Jason reaches out and grabs my arm with one hand and yanks Allie's with his other. Practically stuffing us under his armpits, he drags us towards the back door. "Come on, I've got to get you out of here before the police arrive. *Jesus Christ.* You just couldn't leave it alone, could you?"

He doesn't let me answer, not that I could form words if I tried. "Damn women, always complicating everything. Always getting themselves killed. I can't be responsible for any more damn women getting killed 'cuz they just can't stay out of the damn way." He is now muttering exclusively to himself as he pushes open the back door, Allie and I limp in his arms, too stunned to resist. He shoves us out the door and towards the steps. "Walk," he growls. I nearly pee my pants.

Allie lets out a whimper and I want nothing more than to put my arms around her, comfort her and apologize for getting us into this mess. But my arms and legs are so completely rubbery that I can barely manage to put one foot in front of the other to walk.

I've failed you again, Allie. This time in the worst way imaginable. I couldn't protect you from danger. I am aching to say these words to my daughter who has tears glistening in her beautiful blue eyes. They threaten to burst forward any moment now and smudge the heavily made up face. The face that is simply gorgeous without make–up, but Allie never seems to realize that.

Shit, when was the last time I told her she was beautiful? When was the last time I made her feel good about herself? This may be the last night of her life and I haven't done my job as a mother of a teenaged daughter.

"You're beautiful, Allie," I manage to stammer as we stumble through the Sanders' backyard, Jason shoving us forward. Surprised, she glances up at me and trips on a tree root.

"Oh, for God's sakes," Jason mutters as he pulls her to her feet before she falls flat on her face.

"*What?*" She stares at me incredulously.

"You're beautiful," I repeat, this time with more conviction. If we are going to die tonight, I want my daughter to know that she is beautiful and that I loved her enough to tell her that with my dying breath.

Apparently, Allie is not convinced this is the most efficient use of my dying breath. "Mother, *really?*" And her annoyed tone is accompanied by an eye roll. Daughter, 1, Mom, zip.

"Alright you two, we don't have time for this," Jason complains. "Get in the car." With a forceful grip around our arms, he shoves us towards his car which is now backed all the way up to the garage in the driveway. In the backseat, I can make out two shadowy figures. If I had been scared before, I am downright petrified now.

Stop making this so easy for him, dummy! If you love your daughter, fight! I dig my heels into the pavement in front of me.

"No!" I yell, now frantically searching my surroundings for some way out of this mess. A stick to beat Jason with, a neighbor walking their dog, Roger coming across the street to look for us because we've been gone so long...

Oh, scratch that last one. That'll never happen. Roger has probably assumed Mary and I are having cake and coffee or something like that. He won't look for me until Evan needs his diaper changed. Or he sticks his finger in an electric socket, whichever comes first.

"Mrs. Maxwell," Jason growls in my ear. "We don't have time for you to be difficult. You need to get in the car...*now*." I hate to admit, Jason's warm breath as his lips graze my ear manages to arouse me, even in the face of certain death. But I still am not going to let this gorgeous hunk of a man, who may or may not wear ladies underwear, take me down without a fight.

"No," I repeat, still trying to apply the brakes in my

cheap sneakers. I can smell the rubber burning on the pavement. "I will not go down without a fight. You may succeed in killing me and my daughter, but I certainly will not let you win without a battle from me!" I puff out my chest as much as possible in the current situation.

"Mom!" Allie gasps, obviously appalled. I'm sure I have managed to somehow humiliate her.

At the same time Jason squeaks out in a very unnatural, high pitched voice, "*Kill you*? Why on Earth would I want to *kill you*? I'm trying to save your sorry ass from *getting* killed!"

Okay, this is news to me. "What?" is all I can manage to stammer as I crane my neck to get a better look at him.

Jason shakes his head in disbelief. "Just get in the damn car and I'll explain on the way. Time is of the essence here. You need to listen to me or you're going to be attending your own funeral at the end of the week." He opens the door to the back seat and shoves Allie in next to the two dark forms already sitting there. Then, with his arm still clamped tightly on mine, he guides me around to the passenger side and opens up that door. When the overhead light comes on, I can clearly see that the other two passengers in the back are Walter and Sean. Neither of them appear as if they have been beat up or are being held against their will. True, Walter appears to have been crying, but his wife was just shot to death.

Wait a minute! Do they even know about Mary? Did they even go into the living room and see that Mary had been shot? And Jason had blood on his shoes! Whose blood was that? Mary's? His own?

Confusion swirls around in my brain like a cinnamon bun as Jason hops into the driver's seat and guns the already running car down the driveway. He bounds over the ditch at the bottom of the driveway, nearly sending me airborne.

"Slow down, son," Walter advises in a fatherly tone from the back seat.

"No time for that," Jason replies as we whiz by our house. It looks so quiet and peaceful, nearly every room in the house lit up.

Damn it, Roger. They've got to turn the lights off! What do you think, we own stock in the electric company? You don't pay the bills so you have no idea how much these things cost, I find myself admonishing my husband who is not even there.

Then I remember, I have bigger problems than an enormous electric bill. I turn to Jason and examine his profile as the street lights fly past his window like a strobe light in a dance club. He is a good looking man, anyone with eyeballs in their head can see that. The kind of neighbor any woman wants to have around to watch his rugged form pushing the lawn mower on a Saturday afternoon. But Jason's presence scares me. I have no idea what his deal is, what happened to Mary, what part he played in it, and why he is dragging me and Allie, not to mention Walter and Sean, God knows where. I intend to get to the bottom of this bizarre evening once and for all.

But first, a little motherly housekeeping to attend to.

"Can I use your phone to call Roger?" I ask. "I have to let him know that Evan needs his antibiotic at 8:00 and to put the humidifier on in Colt's room if we're not going to be home by bedtime. Oh and Lexie needs a garbage pail by her bed because if she's throwing up all night, she won't get out of bed and will end up puke all over the floor if there is no garbage can-"

"No can do," Jason interrupts me. "I can't have you calling Roger. The local police will explain to him that we've taken you to a safe place and that he shouldn't worry."

"But I have to explain to him what he has to do for the kids," I wail, tears stinging my eyes for the first time this evening. "You don't understand! He has no clue how to take care of them!"

"Sorry," Jason replies with a shrug. "I'm sure they'll survive. I can't give you my phone. I don't know if it's being tapped or traced. We can't tip anyone off to where we are going."

I take a deep inhale. Typical male. He is not understanding the seriousness of the situation. Roger *literally* has no idea how to take care of his own children. He needs a play by play manual just to watch them when I go to the grocery store. There is a very good chance that out of three children, at least one will be missing, permanently deformed or dead by the time I get home. *If* I get home from where ever we are going.

"Where *are* we going, if you don't mind my

asking?" I inquire sweetly. *You get more flies with honey, Amy,* I remind myself of my mother's sage advice.

"I *do* mind. You wouldn't even have to come with us if you hadn't made it your life's work to snoop," is Jason's retort as he effectively weaves in and out of traffic on Route 1, edging over to the Parkway entrance. I am not a happy camper with his reply. I huff loudly to demonstrate my discord. Jason doesn't seem to care as he is concentrating on the heavy traffic surrounding us. I peek into the back seat.

My daughter is continuing to whimper back there, but other than that, you can just about hear a pin drop in the car. Sean and Walter remain completely stone faced, eyes facing forward. Almost as if they have been *drugged.*

I whip my head around to glare at Jason. "Don't you dare drug us!"

With one eye on the road and one eye staring at me, Jason scowls. "What the hell are you talking about? Why would I *drug* you? Exactly what kind of person do you think I am?"

"I have no idea what kind of person you are!" I retort. "I know absolutely nothing about you other than the fact that you are Sean's father and Walter and Mary's son." *And wear make-up at the mall.*

"Well, that's not exactly correct," comes Walter's voice from the back seat. Jason groans.

"We don't need to get into that now," Jason warns. I turn to see that Walter has scooted up in the seat and is leaning closer to Jason's ear. "You have to tell her, son. It's not fair to drag her along and not tell her."

"Not tell me *what*?" I ask, panic rising in my chest. I am this close to needing a paper bag to breathe into.

"It's going to compromise the investigation," Jason argues, not taking his eyes off of the road.

"What *investigation*? Tell me *what* investigation?" I demand impatiently.

"Son, the investigation is *already* compromised. If it weren't, we wouldn't be in this car headed to the secret location now," Walter reasons.

"*What* secret location?" I ask, clearly panicked. The men continue to ignore me as they banter back and forth.

"Yes, but the less they know, the better off they are. It could save their lives," Jason points out.

"*What* could save our lives?" I demand. "Tell me what you're talking about!" I grab Jason's shirt sleeve and start shaking his arm. Just for your future reference, it is not a bright idea to shake the driver of your vehicle. It tends to cause them to veer out of their lane. *Ooops. My bad.* But fortunately, not one of my 8 mistakes.

"Damn it, Mrs. Maxwell," Jason yelps as he straightens out the car before we can go careening into oncoming traffic. "Don't make me put you in the back seat."

"I just want to know what's going on," I stammer. "I think it's only fair. I mean, where are we going? I have four kids at home that need to be taken care of. Who's going to take care of them?"

"Three," Allie corrects from the back seat. "I'm here with you, Mom." *Oops. Well, at least she called me* Mom *instead of* Mother.

Jason sighs. "You do realize that the information I give you could endanger your life. That means it could get you killed-"

"I know what endanger your life *means*," I interrupt. "Stumbling across a dead neighbor could get me killed, too. I'm pretty sure I'm not 100% safe either way at this point so I'd at least like to have an idea of *why* I'm getting killed if it happens. I like to be well informed. Even in death," I retort sarcastically.

Jason appears nervous as he speeds up to pass a car that is puttering along in the middle lane of the highway. "Okay. I'll tell you. But not until we get there. I don't want to bring the kids into this. It's too dangerous for them"

"Hey!" Allie pipes up, face next to mine as she bounces forward from the backseat. "I'm not a kid! I'm 13."

"Then if you're not a kid, I'm *really* not a kid," Sean mutters. It is the first time I heard Sean speak since we got in the car. I have almost forgotten he is there.

"Absolutely not," Jason replies. "I will speak with Mrs. Maxwell about the situation, but you two do *not* need to concern yourselves with it. This is an adult problem. To be solved by *adults*."

"Well I think we have the right to know what's going on, too," Allie replies grudgingly as she settles back down, crosses her arms across her chest and stares glumly out the window.

Jason continues to weave in and out of traffic, driving in the same infuriating manner that Roger does, impatient and dodgy. It must be a man thing. If I wasn't completely shaken up by the evening's turn of events already, I probably would be slamming on the imaginary brake.

"Put your seat belt on," I tell my daughter before I follow suit and stare out the window, watching the familiar sights fade away as we head off to an unknown destination.

~THIRTEEN~

"What you don't know can't hurt you," Jason tells me as he pats my leg. "But the person you don't know will," he adds in an evil voice, pulling off onto a deserted dirt road on the side of the highway. In one swift motion, he reaches down underneath his seat and pulls out a gleaming meat cleaver. He grins devilishly and I notice his lip gloss. His heavily made up eyes sparkle as he throws his head back and cackles.

Panicking, I turn my head to the back seat, looking for help from Walter, but he is suddenly brandishing his own meat cleaver with the same glint of madness in his eye. He is holding Allie by the hair. She is trying to fight him off to no avail. Sean is cowering on the floor of the back seat, out of the way. I can't tell whose side he is on.

"What are you doing?" I screech as I back up against the door. "I thought you were helping us!"

Jason lets out a maniacally laugh. "You thought wrong then, little lady! You got in the way of our drug ring and now we have to kill you!"

Walter joins in the laugher. "Hehehehe, we're going to chop you up and put you in tiny baggies and throw your tiny pieces of flesh into the river!" Both men hoot in synchrony as they sharpen their knives.

"See, Mom!" Allie calls from the back seat. "I told you so! You never listen to me ever!"

"I'm sorry, Allie! I guess I will listen to you from

now on!" I shout as Jason lurches forward with the meat cleaver…

I sit up with a start, jostled out of my dream, as the car hits a bump in the road. I quickly glance at Jason who is maneuvering onto a gravel driveway, concentrating on the sharp angle of the turn. He does not have a meat cleaver. Still shaking, I realize I must have fallen asleep, lulled into a dream state by the passing headlights on the highway. *It was only a dream, Amy*, I reassure myself. *Only a dream.*

Still, I glance around the car nervously. Allie and Sean are both sound asleep, their heads resting on either of Walter's shoulders. He sits in between them, stoically staring straight ahead, his gnarly hands folded and tucked between his knees. He does not appear to have a meat clever, either. I sigh with relief as I settle back down in my seat.

We are headed up a steep incline towards a dimly shining light at the top. It appears to be a cabin but there are no street lights on the access road and it is now pitch black out so it's difficult to see. I glance at the dashboard clock which reads 10:45. *Holy shit, it's late! We are surely out of state by now. We've been driving almost five hours! I hope Roger got the kids to bed…* The mere thought of Evan, Colt and Lexie chokes me up. *Damn, I miss them already.*

"Where are we?" I ask in a raspy, just woke up voice.

"We're *there*," Jason replies curtly as he pulls up in front of a small cabin with a rickety porch, standing alone on the top of the slope, surrounded by trees. There is an eerie silence in the surroundings; no crickets chirping or whistling of wind through the trees. If this place is supposed to make me feel safer, it's not doing its job. The desolate surroundings cause me to shudder. Every horror novel I ever read starts with an abandoned cabin in the woods. I can hear the narrator now: *Five friends are looking forward to the vacation of their lives. What they don't know is the abandoned cabin they have rented for their relaxing week at the lake is haunted by a Nazi zombie with a predilection for chainsaws...*

I shake that thought from my head as I climb out of the car, stretching my stiff and cramped legs. I swear I see a shadow flit behind the cabin and I back myself against the car until I realize it is just a raccoon. I sigh with relief.

My overactive imagination is certainly getting the best of me tonight. Allie, Sean and Walter also climb out of the vehicle, car doors slamming punctuating the otherwise silent surroundings. Jason scurries to the front door, picking through his ring of keys as he walks. The rest of us shuffle awkwardly behind him, not sure what else to do. It isn't like we have luggage to carry in or anything. We didn't exactly have time to plan for this little impromptu vacation.

Jason pushes the door open and it creaks noisily on its hinges, a true to life horror film. I shudder again as we file into the room, one at a time. Jason flicks on a switch, illuminating a low wattage floor lamp. I blink to adjust my eyes to the sudden light and then take in my surroundings.

The room is sparsely furnished with a threadbare couch that may possibly be a relic from the Lincoln administration, an oversized chair and a warped mahogany coffee table centered between the two. In one corner of the room, there is a heavy oak cabinet/ table with dried and dying flowers in a vase. There are two windows on the same wall as the front door and I assume they look out onto the front yard, but it is too dark to tell and they are covered with a heavy set of mustard colored curtains that remind me of the ones that hung in my grandmother's living room. There is 1970s wood paneling lining the walls; I assume to give it a "log cabin" feel, but instead, it's giving me a retro, sick to my stomach feeling. The floor is hardwood, scuffed up and worn, splinters visible to the naked eye as it groans laboriously under foot as we pile into the room.

Allie is the first one to speak. "Well, I don't like *this* at all." She scrunches up her nose, quite possibly from the smell of garbage that is wafting out of the small kitchenette to the right of the door. In the kitchenette, there is a puce green stove, matching fridge, and a breakfast nook with a cream Formica top and several stools pushed underneath it. There is an empty water bottle sitting in the middle of the otherwise empty nook countertop.

"God damn it," Jason swears under his breath as he stomps over to the garbage can. He knocks the lid off and quickly turns his head to the side with disgust. "God damn pigs. They can't even clean up their own crap," he mutters as he ties the garbage bag up. He tugs it out of the pail and marches past us. The bag is dripping from the bottom, leaving a slimy brown trail from the can to the door. We all turn our heads away as he walks by and Allie makes a gagging noise as Jason bounds out the door, presumably towards the outside garbage can.

Oh please dear God don't let her throw up, I silently pray. Allie gagging reminds me that Lexie is sick and I feel a pang in my chest.

I really hope Roger is taking good care of her. I hope he made her tea and remembered that she likes honey in it instead of sugar. Oh, and that she likes the crust on toast, even though she insists that we cut the crust off of her sandwiches. And she likes the butter melted in the toaster oven, not spread on after the bread has been toasted. Did he know that? Has he called the police yet? I'm sure he realized we were gone, but have the police come to him and told him what happened to Mary?

It is killing me that I have no idea what is going on in my own house. Deep down inside, I know Roger has to be capable of taking care of the children once he realizes he has no other choice, but I am also concerned what he knows about our whereabouts. *Is he worried? Did the police tell him where we are? Do the **police** even know where we are?*

I have a lot of questions for Jason when he comes back in. Meanwhile, I have to clean up that smelly garbage juice trail. I spy a roll of paper towels on the counter and grab it, attempting to rip off a sheet. There is exactly one sheet left. I sigh as I fold it in half to protect my hand from the skanky spill and I proceed to get down on my knees to clean it up.

While I am doing that, Walter moves towards the kitchen and swings open the door to the ancient looking fridge. After peering inside, he shakes his head with disgust and slams the door shut. Then he reaches over the counter and opens the cabinets one by one.

Jason steps back into the house and rubbing his hands together, he remarks, "It's getting cold out there."

"They didn't restock," Walter comments with a scowl on his face.

"Damn it. I gave them plenty of warning!" Jason yells, face contorting with anger.

"Well, give it time-" Walter starts to say.

"No!" Jason snaps. "I gave them four hours notice, per protocol, and they still didn't stock up. What are they gonna do? Wake up the whole house at 3:00 in the fucking morning and start throwing meat in the freezer? I've got two kids here for God's sake. They're going to be starving in the morning and I've got no food for them. I've got nothing! And the assholes from last week left their garbage here. I'm *pissed*." He picks up the empty water bottle from the nook and flings it against the wall in the kitchen. It clatters to the ground, but not before leaving an indentation in the sheetrock. "I'm so sick and tired of this *shit*!"

He plops down onto one of the stools and leans on the table top, cradling his head in his hands. I can hear the unmistakable sound of crying as his shoulders rock along with his sobs.

We are all silent and still. Walter bows his head and Sean pokes at the floorboards with the tip of his shoe, leaving me and Allie staring at each other with *what do we do* looks on our faces. This is certainly an awkward moment for all of us.

Finally, after what feel like an eternity, Walter takes a step forward and gently places his worn hands on Jason's broad shoulders. "I know how hard this is, buddy," Walter tells Jason, while rubbing his shoulders. It seems odd that the man who has just lost his wife is comforting his son. *Or whoever he is.*

"I'm so tired of this happening over and over, Walt! I can't seem to get it right! No matter how hard I try, I fail them every single time. I can't keep doing-" Jason's cries become muffled.

Walter turns to me and speaks authoritatively. "There are two bedrooms at the end of the hall. I'm sorry there are no pajamas or toothbrushes right now, but they should be bringing some clothes and toiletries first thing in the morning. Why don't you guys go pick a room and settle down for the night? Sean can room with me and Jason."

Not meaning to come off as rude, but accomplishing

it anyway, I ask the question burning on my mind, "Who exactly is *they*?"

The answer does not come from either Walter or the visibly distraught Jason. It is Sean who speaks up and replies in a steady voice, "*They* are the DEA."

Allie and I both stare at Sean in complete shock, our mouths gaping open. *DEA?* The idea seems like a joke. I am waiting for *Candid Camera* to leap out. *Well, that explains Jason's penchant for make-up, maybe…*

Allie finally speaks.

"DEA?" She turns away from Sean and yanks on my arm. "DE *fucking* A, Mom!" She stares at me, confused. "What's the DEA?"

"Um, it's like the FBI, but…"

Walter holds up his hand. "No, it's not. It's the Drug Enforcement Administration, young lady."

"Drugs? I'm not doing drugs!" Her words are hostile, but there is fear in her voice. She sounds like she is six years old again and scared to jump off the diving board.

I squeeze her hand, just waiting for her to pull away from me as usual. Surprisingly, she squeezes back.

Walter steps away from Jason who is still acting oblivious to our presence. He leads us towards the threadbare couch. He sits on the coffee table and clasps our hands in his warm grandfatherly like hands. We both stare down at the floor.

"Jason is not my son. In fact, Mary was not even my wife. We are all DEA agents," Walter explains with a grave expression on his face.

"What?" my head snaps up from its hung position. "But you live across the street. Our street," I stammer, as if that would explain everything.

"We did live across the street, but as you may have noticed, we weren't too social. We tried to avoid being in public too much, but we had to maintain the impression of a nice, quiet elderly couple. We were friendly enough, but didn't get involved with the people on our block.

"Anyway, Mary and I were agents and had been friends for many years, both of us widowed, so we were the perfect candidates for the sting operation," Walter continues.

"*What* sting operation?" I ask incredulously. *A sting operation on our block? Seriously?*

"You have to have an operation when you get stung by a bee?" Allie asks, equally disbelievingly. "I didn't know that. Mom, why didn't you tell me that?"

Oh, my dear dumb child... I pat her head and roll my eyes at Walter.

Walter smiles weakly, removes his glasses and pinches the bridge of his nose before continuing. "I guess there is no harm in telling you this since our cover is already blown." He pushes his glasses back up on his nose and leans in towards us. "We suspect that there's a mafia member living on Hartford Ave. He is the leader of the drug ring that we've been trying to take down for several years. Been dealing exclusively to high school and middle school kids. Up until this morning, we weren't sure if we were correct. After the hit on Mary, we

Heather Balog

are certain."

I gasp, unable to control myself. *Holy crap. It **is** about drugs!*

"Who is it?" I question, not sure I wanted to know as I immediately begin scrolling through my mind's neighborhood rolodex for possibilities.

Eddie, the senile, retired bus driver who went out to the store in his underwear last week? Yeah, no, couldn't be Eddie. Bill, the tax accountant who got out the yard stick to place his garbage cans equidistant to the curbs? Hmmm, probably not him. Fred, the butcher who screamed at his wife on the front lawn last month and threw a steak at her? Oh, yes, it definitely had to be Fred.

"That's *so* cool! Who is it?" Allie perks up.

"It is so *not* cool, Allie!" I correct. The kid has watched *Goodfellas* with Roger too many times. "There's a *murderer* living on our block. That is *really* not cool."

Allie shrugs. "I still want to know who it is."

Walter shakes his head. "I can't tell you that. It's confidential information and we haven't caught the suspect yet. As Jason says, we can't do anything to compromise the case."

"We're stuck on a mountaintop a bazillion miles from anyone. My phone is dead and even if it wasn't or I had the charger with me, there's probably no chance in hell I am going to get a signal. You're probably not going to let us go home until after the guy is caught and hauled off to jail and it will be splashed all over the front of the newspapers by that point in time, so tell me, what

~ 218 ~

difference does it make if you tell us or not?" Allie remarks pointedly.

Walter isn't budging. "Nope. Not going to tell you so you might as well get ready for bed."

Grumbling, Allie and I rise to our feet. We trudge down the hall before I realize something and turned back to Walter who now is sitting at the breakfast nook. Jason hasn't lifted his head up, so I don't know if he is still crying or not. "Go ahead," I tell Allie, pointing towards the bedrooms.

She shakes her head vehemently. "No friggin' way. I'm staying with you. I'm not going into that room alone. What if there's an ax murderer behind the door? Waiting to drag me into the woods and chop me into teeny tiny pieces?" *Ugh, not this again.*

Figuring that this is not the time to argue with my teenager, I sigh and pad back down towards the kitchen. Allie joins Sean in the living room where he is now sitting on the couch, staring at his shoelaces, sans expression. They look even smaller than their thirteen and fourteen years sitting there next to each other. Walter and Jason are still at the table, heads huddled closely together. They seem to be deep in discussion.

I step into the kitchenette and stand in front of the nook, hands on my hips. The men glance up when they see my shadow fall across the table.

Walter looks sad, the kind of sad you might see if your cat got hit by a car. But Jason is clearly falling apart. His face is blotchy, his nose reddened and possibly runny. He wipes the underside with the back of his hand. No matter how long I lived with Roger or had two gross little boys, I can never get used to that. I shudder before speaking.

"Listen, I need to know one more thing…"

Jason sighs. "Mrs. Maxwell-"

"Amy," I correct him.

"What?" he replies, furrowing his brow.

"Call me Amy. If we're going to be stuck together for God knows how long, it's ridiculous for you to keep calling me Mrs. Maxwell." Jason nervously runs his fingers through his hair. I notice a small clump interwoven in his fingers. Maybe the idea of being stuck with me till the end of time is torture to him. "Besides, we're neighbors anyway. Well, I guess we're neighbors until you figure out who the neighborhood criminal is."

Jason nods. "Yeah. I'm sure we will be getting another assignment after that."

"Which is exactly why I'm wondering…who *are* you exactly?" I raise my eyebrow. "You're not Walter's son. Walter's not Mary's husband. So who are *you*? And," I glance over towards the couch as I lean in to whisper. "Who is Sean?"

Nobody is who they claim to be, so what are a bunch of undercover agents doing with a fourteen year old autistic child? If he is in fact, autistic. Shit, for all I knew, he could be a twenty-two year old undercover college student. Hell, the kid was big enough and he looks like he shaves.

Jason glances at Walter nervously. Walter shrugs and remarks, "Hey she's involved whether we like it or not. Can't really leave her in the dark."

Sweat is beading around Jason's hairline as he runs his fingers through his thick hair again. I know it sounds crazy, but I am actually getting a little giddy from making him so uncomfortable. It seems like I have the upper hand in this conversation, even though that probably isn't true.

"Mary really *was* my mother. I was never married to Stacey, Sean's mother. She was actually an FBI agent with whom my mother got really close to. She lived next door to my mom for about three years, but since I was busy with work, I didn't often get to visit Mom. I usually came by for holidays and Mother's Day, but I'm ashamed to admit, I didn't see her as much as I should have.

"All that changed one day when I stopped over in the middle of the week because I was working in the area. That's when I met Stacey Sanders and I fell madly in love with her. Sean was nine at the time and becoming a real handful because he was almost bigger than her. Sean would go into violent rages and become uncontrollable, hitting her and cursing at her. Stacey even had to call the police once when he threw a chair at her and ran out of the house. She was terrified that he would get kidnapped or hit by a car. She was always worried about him; never herself. His deadbeat father had disappeared long before he was born and Stacey didn't have any family nearby to help her with Sean which is probably why she connected so much with my mother."

Jason glances up at me, lids brimming over with tears. I can't take my eyes off of him; this child he is describing seems nothing like the mild mannered Sean who is sitting in the next room.

"Mom had taken Sean and Stacey under her wing. I found myself visiting even more often and Stacey and I ended up dating. I moved in with them soon after, selling my condo. We were going to get married. I was going to adopt Sean. He had calmed down tremendously since I moved in." Jason just shrugs. "Maybe half of his problem was just the fact he needed a male role model in his life.

"So one day, three years ago *tomorrow*, believe it or not, I got a call from my supervisor that he needed me downtown in his office immediately. He didn't say what it was about, so I assumed I had a new case. I remember it was an unseasonably warm Indian summer day and I had been jogging in the park. I normally would have gone home to change first, but I didn't because he had sounded urgent. So I rushed to work instead of stopping home. And the boss did have a new case for me, so I didn't go home until later that evening when I got the phone call."

Jason pauses in his tale and swallows hard. He lightly touches his hand to his forehead. "I always wonder what would have happened if my boss hadn't called me; if I had gone home after my run. Or if I hadn't gone for a run at all. I know in my heart it probably never would have changed anything, but I always wonder-" His voice breaks off; he is swallowing more now in attempts to control his sobs. Walter is obviously uncomfortable as he clumsily pats him on the back. I shuffle my feet, not sure if I should try to comfort Jason or if he would rather that I don't acknowledge his grief. Finally, Jason waves Walter away.

"Stacey had been working in the backyard where she had made a small garden. She loved that garden, she said it gave her so much peace from her life that she worked on it every day, rain or shine. That day she must have been weeding because they found the pile of weeds next to her. Shot in the head. She had worked on a particularly gruesome case many years ago. Serial killer she had put away for 113 years. The wife of that guy was distraught. She had been hysterical in court; screamed she couldn't live without her man. Didn't care he was a criminal mastermind who would have killed her too. The woman found out where Stacey lived. She waited till nobody else was home and shot Stacey and then killed herself."

Jason's face is blotchy from emotion and tears; his hands shaking. I am silently hoping that is the end of his story, but he continues on.

"Thank God Sean wasn't home. I was so worried about him and the trauma he might endure that we moved out of that house. Stacey had recently named me as Sean's guardian in her will, so without another parent or family to contest that, he came to live with me. I'm in the process of formally adopting him.

"Mom moved out of her own house shortly afterwards. Stacey had been like a daughter to her and she said it broke her heart every time she looked into the backyard where the garden used to be. Mom was so shaken up and distraught, she felt the only thing that would cure her was throwing herself into her work. Despite being almost 60 years old, she requested a long term assignment. She thought if she kept busy with work, she would forget about Stacey.

"The agency balked at that idea. Mary was at retirement age, not the type of person to put on such an assignment. In fact, she hadn't been on a long term assignment in years. They actually were pushing her to retire, but Mom was a stubborn woman and she refused. But then, this case fell into their laps and she was perfect for it." Jason jerks a thumb towards Walter. "They paired her with Walter, they decided to call themselves the Sanders in honor of Stacey, and the rest is history." He shrugs again, a scowl on his face replacing the sadness.

I feel like I need to sit down. This is all an overwhelming amount of information to process in one night. I grab one of the remaining stools and hop onto it, staring at Jason before I speak. And all I can manage to mutter is, "Wow."

Allie pipes up with, "But how did *you* end up living there? I mean, I get you're DEA, but it wasn't your case. It was your mother's." She is standing behind my stool, leaning her elbows on the counter. *Oh, that was true. Smart kid I have there. I thought she was in the other room, though...*

"Anyway, I was assigned to the case too at my

request. I was only supposed to stop in and do 'son-like' things, visit and stuff like that but I was nervous about the assignment. Mom was 60 years old and essentially living with a stranger." He gives Walter a sheepish look. "Sorry. It wasn't you. Just the whole case freaked me out."

Walter throws his hands up, almost in defeat. "Hey, I can't blame you. You didn't know me from Adam. Even though Mary and I were colleagues for years and we have to endure intense security scrutiny on this job, you never know. I applaud you, son, for taking charge."

"Thanks," Jason remarks with a shy grin. I can tell he is pleased by Walter's approval. I wonder what had happened to his own father. *Was he an agent, too? Jason said Mary was a widow; did his father get killed?* I can't help wondering if Walter had been like a father figure to him in the few months that they were living together.

"When they thought they had a break in the case, I moved in. The agency didn't know about Sean living there, so we kept him kind of hidden, home schooling him and everything until the day he got out and wandered over to your house."

Ooo, so that's why we never saw him until Colt's party. It makes sense now!

"After that, the cat was out of the bag and we had to incorporate him into our cover, officially enrolling him in school and all. The DEA flipped out as you can imagine, but I wasn't about to abandon my mother."

His face clouded. "But in the long run, it didn't accomplish what I had set out to do in the first place;

protect my mother." His voice drops to a low and raspy octave. "I failed my mother, just like I failed Stacey."

"Stacey wasn't your fault," I interject, realizing I shouldn't have said anything as soon as the words escaped. *Shut up, Amy. You didn't know Stacey and you barely know Jason.* "I'm sorry," I apologize immediately.

"It's fine. I know that I am probably the reason my mother got killed," Jason replies with a shrug. Walter stands and places both hands on Jason's shoulders.

"Stop it, son. Your mother knew what she was getting into. She wanted to take the risk. Hell, she *welcomed* it. She was a very strong willed woman. I may not have been your mother's husband, but I certainly got to know her in the few months we lived together." Walter adds a chuckle that causes Jason to whip his head around and glower at the older man. "Oh, not like that," Walter stammers when he realizes what he has implied. "We were friends. Very good friends and nothing more. I will miss her tremendously." He squeezes Jason's shoulders affectionately.

Out of the corner of my eye, I can see Sean getting up from his spot on the couch. He ambles over to the table where Jason and Walter are and timidly places his hand on Jason's shoulder. Jason turns his head towards Sean, offering him a grateful smile, placing his own hand on top of Sean's and they remain still, no words escaping from any of them.

I back away slowly from this family who is not really a family but still seemed to support each other more than my own family did. I wished I knew what I was doing wrong and what they had done right.

~FOURTEEN~

Jason is smiling down at me when I wake up; the sun is streaming in the dirty windows.

"Hi," he says with a charming smile that causes my insides to melt like a crayon left on the sidewalk on a hot summer day.

My mouth feels dry and cottony, as if I drank too much the night before and I find that I can't speak as I struggle to sit up. In Jason's hand a bottle of Perrier appears.

"You look like you could use some water," he purrs as he holds the bottle up. He twists off the cap and hands it to me with the same adorable grin. God, how he makes his dimples dance! So tantalizing!

"How did you sleep?" he asks while lovingly stroking my hair. I am paralyzed in awe of this gorgeous man.

"Um, I slept well," I manage to stammer, remembering correct grammar. Oh, how my mother would be so proud of me!

"They caught the suspect," he whispers as he sits on the bed and leans closer to my ear, his warm breath causing a chill to rip through my body. "He's in custody."

"Oh, that's excellent," I manage to respond in a raspy voice. Water. I need water. I take another sip of

water to lubricate my parched throat.

"I've sent everyone else home," Jason murmurs, practically nuzzling my ear. My overtired body trembles with desire, energizing my limbs. I can feel stirrings in regions that haven't felt such sensations in four years.

"Oh," I reply, trying to prevent my voice from squeaking. "Everyone?"

Jason nods as he cups my face in his hands and stares lovingly into my eyes. I feel as if I can see into the depths of his broken and damaged heart and soul through his eyes. "We're all alone. It's a rainy day, too. You know what rainy days are good for? Staying in bed...all day."

"Alone?" I repeat in disbelief. I haven't been alone in ages. I'm not sure I even know what alone is anymore. And what would one do if they find themselves "alone" with a handsome, mysterious neighbor who isn't really a neighbor but an undercover agent who fights the bad guys?

"Yes," Jason says as his hand brushes the side of my face from the top of my cheekbone down to my chin. "Alone. Together." He leans in and his lips touch mine-

"Amy!" Jason is standing over my bed wearing a scowl. "Are you getting up at some point today?"

I struggle to sit up, my eyes bleary and my head foggy. I glance around the room and discover that Allie is not sleeping in the twin sized bed next to me and the cabin is quiet except for the sound of rain pounding on the roof. And Jason.

Gone is the soft and vulnerable Jason that revealed himself last night. In his place is a hardened looking man taping his foot and glaring down at me, causing me to think I may have dreamt up his tears the previous evening.

"I need you to get up and keep an eye on the kids. Walter and I are being debriefed this afternoon so we are going to be gone for a while and I want to make sure that you-"

My throat is scratchy, but I manage to sputter, "You're leaving us here? Alone in the woods? With no cell phone?"

Jason shakes his head. "You'll be fine. The perps aren't after you and Allie, or Sean."

"Oh really? Then why did we have to be dragged all the way up here then?" I snap as I leap from the bed, forgetting that I have been sleeping in a tee shirt and my underwear. I had tried to fall asleep completely clothed and I just couldn't, so I ended up peeling off my jeans around 3 am after tossing and turning, worried and appalled about the whole situation.

Jason's eyes widen and his head jerks back in surprise at my attire. Mortified, I rip the top sheet off the bed and wrap it around my lower body; my face feeling like it was going to burn off from the heat of my blushing. Jason appears to be averting his eyes as I struggle with the sheet and try to remember what I had wanted to say. *Shit, this is embarrassing.*

"If they are going to take out anyone, it would be someone with evidence against them," Jason explains, still not looking me in the eye. *Oh yeah, the perps.*

"Well, then why are we in hiding?" I ask again, recalling the whole point of my concern.

"Because they still may think you saw something or know something because you were at the house. They probably did *not* see you, but if they have someone watching the house, there's still that minute chance and I don't want to put you or your family in danger by letting you roam around your neighborhood," Jason replies with a triumphant tone.

"So, then they still may come up here looking for me and Allie and Sean because they *think* we know something," I point out. Jason flushes. Apparently he hadn't considered that.

"Fine," he stammers. "I'll get an agent to stay here and babysit you. You can go shower; nobody's in there right now." He turns to storm out of the room with a huff.

"Don't do me any favors," I call to his back, agitated that he first of all, didn't think to get someone to protect me and secondly, that he referred to me needing to be babysat. Yes, I know. Conflicting thoughts, but all I seemed to be able to think around Jason were conflicting thoughts. The man infuriated me and delighted my senses at the same time. I simultaneously wanted to wring his neck and cover him with kisses. *Poor Jason is a lonely guy with a broken heart. He needs a little TLC. Bet I know exactly what would make him feel-*

Stop it, Amy! You are married. *You love Roger. Roger is your husband,* my conscience is practically screaming at me while I ogle Jason retreating, his rear end looking *oh so good* in his nice butt hugging jeans.

I shut down my impure thoughts immediately. I can swear that my loins are speaking to me instead of my rational 16 year old, er, 30 something year old brain.

Get a grip, Amy, I command myself as I close the bedroom door. Between being confined to this cabin with no way to contact the outside world and the shocking events of the last 24 hours, my brain is fried. It isn't even making sense anymore.

Sighing, I step over to the ancient dresser in the corner that has a mirror perched atop it. I am immediately horrified by the face that is staring back at me.

"Ugh, what a mess," I growl at my reflection. I know that I am not beautiful by any stretch of the imagination, but most days I manage to keep it together enough to look *presentable*. I stare at myself in disgust. I can't believe I just faced my heart palpitation inducing neighbor in my current state.

Do I really look this bad when I woke up every day or is today particularly horrible? It makes me wonder what the heck Roger has been thinking all these years. My hair, which is in dire need of a dye job, is matted on one side of my head and sticking straight up on the other. It looks like I have a compass on my head pointing due North. My eyes are bloodshot with dark purple moons underneath. My skin on my face is pale and sallow. My lips are dry and cracked. *I need make-up...* I chuckle to myself as I wonder if Jason has any make-up he can share with me but my thoughts are interrupted by a nauseating odor. On a hunch, I sniff under my arm pits. I am pretty ripe.

You really should take that shower, Amy. Jason could probably smell your stench from where he stood. Telling you to shower was a not so subtle hint that you stink, I consider as I reach down on the floor to retrieve my jeans from the place I tossed them. I sniff them; they do not have that "fresh from the dryer" scent. I wish I had clean clothes. I really want to take that shower but the only thing worse than *not* having a shower, is putting dirty clothes on after a hot, relaxing shower.

Instead of bathing, I drop the sheet and pull my right leg into the jeans. I am hopping around the bedroom trying to get my left leg in when there is a soft knock at the door.

My stomach tenses into a knot. I really don't want to see Jason again looking the way I do. I would kill for a toothbrush right now. It bothers me as I realize that I would be the first person voted off the island in *Survivor* and that would make me very happy.

"Amy?" It is Walter's gravelly voice at the door, not Jason's. I let out a sigh of relief.

"Just throwing my jeans on," I call back as I continue to bounce around the room. It's like my skinny jeans actually got skinnier overnight, but I have not had the same luck. I suck in my flappy gut as I zip up.

Damn, how did I get into these yesterday? Had I known that I would be wearing them for a few days, I would have put my mommy jeans on. Or sweatpants. *Ah, sweatpants.* How I long for my favorite sweats and a cup of coffee, snuggling up on the couch with Evan, watching *Live with Kelly and Michael.*

The thought of Evan and what I am now considering to be "my former life", causes me to choke back a sob.

I wonder what Evan's doing right now. Did Roger have to take the day off of work? Did my mother come over to watch him? Did Colt cry when I wasn't there to take him to school? How many times did Lexie visit the nurse today? Did anyone even tell the kids what happened? Did Roger even notice that I haven't come back yet????

Suddenly, I'm angry at Jason all over again for some bizarre reason that only makes sense in my head. I throw open the door to see Walter standing there, an apologetic expression on his face.

"I'm sorry to have bothered you, but Jason and I are leaving in a moment," he explains, staring down at his shuffling feet.

God, how awful do I look that this 60 something year old man can't even look me in the eye?

I don't even thank him for the information. Instead, I abruptly ask, "Where *is* Jason?"

Walter points in the direction of the kitchen and I promptly storm off towards it, my feet bare. Jason is securing the lid to his travel mug as I round the corner in a fury.

Out of the corner of my eye, I notice that Sean and Allie are lounging on the couch, listening to a radio that is somewhere in the room. Both of the teenagers now wear vacant expressions on their faces as the static of the radio station completely obliterates the peppy pop music. They're probably miserable being trapped here in the pouring rain, no cell phone or TV. I actually feel sorry for them.

But I don't have time to think about it now. "What did you tell Roger?" I demand from Jason. He obviously did not know I was in the room because his hand shakes as he glances up, startled. A stream of brown coffee pours down the side of the mug and over his hand.

"Shit," he exclaims, practically dropping the mug back down on the counter. He glares at me accusingly. "Thanks a *lot*, Amy."

"Sorry," I reply, not meaning it. And then I immediately proceed to hound him again. "What did you tell Roger? I assume *somebody* told Roger something, right? He's not sitting there looking out the window, waiting for me to come home, is he?"

Jason looks at Walter who offers him a half-hearted shrug.

"Oh for God's sakes, nobody explained *anything* to Roger? Are you *kidding* me?" This is exactly why women need to be in charge of everything. Men completely forget to take care of the "details".

"Actually, he called in a missing person's report last night," calls out a new voice from the doorway. I spin on my heel and see a middle aged man with a very broad neck and a military style haircut in a beige dress shirt, mint green tie and dark brown khakis standing in the doorway, arms crossed over his formidable chest. There are puddles forming underneath his size 14 feet.

"Who the hell are you?" I ask. Okay, rude. But I am done with being the polite one here. Let's recap, shall we? In the past twenty four hours I have been dragged through the ringer at my son's school, been puked on by my ten year old, thought I discovered my daughter was doing drugs by snooping through her phone, stumbled upon the corpse of my elderly neighbor who was in fact an undercover agent, taken to a remote and desolate area of the woods by my other neighbor for "my safety" and discovered no one on my block seems to be who they say they are. Oh and I slept in my clothes and my drool worthy hottie neighbor saw me in my underwear. And I smell. Am I forgetting anything? So please, forgive me if I've been rude to this stranger who is invading my so called "safe place".

"This is Agent Harding," Jason replies drily. "Your babysitter for the day." He reaches for the coffee pot and pours more coffee into his mug to make up for the bit he had spilled at my expense.

Agent Harding balks at Jason's description. "What? No. I didn't know I was babysitting. I'm just supposed to be-"

I cut the agent off and continue to grill Jason. "Okay well that's fine, but you didn't answer my question. Don't *think* I forgot about my question." I shake my finger at him before I whip my head back towards the new agent. "What do you mean he filed a missing person's report? Jason told me the police would tell him what happened." I turn to glare at Jason accusingly.

"Ha," Agent Harding scoffs. "The police couldn't tell him that because the police don't *know* anything." His lips are hardened into a hair-raising grin.

My hands suddenly feel cold and clammy. *Is Jason lying to us? Did he make the whole agent thing up to lure us to this cabin?* In the back of my mind, I recall the whole meat cleaver dream. I glance around frantically, wondering how I can catch Allie's attention and get us both to safety. I tremble as I realize I am no match for these goons.

Jason glowers at Agent Harding. "The police know there is an undercover operation, but they don't know *why* we took you. They may be under the impression that you are, um, a suspect. Your fingerprints are in the house."

"What?" I screech much louder than I have intended to. Allie and Sean's heads snap up, trance broken and they stare at me, mouths hanging open. I clench my fists angrily at my sides, seething at Jason.

Oh man, how I want to pummel his gorgeous face right now. Break his straight and perfectly proportioned nose. Give his crystal blue eyes a nice round shiner. Split his soft lips that are probably so delightful to kiss...

Jason screws the cap on his travel mug again. He picks it up and strides over to where I am standing, hands indignantly parked on my hips. "It's fine. It's only temporary. We *know* you didn't do it. It's just to throw the real perp off." His pats my elbow patronizingly, sending shivers up my arm and throughout my body.

Stunned by his apathetic attitude, I ignore the sexual chill and call after him, "You're sullying my good name!"

Jason snorts as he raises his eyebrows at Agent Harding. "Good luck with this one. She's feisty," he remarks as he heads out the door, Walter trailing behind him.

"Hey!" I call after him as he and Walter retreat down the steps. "I resent that!" I rush to the door to follow them, but Agent Harding steps in front of me and closes it before I can finish screaming obscenities at Jason's back.

I frown at his hulking form before flopping down on the chair like a petulant child. I cross my arms over my chest, fully intending to sulk until Jason returned.

"I brought toothbrushes and shampoo and stuff," Agent Harding reports as he holds out his arms, hands full of *Target* bags.

Allie's head snaps up again. She leaps to her feet and races over to Agent Harding who is now explaining to me that he didn't know our sizes exactly but he had to estimate based on Jason's description. After riffling through the bags, Allie loops a bag over her wrist, apparently full of clothes for her. She then throws one of the remaining bags at me and gathers up shampoo and body wash into her arms.

"Dibs on the shower," she calls while speed walking towards the bathroom.

Well, I've gone more than twenty four hours without a shower now. What's a few more hours? Allie is notorious for spending hours in the shower. *Literally,* hours. Roger took the door off the bathroom once when she was in there for an hour and a half, after flushing the downstairs toilet and banging on the door had not gotten her out. She screamed like an absolute crazed maniac about calling DFYS but it cut down her shower time considerably. I am hoping that this cabin has a decent sized hot water heater, otherwise I'm certain that I will be a Popsicle after my shower. When I finally get one, that is.

Agent Harding settles down on the uncomfortable looking wooden chair positioned near the door. I didn't notice it the last night so Jason or Walter must have put it there for him when they found out he was coming to babysit. Hardly seemed fair that he needed to sit in such an uncomfortable way for heaven knows how long. I guess he is used to it because he clasps his meaty hands together, tucks them behind his head and leans back slightly, staring straight ahead on full alert.

Dumping the bag that Allie has tossed to me on the breakfast nook, I peek inside and inspect its contents. The first thing I pull out is a college sweatshirt, size XXL. As

I hold the ridiculously oversized sweatshirt up against my relatively small frame, I glower at Agent Harding who is now an interesting shade of eggplant.

"I *told* you I only had Agent Collins' description to go on!" he stammers.

"Who the hell is Agent Collins?" I ask, infuriated now. My ego has been bruised. I know I'm not skinny, but hell, an XXL? *Roger* would be swimming in this thing and he is a professional couch potato with a penchant for deep fried Oreos. And deep fried Twinkies. In fact, deep fried anything.

"Agent Collins? *Jason* Collins?" Agent Harding stammers.

Oh. Jason. I didn't know his real last name. I clamp shut my open mouth. I can't be mad at Agent Harding then. Obviously Jason gave him a glowing description of me that incited him to think I was 400 pounds and a fan of…I turn the sweatshirt over in my hand…*Bootylicious U??? Ugh. I can't wait to see the underwear he bought. I am envisioning a thong that could double as a parachute.*

Throwing the sweatshirt back into the bag with disgust, I lean my elbows on the countertop and rub my temples. I have a throbbing headache and I feel nauseated. Maybe I will feel better after a nice, hot shower. And a meal. *Ah, what I wouldn't give for a nice filet mignon with a side of garlic dill potatoes right now. And a nice fat glass of Shiraz.*

My stomach growls in agreement and my eyes fly open, glancing at Agent Harding with embarrassment. It isn't necessary though, because in the brief thirty seconds I had *my* eyes closed, he has managed to drift off to sleep, head lolling to the side, drool drip out of the corner of his mouth.

"Some babysitter," I scoff as I straighten up. My stomach feels like it is starting to eat itself. We never ate dinner last night and although the stress of the evening had disguised my hunger, it is catching up with me now. Hopefully someone brought some food. I putter off in the direction of the cabinets, annoyed at Agents Harding *and* Collins. And whatever Walter's real last name was, just for associating with them. I yank the cabinets open with unnecessary brute force and stare glumly into them. Boxes upon boxes of cereal stare back at me, grinning rabbits and dancing leprechauns adorning their sides. "Just peachy," I growl as I select the box with the least offensive amount of sugar. Then, I open the other cabinets, searching for a bowl or something to put the cereal in. Groaning, I discover that the bowls are on the top shelf of the cabinet. I am about to hoist myself up on the countertop to retrieve one when I hear a voice behind me.

"I can get that for you."

I turn sharply to see Sean standing behind me. He is a good three inches taller than I am and easily reaches the top shelf to bring down two bowls. He hands me one and then reaches up to retrieve an additional bowl. "In case Allie wants cereal," he remarks shyly. As an afterthought, he grabs another one and jerks his thumb towards the agent who is now nearly falling off his chair. "And that guy, too."

"Thanks," I say with a smile, opening the fridge to look for the milk. Obviously a man has shopped for us because there is nary a fruit or veggie in the fridge. It is stocked with lunch meat, pudding cups, string cheese and soda. And whole milk. *Gross.* I shudder to think what must be in the freezer. Probably stacks of frozen waffles and TV dinners. Men knew nothing about nutrition. Especially DEA agents who probably lived on coffee and diner food.

As I rummage through the drawer for spoons, Sean hands me a box of cereal. "Can you open this?" he asks pleadingly. "I have a hard time getting the plastic apart without destroying it."

Nodding, I take the box from his outstretched hand. This is the most I have ever heard Sean speak since that first day when I dragged him away from Colt's fort. After I open the box for him, we both pour our cereal and sit at the nook in silence, crunching away on the puffs mixed with color infused marshmallow hearts and stars floating in the milk. I am thoroughly grossed out by the time I'm done eating and dying to brush my teeth.

Allie comes bounding down the hallway, happier than I have seen her in ages, hair wet and hanging limply on her shoulders. She is wearing an off the shoulder sweatshirt (her favorite), skinny jeans (wayyyy too skinny jeans) slung low on her hips and her Uggs that she had on yesterday.

I frown at her outfit, but am thrilled that she isn't in a cranky mood for once. *Ahhh, the power of a hot shower.* Which, judging on the steam pouring out of the bathroom behind her, I undoubtedly will not get.

"There's cereal?" she asks as waltzes into the kitchen.

I nod and point to the cabinet. "Yes. And Sean got you a bowl," I remark between bites.

Allie offers Sean a slight smile of gratitude as she inspects her cereal choices. She isn't a fan of sugary cereals, either. I'm certain that she's going to put up a stink.

Instead, she pulls down the same cereal we're eating and pours it into her bowl. The milk is still sitting on the table so she grabs it and drizzles it over the cereal. Pulling out a stool, she sits down and begins to spoon the marshmallows and puffs into her mouth feverishly. I guess she's as hungry as I was after missing dinner last night.

I place my bowl in the sink, resisting the urge to pour another, not because it was good, but because my stomach is still growling from hunger. "I'm going to shower," I announce to the two teenagers who are rapidly shoveling spoonfuls of cereal into their hungry mouths, milk dripping off their chins. They wave me away as they both stare at the back of the cereal box for entertainment and I wonder how long they are going to be able function without cell phones and other electronics. I'm certain that Allie is going to start developing a twitch from not being able to text Victoria or update her Instagram account very soon.

Who knows? Maybe this little trip into the boonies might be good for her. Maybe I'll actually be able to have a conversation with my daughter that consists of more than grunts or a screaming match. One could always dream, right?

I throw open the bathroom door to discover that it is not much better than an outhouse. There is a small sink angled into the corner and a toilet with a faux wooden lid huddled practically on top of the sink. The shower isn't much larger, tucked into the opposite corner with a ratty shower curtain drawn across the front. I can feel the cold seeping in through the wood the second I open the door, despite the steam that is dissipating from my daughter's shower. I can actually hear the wind howling outside, shaking the tiny window in the corner of the room. It is still pouring and the rain is hitting the panes of glass. I shiver as I close and lock the door behind me.

Allie have better left some hot water, is all I can think as I strip down to my bra and underwear and pull back the shower curtain. I reach for the knob to turn the water on and promptly let out an ear piercing, bloodcurdling scream.

Within seconds, the doorknob clatters to the floor and the bathroom door flies open, revealing Agent Harding with his gun poised midair. He glances from side to side, looking for the perpetrator, the reason for my hair raising screams.

I snatch a towel from the rack and cover myself quickly. *How embarrassing, two undercover agents see me in my underwear in one day. What are the odds?*

"What happened?" Agent Harding asks suspiciously, eyes still darting around furtively. "Was there someone in here?"

I grip my towel tightly with one hand and with the other, stick out a shaking finger towards the faucet. "There…" I stammer.

Agent Harding whips his body and his gun around towards the shower. And then, he discovers the source of my distress. "Awww, shit," he groans as he lowers the gun. "Are you shitting me?"

"Get it, get it!" I squeal as I step back farther into the corner. The golden colored daddy long legs is crawling up the side of the shower at a rapid pace.

"Shit," Agent Harding repeats as he holsters his weapon and slides over to the shower. "It's not bad enough I gotta do this at home for my wife and daughter, I gotta be on spider patrol on the job?" he grumbles as he opens the window, grips the spider by one of its ginormous legs and tosses it out the window in one swift motion. "What am I? Freakin' Spiderman?"

He stomps out of the room, leaving the window open and my dignity shattered. I quickly close the window before I freeze to death and attempt to lock the bathroom door, only to discover that Agent Harding broke the doorknob to get in. I stare at it as it rolls around on the floor, stirred up in the agent's wake. Sighing, I push the door so it is practically closed. *Well, at least I know he is protecting me. Even in his sleep.* It eases my mind slightly, but not enough to make up for the fact that I now have to shower with the door ajar.

Shivering, I timidly reach for the faucet. I glance around suspiciously, on the look-out for Mr. Spider's family members to come crawling down the water spout at any moment. The words to *Itsy Bitsy Spider* come to mind and I swallow hard, trying not to think of Evan. He giggles like a lunatic whenever I sing it and creep my fingers up his cubby little belly.

I step into the shower stream to find that indeed my daughter has used up all the hot water and I won't be getting any. I shiver as I quickly soap up, eyes darting around nervously for arachnid friends. I reluctantly stand under the freezing water that is hitting my body like little ice pellets and rinse off as hastily as humanly possible.

Screw my hair; I'll wash it later, I think as I turn the water off. There are goosebumps erupting all over my flesh and I want warm, dry clothing immediately.

Grabbing for the towel that I had previously wrapped myself in, I step out of the shower and onto the ice cold bare floor. Shuddering, I tuck the towel firmly around my body before emerging from the bathroom. Cautiously, I scan from left to right down the hallway, not wanting to bump into any of the DEA agents that might possibly be running around the house. With my luck, I would probably drop the towel.

I dash into the bedroom and quickly get dressed, the

chill permeating through my body all the way to my bones. Still shivering from my frigid shower, even after I am fully dressed in clothing that is way too large for me, I head out the bedroom door and down the hallway.

What I spy when I round the corner to the living room stops me in my tracks. Allie and Sean are both kneeling on the floor, crouched over a dented and lopsided box sitting on the coffee table. Allie is riffling through it as they both peer inside.

"Oh wow, what about this one?" Allie squeals as she pulls something from the box. It looks like...*a record*?

"Okay," Sean agrees and they both clamor to their feet. I step back behind the wall a bit so that they won't catch me watching them.

What I thought was a cabinet/ table the previous day, turns out to be an old fashioned radio and turntable. Allie lifts the lid and a pang of nostalgia hits me as I am instantly reminded of my grandmother's similar record player. She used to let us play her records on it whenever we slept over. Sometimes, we even remembered to bring our own records and Sesame Street always sounded so much better on the large speakers rather than our dinky Fisher Price turntable.

Sean removes the record from its sleeve and drops it expertly onto the turntable. Allie lifts the needle arm and places it gingerly onto the record.

How the hell did she learn how to do that? We certainly haven't had a record player in our house since she's been born. Curious to find out what they've chosen, I inch forward to hear the music playing. I recognize the song right away. It's "Piano Man" by Billy Joel, who was one of my favorite artists growing up. It seemed to be just about the only thing my mother and I could agree on as a teenager. We would spend hours listening to his tapes. And then afterwards, we'd spend hours arguing over ridiculous minutiae.

"I love this guy," Allie gushes as she sways along with the music. *She does?* This is news to me. I smile. *Maybe Allie and I do have a common ground after all. Maybe there was something we could bond over. Why, I could introduce her to some of my favorite-*

"My friend Victoria is like *the* biggest Billy Joel fan," Allie explains to Sean. *Uh, what? No she's not! I am! I've even seen him in concert. I bet Victoria can't say that!*

Allie is still boasting about Victoria, the President of the Billy Joel fan club. "She totally turned me on to him, like, months ago. I've downloaded all his songs onto my ipod." *I highly doubt that, Allie. His collection is like a bazillion songs.*

She leans her elbows on the cabinet, propping up her chin with her hands as she gazes at the record going around and around, music piping out of the speakers. Sean is silent, but he follows her lead and they are both leaning there, staring. "It's so awesome that they have these old records here since we have nothing else to do." Allie starts singing and I am surprised that she actually knows the words. I have the urge to join her and sing along, but I am afraid if she thought I liked something that she did, she would run for the hills.

"I like the Eagles," Sean remarks in a soft voice. *He does? Did kids these days even know who the Eagles were?*

Allie scrunches up her face, thinking. "I never heard their music but I think I saw an Eagles record in the box. Let's look. I'd love to listen to them." She gingerly takes his arm like he is an invalid and leads him back over to the coffee table where they start riffling through the records again.

I pull my body flush against the wall so that they don't see me because I certainly do not want to interrupt this touching scene unfolding before my eyes. I am impressed, not only with Allie's taste in music, but how kind she's being towards Sean. Gone is the demanding and selfish Allie I have grown accustomed to over the last few months and in her place is a considerate and thoughtful Allie. Maybe it's because she doesn't have her phone and her Facebook and her Twitter and all her bitchy friends surrounding her, but I like what I am seeing, even if it's only temporary. It means that she has the ability to be a kind person.

I spin on my heel and head back to the bedroom. With nothing to do, I'm just as bored as the kids. I stare longingly at the bed, wanting to crawl underneath the covers and drift off to sleep. I'm starting to get one of those nagging headaches, right behind my eyes, probably from not getting enough sleep. A nap would be fantastic, but I can't just take a nap in the middle of the day.

Well, why the hell not, Amy? You have nothing else to do. No endless piles of laundry, no diapers to change, no toddler to chase after.

I feel a sob choking up in my throat. I miss the other kids tremendously. Bizarrely, I am aching to have them around me. *How many times in the last thirteen years have you wished for just this, Amy? Solitude, with no distraction? Peace and quiet? A day to just relax, no housework to do? No chauffeuring around, no schedules to keep? And here it is, staring you right in the face and you're not even taking advantage of it.*

I lower my body onto the bed and pull the covers up around my head. *Maybe just a little nap...*

~FIFTEEN~

I wake up to a God awful glare created by the setting sun as it streams in through the rain droplets on the window and bounces off the mirror. Shielding my eyes, I push myself up into a sitting position.

I must have been sleeping for a good three or four hours at least because I now feel like a bus hit me. And then backed up over me. Groaning, I throw off the covers and sit on the side of the bed.

If that's what naps feel like, I'd rather not do that again. No wonder why Evan always fights me about napping. Refreshed my ass.

I stumble to my feet and lumber towards the door. Once I fling it open, I hear voices chattering loudly and pots banging in the kitchen. There is the distinct noise of an oven timer going off and the sound of the refrigerator door opening and closing. If I didn't know better, I would think dinner was being prepared.

Rounding the corner, I have to rub my weary eyes twice. I have been correct in my assumption. Dinner *is* being prepared. Allie is standing at the stove, large pot of water bubbling in front of her. In her hand, she holds a fistful of spaghetti which she is breaking over the pot.

Sean is at the counter, carefully cutting a cucumber while Agent Harding sits on a stool at the breakfast nook, sprinkling garlic over slices of bread and butter laid out on foil.

What the hell is going on here? They took initiative to start dinner without waking me up? Is this an alternate universe I've stumbled upon? Am I having one of those dreams again?? I pinch my arm to make sure I am awake.

"Um, hi," I call out to the busy little bees as I step cautiously into the kitchenette. "What's going on?"

Allie turns away from the stove and rolls her eyes. "We're tap dancing, Mom. Duh." *Ah, snarky Allie is not lost. Only bitchy, sulking Allie is missing. I'm certainly not putting that face on a milk carton.*

"*Okay…*" I carefully rephrase the question. "What are you *making?*"

"Breakfast," Sean pipes up, grinning at Allie. She snorts with delight. *Did she tutor him in sarcastic comments while I was sleeping?*

"Funny," I reply. "Everyone's a comedian."

"Spaghetti and meatballs. It was Allie's idea," Agent Harding replies without sarcasm or humor.

"What?" I stare at Allie. "You don't know how to make spaghetti and meatballs! And it's time consuming and-"

"Relax, Mom." Allie rolls her eyes. "There were frozen meatballs in there and jars of sauce. I think I can handle that and boiling water. I took Home Ec, remember? *Geez.*" She tucks a strand of her dark hair behind her ear.

Yes, Allie and I remember you getting a C in Home

Ec, I think to myself. *Don't be negative, Amy. She's trying to help. And she let you sleep! That's amazing! Don't be such a control freak. One of your kids is actually helping!*

I smile as I join her at the stove. "Need me to do anything?" I offer.

"Can you put the sauce on?" Allie asks as she stirs the spaghetti and blows her wispy multicolored bangs out of her face.

"Uh, sure," I reply, not used to being demoted to sous chef in the kitchen. I cringe as I reach for the jar of sauce that was sitting on the counter. In all my years as a wife and mother, I have never once made sauce from a jar. Only homemade sauce for my family. There were certain things I deemed unacceptable in my life as a stay at home mother; not many, but jar sauce was one of them. I know, not what you would expect from the woman that orders take out at least three times a week, but I did have *some* standards.

"And could you put the meatballs in it?" Allie calls out to me as I twist the jar open with a pop. She cocks her neck towards the bag on the counter. *Oh dear Lord. Frozen meatballs. My Italian grandmother is rolling over in her grave right now.*

We are finishing up the preparations for dinner when I hear the crunch of tires on the gravel driveway out front. Agent Harding's hand flies to his gun and he is crouched down by the window before I can even register the word *car.* He parts the heavy draperies with the tip of his gun and lifting his head slightly, he peeks through the window.

"Just Collins and French," he informs us as he stands at full height and strides back into the kitchen, serious expression on his face. "Nothing dangerous, like a spider."

Allie and Sean let out hoots of laugher as Agent Harding smirks.

"Very funny," I mutter as I gathered plates from the cabinet, adding two for our returning guests. I am guessing that Agent *French* is Walter. At least I'm hoping it is. I don't need any more agents to keep track of.

Jason flies through the front door and storms into the living room. I can immediately see that he is aggravated. He stomps his boots off on the mat by the door and blows on his cupped hands. Puffs of breath emerge from his mouth; it has obviously gotten much cooler since last night. Walter follows closely behind, shutting the door after he enters.

"Just in time for dinner," I call out to them as I place the plates on the nook. "We're having spaghetti and meatballs."

Walter appears enthusiastic about my announcement but before he can join us, Jason waves me off. "We don't have time for that now." He crooks his finger at Agent Harding. "Harding, a word?"

Agent Harding, who is already heaping food on to his plate, appears crestfallen. Sighing, he lowers his dish to the counter top and joins the other men at the door. They huddle together, whispering amongst themselves, Jason's voice occasionally rising in agitation.

The kids and I continue to sit and start to eat, all the while, our eyes glued on the agents and our ears perked up to listen in on their conversation.

Through our slurps of the saucy spaghetti and chewing of the rubbery meatballs, I manage to catch words like, *flee*, *wife*, *tipped off*, *bank account* and *surveillance*. And Jason isn't smiling. Filling in the gaps, it seems their suspect has emptied out his bank account and taken off, possibly tipped off by his wife and now she is under surveillance. This does not bode well for us to return home anytime soon.

And then I hear something that sends chills up my spine. *Donoghue.*

Holy crap! Do they suspect the senior Jimmy Donoghue?

And suddenly, everything makes sense. Jimmy works in the high school. He's our neighbor, almost directly across the street from the Sanders or Collins or French family or whoever the hell they are. *That's probably what Jason was looking at that morning that I caught him with the binoculars! Not Allie but Jimmy Donoghue next door!*

My pulse quickens as I try to strain my ear to hear more of their conversation, but it is even more difficult to catch the words.

At last, Jason lets out a final sigh of exasperation and

Agent Harding pats him heartily on the back. He then turns back toward the kitchen, over the whole meeting and seemingly eager to return to his abandoned meal. Walter trails behind and I leap to my feet to get him a plate. Walter accepts it with a grateful nod. "Haven't eaten all day," he comments.

Expecting Jason to be close behind, I hold out a second plate like a dummy until I realize that Jason has just left through the front door. Placing the plate back on the counter, I feel a twinge of disappointment. The man infuriates me, but I still crave his presence for some sadistic reason. Plus, I'm dying to grill him about Jimmy Donoghue. I hate Cammi so much; how awesome would it be if her husband got thrown in jail? *That's terrible, Amy*, I admonish myself.

"Where's Jason going?" I ask, trying to appear casual as I hand Walter a piece of the Agent Harding invented garlic toast. In my opinion, it tastes like a dish sponge, but Walter doesn't hesitate to scarf it down.

"Phone call," Walter mumbles between bites, crumbs flying from his lips.

I nod. *Okay, so he's coming back in. He's not leaving us alone again.*

That cheers me up until my conscience starts to nag at me. *Why do you care, Amy? Agent Harding has done a superb job at keeping you and the kids safe this afternoon. Even from spiders. And I'm sure Walter, despite his advanced age, is also quite capable. Is it because you enjoy the eye candy Jason provides you with?*

I shake off my prudish subconscious that is taunting me and start to clear the empty plates. The kids have finished their meals and have headed back into the living room to pour over the records. From the window over the sink, I can see Jason pacing in front of the house, cell phone at his ear, talking animatedly and gesticulating wildly. I absentmindedly pour soap into the dishpan as I watch him. His forearm muscles tense as he grips the phone, his clenched teeth accentuating his dimples. After angrily punching the end button on his phone, he stomps towards the house, obviously agitated. He definitely is adorable when he's mad.

You look adorable when you're mad, too, Amy, he whispers in my ear, suddenly standing behind me at the sink, his body dangerously close to mine. I jump, but I don't dare move as he presses his chest against my back, his erection evident from the hardness against my lower back. I can feel heat radiating from him, desire seeping from his pores as he tilts his head towards my neck, sweeps my hair away and leans his lips closer...

"Mom!" Allie calls out, startling me and causing me to drop the mug I have been holding in my hand. The ceramic shatters as it hits the sink.

"Shit," I mutter under my breath, mortified at being caught daydreaming by my daughter. I spin around and paste a fake smile on my face. "What's the matter, Allie?"

She shakes her head. "Nothing is the matter. It

stopped raining so Sean and I are going to go outside to check the rest of the place out-"

Horrified, I cut her off. "No! Don't go outside! It's nearly dark out now! And we are in the middle of the woods! There's bears and skunks and mafia men out there!" After I open my mouth, I realize how ridiculous I sound.

Allie rolls her eyes. I'm glad I can always count on that good ole eye roll when I've lost my sanity.

"Don't forget the spiders!" Agent Harding reminds me from his spot at the nook. He is on his third helping of dinner and I am tempted to make a joke about his weight, but I doubt that will work in my favor if I need saving any time soon. So I bite my lip and return to furiously scrubbing dishes that don't need to be scrubbed because I can see a dishwasher in the corner of the kitchen. No freakin' TV, but we've got a dishwasher.

"Spiders?" Jason asks and I realize he is back in the house and reaching for the plate I took out for him earlier. I nearly jump out of my skin because his arm grazes mine as he scoops spaghetti onto his plate at the stove. *Slow down, heart,* I order. *He can probably hear you slamming around in there.*

"Oh, yeah. We have lethal spiders in here," Agent Harding deadpans. I ignore him and scrub the plate so hard that the paint flecks off.

"Come on, Mom," Allie is practically whining in my ear. "We've been cooped up in here all day. I can barely breathe from inhaling cabin air. You don't want me to have an asthma attack do you?" She gives me a pouty little look. Leave it to Allie to pull the asthma card.

"Stay close to the cabin," I tell her and I immediately hear her footsteps dashing to the front door. I call after her, "Don't forget your jacket." The door slams and I know she doesn't have a jacket on.

If I crane my neck to look out the window, I can see Allie and Sean in front of the cabin as they walk over to one of the many large oak trees lining the driveway. Allie leans her back against the tree while Sean stands awkwardly off to the side, snapping a loose branch in his hand. I see Allie pull something out of her pocket and glance around furtively before she cups her hands over her mouth and leans forward.

"Son of a bitch," I shout. She's smoking a cigarette! I wipe my wet hands on my jeans as I roll down my sleeves and spin on my heel. I am going to beat that child. I've caught her red-handed. I smack head first right into Jason's intimidating chest. As I step back, I catch a whiff of his intoxicating manly scent which causes my knees to buckle.

He grabs my forearms lightly, causing my skin to feel as if it is going to melt off of my body. *Breathe, Amy.*

"Easy there, killer," he jokes as he attempts to steady me.

"Going to kill my daughter," I mumble, trying to remember how to speak.

"I'm pretty sure I can't let you do that," Jason replies with a cocky grin, the first I've seen in at least twenty-four hours.

"You don't understand…"

"I'm sure she will be fine out there without a jacket," Jason tells me.

I shake my head. "No, that's not it." I storm back over to the window and point my finger accusingly at the glass towards my daughter with puffs of smoke coming out of her mouth. Sean also has smoke coming out of his mouth. "Look! They're smoking!" I turn back to Jason triumphantly.

He is trying to hide his grin and it turns out appearing like a smirk. "No they're not!" He grips my shoulders and spins me back around. "It's cold out, Amy. That's air coming out of their mouths. You do know that's what happens when we breathe outside in the cold? Or are you new to this kind of weather?"

I squint as I peer out the window. Allie offers a piece of gum to Sean, who is still snapping twigs. Neither of them are holding a cigarette. And there is still "smoke" around their mouths. My shoulders slump in a combination of relief and defeat.

Now I am mortified at my mistake as I try to explain to Jason, "You don't understand. I've caught her smoking before. And she was cupping her hands over her mouth…"

"Probably to warm them up," Jason reasons. "It's dropped into the thirties according to the thermometer on my dashboard."

I stomp my foot like a petulant child. "Ugh! That's

exactly why I told her to put her jacket on!"

Jason purses his lips and I can tell he's trying not to laugh. "I can see that you're frustrated-" he begins, but I cut him off rudely.

"Don't try to placate me. I was a psych major. I know what you're doing.*" Okay, so only for one semester, but Jason doesn't need to know that. Unless…oh crap. What if he knows that already? What if he did a background check on me?*

I nearly start to hyperventilate as Jason gently grips my wrist and steers me towards the couch. My heart is hammering in my chest like it is building a little cabin to enclose itself in. *Oh dear Lord, that sounds insane. I really need to get out of here. I am officially losing my mind…*

"Amy," Jason says quietly, as he sits me down and joins me on the ancient relic of a couch. His eyes are soft and caring, with crinkles around the edges. *The kind of eyes I can probably stare into lovingly for an entire day, a year, a lifetime…*

I abruptly halt my obnoxiously perverse thoughts before I go off onto a tangent.

"You're doing a good job," Jason tells me, his hand innocently brushing my thigh. I tense up, desperately trying not react to his touch, no matter how *good* it feels. *Think of something else, Amy. Focus on something that doesn't feel good.*

And then I remember the XXL sweatshirt emblazoned with Bootylicious U and the balloon sized panties bunched up underneath my jeans. I have no problem feeling pissed at Jason again.

"Pray tell, exactly *what* am I doing a good job at?" I ask, practically spitting venom at him.

He recoils slightly from my less than cordial reaction, but explains. "Parenting. It's a tough job. But you're doing it right."

"What do you know?" I scoff as I slump back on the couch. "Apparently my kids don't agree."

Jason drapes his arm over the back of the couch, dangerously close to my shoulder, scoots his hip back against the couch and turns to face me. I inch even farther away, nervous that I will succumb to his not so innocent touch and his wily handsome man charms. He *knows* what he is doing; he's working me to the point that I am putty in his hands and I follow his every order. That way he doesn't have to deal with a hormonal, neurotic woman. I'm not dumb and I was *not* born yesterday. Roger pulls the same crap when he wants me to cooperate.

If Jason is offended by me moving away, his face doesn't show it. "Your kids will always be the last ones to tell you that you're doing a good job."

"It's not just them. I *know* I'm doing a lousy job. I've got this one telling me off," I sweep my hand towards the door where Allie is outside. "Not to mention the smoking, the younger one getting into fights, the one that doesn't shut up, and a toddler who won't stay still. I'm *not* doing a great job. I can't even get it together. And half the time, I'm so frustrated, exhausted and overwhelmed that I'm not even enjoying them. In fact, the only time I enjoy them is when they're sleeping and I know that makes me a horrible mother but I can't help it because I'm just so damn tired."

I gasp for air and am instantly mortified. What the hell was that? *Diarrhea of the mouth? Why would you share that with a stranger? You don't even say that sort of thing to your friends! What the hell were you thinking, Amy?*

I see a grin playing on the corners of Jason's mouth and I cannot believe I just spouted all that out to him. And what's more, it looks like he thinks it's a joke.

"I'm sorry," I stammer, rising to my feet, eager to get away from him.

Jason grabs my hand as I try to escape and pulls me back to the couch. Suddenly, I feel that damn tingle shudder through my body again. His hand makes me feel safe and wary at the same time.

"It's fine, Amy," he tells me as I land back on the couch with a plop. The pillows make a little farting noise.

Wow, can we add any more embarrassment to this day? I was in my underwear in front of two undercover agents, overreacted to a spider, thought my daughter was smoking when it was just her breath coming out of her mouth, revealed my deepest insecurities to my hot as hell neighbor and now I've made a farting noise in his presence. Maybe I should just round up some of my class pictures from when I was in middle school to cap the day off. The ones with the braces, awkward expressions, pimples, and bad hair.

"I've only got the one kid and damn, every single day I am convinced I'm doing it wrong." Jason is still holding my hand and in my mortified state, I can't detach my hand from his. Besides, it stops the shaking a little. "There's not one day that goes by that I doubt something I did and beat myself up over it. It's not just you."

I shake my head in disagreement. "I'm screwing up four of them. You would think I would get it right after the first or second one, but every day I'm reminded that I'm fucking it up a little more. Until one day, they're going to all be on drugs and homeless and nobody is going to want to come visit me in the nursing home." I choke back the tears I didn't even know I were threatening to fall.

Jason now starts to laugh. I shoot him an icy glare; he immediately stops but screws his lips together to prevent further chuckling.

"I'm sorry, but I think that's a little extreme. I'm pretty sure your kids are going to turn out fine. Or at least the odds are that 3 out of the 4 will be fine," Jason informs me as he hands me a tissue that seems to have appeared out of nowhere.

"What happens to the fourth one?" I ask as I dab at my eyes.

"Oh, they become assholes, do drugs, end up living in a refrigerator box. You know, that sort of thing," Jason tells me, grin creeping back on to his face.

Seeing his dimples, I can't help but smile. And snort. Of course, I snort. I need to add to the level of embarrassment for the day. Before I know what is happening, I am laughing hysterically, Jason joining in. After I am to the point that my sides are hurting, I stop and take a deep breath, wiping the tears of laughter from my eyes, thanking God that I haven't wet my pants like I usually do when I laugh that hard.

"Thanks," I tell him as I stand up. He has just said everything that I had silently begged Roger to tell me for years.

Jason reaches for my hand again, but this time he doesn't pull me back down towards the couch. Instead, he gazes up at me. I find my breath catching in my throat. I can't remember the last time anyone ever looked at me like this and the fact that I enjoy the way it makes me feel is very uncomfortable.

"Amy, your kids *will* appreciate you some day. I knows it's really overwhelming and if it means anything, *I* think you've got it together." He winks and squeezes my hand before letting it go. I can barely remember how to put one foot in front of the other as I offer him a half-hearted wave and stumble back to the sink, hoping to banish the dirty thoughts that I am now having about one Agent Jason Collins.

~SIXTEEN~

I am cutting up carrots in the kitchenette, putting together a salad for our lunch. Come hell or high water, I'm going to get the occupants of this cabin to eat a little healthier. From my spot at the counter, I can see Allie and Sean, leaning against that tree in the front yard, deep in conversation. I smile to myself, pleased that Allie has made a new friend.

Jason slips in the room behind me, wearing an expression of deep concern on his face. I put the knife down and turn to face him.

"What's the matter?" I ask. He seemed much happier at breakfast time after taking a jog. Apparently there is a lake with a trail not too far from our cabin. He had taken off before any of the rest of us were awake and when he came back in, I did my best to avert my eyes as he stretched in his running shorts and cut off tee that accentuated his defined muscles, glistening with sweat. Instead, I set to work on making everyone breakfast. We had all laughed over Eggs Benedict and orange juice. And then, after a shower, he had gotten a phone call from his office, which he took outside as usual. And now when he came back in, that grim expression is back on his face.

"Can you come with me please, Amy?" he asks. But any idiot could tell he wasn't asking. He is telling me that I have to go with him.

I nod as I step away from the cutting board and dutifully follow him out the front door, heart hammering in my chest. My mind is racing, trying to figure out why he wants to see me, what have I done wrong? Do the police really think I am a suspect in Mary's murder? I was an idiot touching everything in the house that night. Why my fingerprints must be all over everything! I shake with uncertainty. I don't know anything about law enforcement; I have no idea what the procedure for handling one suspected of a crime would be.

The kids are off to the left of the cabin, so Jason steers me toward the right side. The woods are thicker here, the trees more densely packed together. Jason continues to lead me into the wooded area where it is actually much darker than it is by the cabin.

My heart is still flopping around in my chest, my mouth dry, and my tongue thick. I am frantically scrambling to organize my thoughts.

Jason comes to a halt when we are well into the heart of the woods. I should be scared of being alone with him, but suddenly, I'm not. My pulse slows down as he grabs me by the wrist and pulls me towards his chest. I gasp from the surprise.

"Amy," he murmurs in my hair, his lips gazing my ear. "Do you know why I've brought you out here?"

I flutter my eyelids as I gaze up at him. "Is it because I've been a very bad girl?"

A sly grin crosses Jason's face. "Yes, you've been a naughty, naughty girl. Do you know what undercover agents like myself do to naughty girls like you?" He arches his eyebrows as he speaks, sending an erotic tingle down my spine. Oh man, I want him to punish me for being the bad girl that I am...

"Amy!" Jason is standing next to me as I chop the carrots absentmindedly. "Amy! You're going to chop your finger off!" he yelps as he snatches the knife from my hand.

"Huh?" I am clearly coming out of a daydream and as I glance at Jason, a blush spreads from the roots of my hair all the way down to my toenails. *Shit! What was I just thinking about him?*

Jason sighs as he runs his fingers through his hair. "Maybe you shouldn't use knives if you're not really paying attention," he advises with a stern look of admonishment.

"Um, yeah, you're right," I reply, trying desperately to forget the impure thoughts I was just having. It was seriously getting difficult to live in close quarters with this man if I couldn't get him off my brain. I awkwardly wipe my sweaty hands on my jeans. "What's up?"

With a grimace, Jason cocked his head towards the front door. "Walk with me?"

What? Shit. Can undercover agents read your mind?

"Uh, why?" I manage to stammer, backing up against the countertop.

He leans in towards me and his tantalizing scent assaults my nostrils, making my knees feel jello-ish. "I need to talk to you…*alone*."

He arches his eyebrows and I feel as if I may faint. This must be *the vapors* that Victorian women were always talking about in books. Swooning and the vapors.

I guess he can tell I am reluctant from my expression, because he adds, "It's about the investigation and I don't want the kids to overhear."

"I thought they were outside?"

"They are, but you never know when they're going to come back in. Can you just not be difficult for two minutes and follow me?" Jason asks, clearly agitated.

Well excuse me, *Mr. Agent Man. I wouldn't dream of being difficult*, I feel like saying, but instead, I clamp my mouth into a thin line and follow Jason out the front door. He turns right towards the woods, just like in my dream and I am starting to wonder if I really might be psychic.

Jason glances around nervously as he leads me into the wooded area, tromping through the knee high grass. I am growing increasingly alarmed and annoyed at the same time. I rained all day yesterday so my sneakers are squishing into the mud, causing an obnoxious farting like noise when I pull them up. Jason's boots are doing the same.

Finally, when we can no longer see the house, Jason grinds to a halt. "Okay, I think we're good here," he tells me, eyes still darting around nervously.

His lack of ease is unnerving me and I blurt out, "You look like a man who is scared of his own shadow. You're not exactly instilling confidence in me…*sir*. Or should I call you ma'am?" I add a little smirk at the end because I am petty like that. I don't know why I feel the need to stick it to Jason whenever possible, but it's like guys having a pissing contest. For once, I am able to participate in the contest.

Jason's face hardens into a scowl. "Why would you call me that?"

I stifle a laugh. Damn. I hadn't meant to bring this up, but, hell, I said embarrassing things last night, so he could hardly be horrified if I mentioned something that my own daughter witnessed at the *mall* for cripes sake.

"Because you wear make-up?" I volunteer with a smirk.

"What?" Jason yelps and leaps back, nearly tripping over a log. "What makes you think that?" He is clearly insulted.

"The reason we were over your house to begin with the other day was because I read my daughter's text messages from her friend," I confess.

Jason simply nods.

"Her messages confused me and I thought she was doing drugs. And after you had said to keep an eye on her, I thought maybe you knew something about it."

"I was speaking hypothetically, Amy. Because this drug ring was targeting high school students and our suspect had access to high school kids. I didn't mean that I had knowledge of her actually-"

"I know," I cut him off. "It was an assumption on my part. It turned out the friend was texting about *make-up*, of all things. But when I asked her about it, when I still thought it was drugs, she said she saw *you* doing it at the mall. And mind you I was still thinking drugs…"

"Wait a minute! She said she saw me doing *drugs* at the mall?" He is scratching his head vigorously.

"No, no. She was actually talking about make-up. And she said that she didn't do it, but she saw the *neighbor* do it. Which I don't understand why she was hiding it from me to begin with. None of it made sense."

Jason's face brightens. "She said the *neighbor*?"

I nod. "And I assumed it was you."

He shakes his head. "I think you need to have another little chat with your daughter, Amy. You'll find that things make a little more sense when you talk to her and find out what she was *really* texting about. I think I have a pretty good idea of what it is."

"Oh." I am stunned. *Did Allie lie to me again? Her story made no sense…why did I believe her?*

I turn to walk back to the cabin when Jason grabs my hand.

"Where are you going?"

Anxious to get to the bottom of this, I point toward our origin.

"Listen, I brought you out here to tell you something. I'm thinking that the cabin might be bugged," he explains, eyes gazing upwards, scanning the surroundings like a swat team might descend upon us from the tree cover.

"Well, shouldn't it be? It *is* a secret hideout, right?" I

am confused. The idea that the cabin was bugged was pretty much something I had assumed all along and I'm just a lowly civilian housewife. It boggles my mind that this thought has just occurred to my agent man/knight in shining armor.

Jason shakes his head. "No, I think it's bugged by a member of the…" he pauses and bites his lip, obviously searching for a word that a neophyte woman on the run like me would understand. "…drug ring that we are chasing. It seems like they have been one step ahead of us the past few days and I can't for the life of me figure out how."

He has now moved on from scratching his head to twisting his hair around his finger and tugging at it violently. The mother in me is afraid that he is going to pull his hair out, and I cannot resist reaching out and taking his hand away. He stares at me as if he can't believe that I just did that. I can't believe I did, either.

"Sorry," I mumble, staring down at the boggy ground that is seeping into my cheap sneakers and chilling my feet.

"Uh, it's fine. Thanks, actually. I have a twiddling habit…" Jason explains, face turning crimson.

"A *what?*" What he has just said sounds extremely sexual.

"I twiddle my hair when I'm nervous. My mother yelled at me for years about it." At the mention of Mary, a wretched look crosses Jason's face and I feel as if my heart is going to burst with sorrow for. It was bad enough finding Mary like I did; I can't imagine what it was like for Jason, seeing his own mother like that.

Suddenly, without warning, I am overwhelmed with a desire to see and speak to my own mother. It comes out of nowhere, a feeling I don't ever recall experiencing before. In fact, one summer when we went to sleep away Girl Scout camp, I remember Joey and Beth crying at night for Mom and I just stared at them in disbelief, laughing.

Still, I can't very well bring that up now, can I? Jason just lost his mother and he brought me out here to tell me something...Wait a minute, what was he just saying to me? My brain is short circuiting all over the place; I have forgotten what this whole conversation was about.

Fortunately, Jason is determined to keep me up to speed. He shoves his hands deep in his pockets, quite possibly to prevent himself from twiddling his hair, and stares straight into my eyes. His gaze is unsettling, so I look back down at my ruined shoes.

"Anyway, there's either a bug in the cabin or a mole somewhere. So I need you to make sure you're not discussing *anything* you know about the case. And don't ever say we are gone or anything like that. I don't want anyone to know that you're alone-"

"Wait a minute. You're going to leave us alone again?" My voice squeaked at the end. It is darker in this part of the woods and a light breeze is shaking the trees. I feel a chill and all of sudden, I'm more nervous and frightened than I've ever been. *I want Jason to wrap me in his strong arms and...stop, Amy!*

Jason shakes his head. "I'm not planning to leave you *alone*. I will always leave you with an agent, whether it be Walter or Harding. But bear in mind, one agent is not as much of a threat to these guys as three agents are." He raises an eyebrow at me. "If you are alone with one agent, they may seize the opportunity to take you and them out when you're most vulnerable."

I do not like Jason's words. He is making this real right now and I don't like it one bit.

He senses my apprehension and takes a tentative step towards me. I don't move away as he reaches out and lightly brushes the hair off my shoulders with the tips of his fingers. His touch does nothing to control my trembling; if anything, it intensifies it.

In a low murmur, Jason explains to me, "Amy, please don't worry. We are trying desperately not to put you in harm's way. This whole thing is just a precaution, maybe not even necessary. We like to err on the side of caution at the agency, you know?"

As he speaks, he steps closer to me, his body so near that I can not only smell his scent, I can taste it. I feel heat radiating off of him and I don't want him to stop touching me, but at the same time, I don't want his hands on me. I am under a spell when he is near me and it frightens me.

Afraid to look into his eyes, I stare down at the ground, my heart hammering in my chest, my breathing becoming labored and difficult. He slips his hand under my chin and lifts my face so that I have no choice but to look at him.

His eyes are darker than usual, maybe because of the light, but somehow, it makes him look softer, more vulnerable. He says nothing to me; instead, he lowers his face to mine and without even thinking about it, I find my own eyes closing, my lips puckering in anticipation of his.

His kiss is soft and delicate, not at all what I would have imagined. His arms slide off my shoulders and he pulls me in for a deeper embrace. I find myself hungrily accepting his lips, his affection, my brain screaming at me to stop and my body completely ignoring its commands.

As quickly as it began, Jason's kiss ends and I feel him backing away from me. My eyes fly open, startled at the abruptness. Jason's expression is a mixture of concern and remorse.

"Shit," he mutters as he runs his hands through his hair, stopping to feverishly tug at the ends. "Shit," he repeats as he leans against the nearest tree as if he is trying to steady himself.

I am having no problem steadying myself. The shaking has completely stopped. Now I'm just frozen in place, in complete disbelief of what just happened. *Did I really just kiss a man who wasn't my husband? My hot neighbor? The undercover DEA agent? In the middle of the woods?*

I look to Jason for guidance, an explanation, anything. His expression is akin to being slapped. "Shit. Amy, I'm sorry. I can't…I didn't mean to…" This is the most flustered and unraveled I have ever seen him. And for once, I don't want him to be that way. I want him to take charge and tell me what to do, damn it! I want him to explain to me, what just happened and what does it mean? But I can tell, he doesn't know either.

"I've got to go," he says in a clipped tone. "I've got a meeting. I'll be back later." Without another word, he spins on his heel and retreats out of the woods at a breakneck pace.

At first I am stunned by his hasty retreat, but then I realize, I have to follow him quickly or I will be lost in the woods and not have any clue how to get out. And God knows what's in these woods. *All sorts of dangerous creatures; bears and snakes and leaders of drug rings*, I think to myself as I squish through the marshy ground. *And don't forget DEA agents, Amy.*

~SEVENTEEN~

As I approach the cabin, I lightly touch my fingers to my mouth, feeling where Jason's lips had been not ten minutes ago.

"Hi, Mom!" Allie pipes up from the corner of the porch. I startle, not expecting to see her there. She is reclining in an Adirondack chair that I had not noticed before, her feet propped up on the railing. In her lap is a giant sketchbook and she is holding a charcoal pencil in her hand.

"Oh, hi," I reply, hoping she didn't see me touch my lips and wonder why I was doing that. "Where did you get that?" I ask, gesturing towards the sketchbook. When she was younger, before she went into middle school, Allie had a book just like that. She would lounge outside for hours, drawing her siblings, insects or trees. Anything, really. She would slip into an artistic trance, sketching for hours. Once she started middle school however, she stopped drawing. I had asked her about it and she had gotten really snippy and told me to mind my own business. What else is new, right?

Allie's cheeks flush. "Sean got it for me." She stares back down at the page, obviously embarrassed by this revelation.

"Well, that's nice of Sean, but...where did he get it from? We're in the middle of the woods."

Allie starts scribbling away on the pad. "Um, he said

it was in the car. He bought it last week to give to me for my birthday." she mumbles, hair falling into her face so that she is barely audible. I'm not sure if Allie is more embarrassed by the fact that Sean went out of his way to get her this gift he thought she would appreciate or the fact that she is relishing his gift.

"That's right. Tomorrow is your birthday," I recall with gloom. *Wow. It's really going to suck if my daughter has to spend her fourteenth birthday here, holed off from the world.*

She nods glumly, obviously thinking the same thing. Then, she turns her attention back to her drawing.

Plopping down in the chair next to my daughter, I lean back and shield my eyes from the bright sun.

"We never actually finished our conversation the other day," I remark.

"Uh, which one?" Allie inquires as she studies a pinecone she has propped up on the railing.

"The one about the make-up and the neighbor? I was wondering why you would be so secretive about make-up, but Jason has suggested that I may have completely misunderstood what you were trying to tell me."

Even out of the corner of my eye, I can see her flush.

"Mom, I'm really sorry about that," Allie replied, chewing her lip nervously.

Patiently, I lay my hand on top of hers. "You want to tell me the whole story?"

She nods, laying down her charcoal pencil. "Victoria stole that make-up. She's been…stealing things. A lot."

Allie stares at her fingernails as she explains.

"Oh?" This is not what I was expecting.

She glances up at me. "I swear I never stole anything, Mom. She wanted me to. She even pointed out Mrs. Donoghue stealing a make-up and a Coach bag from Macy's last week and said that everyone does it…"

Mrs. Donoghue? Cammi? That's the neighbor she meant?

Suddenly, everything is starting to make sense. *The reason Cammi and Jimmy can afford expensive things, his job at the high school, her shoplifting. He's running a drug ring and she's giving herself a five finger discount! Shit! This is why Laura doesn't want Kaitlyn hanging out with Allie! This is why Kaitlyn stormed out and why Allie's friends consider Kaitlyn uncool! All this happening under my nose! I knew something was wrong…just didn't fit the puzzle pieces together properly.*

Allie clears her throat and I remember that she is still sitting there, looking like a lost puppy.

"Please don't make me give up being friends with Victoria. I know she's a little rough around the edges, but she's had a tough home life. Her mom walked out on them when she was a baby and her older sister raises her." She gives me a pleading look with those beautiful, truthful eyes that I haven't seen in years. "She needs a friend like me, Mom. I promise I won't ever steal anything."

I pat her knee affectionately. "I hope so, Al."

Just then, Sean comes bounding towards us, arms

bearing gifts of leaves and other relics of nature. "Got you some things to draw, Allie!" he calls out enthusiastically. Allie beams as he drops the presents at the base of her chair.

I clamor to my feet, avoiding eye contact with my daughter, not wanting to embarrass her. She and Sean are content and occupied; my job is done here. For now. Roger and I can speak to Allie about Victoria and the shoplifting at another time.

I head into the house and sigh as I notice my abandoned salad prep. I open the fridge, half expecting a bottle of water to magically materialize and I sigh as I see there is still only soda.

Should have told Jason to pick up wine and rum and vodka on his way home. And a cake for Allie's birthday. Too bad he dashed off so suddenly, I think to myself as I realize that I am the reason he dashed off.

I pour some soda into a glass and then wander out of the deserted house onto the front porch.

Sean is crouched on his knees, inspecting the ground for heaven knows what. He is creeping around, occasionally picking up a leaf and inspecting it, before tossing it aside or tucking it in his pocket.

Walter and Agent Harding are standing by the tree I thought that Allie and Sean were smoking next to last night. As I pass them I can see the men are deep in conversation, Walter facing me, looking rather animated, and Agent Harding with his back to me.

I wonder about him, I muse as I slowly sip the

noxious drink and wander towards the side of the house, out of sight. *Wonder how old he is and where he lives. He mentioned a wife and daughter, but does he have other kids? Hell, I don't even know what his first name is. I should ask him…oh Amy, who cares?*

I know I am just distracting myself from thinking about what just happened with Jason. I lean back against the house; the sun is just starting to graze the horizon. Within the hour it will be dark. I close my eyes, letting the last bit of the October sun warm my face. And the lips that Jason has just kissed only an hour ago.

Roger and I have been married for well over fifteen years. When we first met, I swore it was love at first sight, even though, Roger wasn't anything extraordinary. In fact, many of my friends turned their noses up when they met Roger, telling me I could certainly do better. But I was drawn to that man like a moth to a flame, to borrow an overused cliché. He fascinated me for some unknown reason and I wanted to be with him. I craved him when he wasn't around; my wandering thoughts always turned to him when I wasn't with him during the day. In my mind, this was love.

Maybe it wasn't him, per se, but the way he perceived me, the way he treated me. Nobody had ever really taken such an interest in *me* before. Most of my high school boyfriends had only one goal in mind and while I claimed that was fine back then because I was as horny as hell too, maybe I was really looking for someone who got *me*. At one point in time, Roger, the man who couldn't understand *why* I didn't appreciate his dirty underwear on the bed, got me. He was capable of getting me to think on a level I never thought possible and what's more, he understood me. He made me feel safe, secure, loved and understood. And all at once, that was gone. Did he still get me? And who was I anymore? Was I completely overwhelmed with the daily minutiae of my life that I wasn't even a real person anymore? If *I* didn't get me, how could I expect Roger to get me? And if he didn't get me anymore, what did we have left?

I shiver as a gust of wind whips past, but somehow, I have the feeling that is not the only reason for my goose-bumps. I open my eyes and see that it has become extremely overcast and the sun is completely gone.

I wrap my arms around myself as I hear a high pitched scraping sound, like a chair being moved across a patio. My pulse quickens as I crouch down. I find myself creeping towards the back of the house, curious, despite my mind screaming, *what are you doing, Amy! Are you trying to get yourself killed? That's why you have agents watching over you!*

Even with my logical brain warning me, I continue to creep towards the back of the house. I hear the sound of a cell phone ringing and then a very quiet whispering voice.

"Yeah, he's gone," says the voice. It is vaguely familiar, but because the person is speaking in such a low tone, I can't place where I know them from. *Is that Jimmy Donoghue?* I've only spoken to him twice. Once when I hit his rosebush while backing out of the driveway and once when I asked him if recyclables were being picked up on Christmas week.

I chew my lip trying to remember if this particular voice is his. The wind is picking up, disguising the voice even further. I can barely make out the words, let alone figure out where I've heard that voice before.

I crane my neck, resisting the urge to peek around the corner and see who it belongs to. "Yeah, he's going to the office to meet with Anderson. You need to warn him that they're getting close to his location. They're trying to…" the wind starts howling at this point in time and I can only make out snippets of the conversation. But what I do hear crystal clearly is, "Well, I'll kill Collins if I have to. He certainly won't be as easy as the old lady was. She was just sitting there, taking a nap. Simplest hit ever."

My blood runs cold as my body locks up, unable to move. *Run, idiot! Run! Get Harding and Walter so they can catch this creep! He's obviously the one who killed Mary. And he's part of the group they are looking to catch and he's HERE! And you're standing still like a moron, Amy! Run!*

I'm not sure how, but my legs loosen up and I find myself putting one foot in front of the other, albeit in slow motion. I soon reach the front of the house and I peek around the corner, looking for Harding and Walter. They are no longer standing in front of the tree. In fact, the kids are gone from the front porch, too. Now I start to panic, thinking that whoever was talking on the phone has somehow gotten to them already. They are probably like Allie fears, chopped up and stuffed in plastic sandwich bags and thrown in the river.

Allow me to pause at this juncture in my story in order to point out how illogical this thought process is. The only entrance to the house is in the front. There are no windows in the back of the cabin, either. On the other side of the cabin are tall trees and an assortment of bushes. The only way for the person behind the house to have reached the front first without passing me, would have been to fly. And as we all know, people can't fly. Duh. Oh, and also, I don't think there is a river around here either.

Now trembling with fear, I cautiously step on to the porch, the boards groaning under my feet, protesting my presence. It suddenly starts to drizzle and the wind is blowing furiously, the trees beating against the window panes. My hand is poised on the screen door when I hear the sound of gravel crunching under tires behind me and I swivel my head in the direction of the driveway.

Jason's car is pulling up in front of the house and relief washes over me. As he climbs out of the car, I rush towards him, taking the porch steps two at a time.

"Amy?"

"Oh my God, Jason! The killer is here I heard him talking on his cell phone in the back of the house and I don't know where anyone else is because I came around the corner and Allie wasn't drawing and the other guys weren't by the tree and now I'm afraid to go in the house and why are you here didn't you have a meeting?" I take a deep breath after my run on sentence. I can tell by his expression that Jason is extremely perplexed.

"What? What are you talking about? What killer?" he asks while I drag him towards the house.

"Mary's killer! He's *here*!" I shout with exasperation. *Geez, for a secret agent he was kind of slow witted.*

Jason's hand covers his vest, reaching for his weapon. "How do you know? Why didn't you tell Harding? Or Walter?"

"He was behind the house. I heard him talking on his phone, telling someone he killed Mary. I went to go tell them but I couldn't find them. And then you showed up," I explain, suddenly lowering my voice as we approach the front door.

"You heard him say *I killed Mary* on his cell phone?" Jason asks incredulously.

I shake my head. "Well, not in so many words. I heard him talking and it sounded like he couldn't me trusted. He said, and I quote, *the old lady was the simplest hit he's ever done...*" Or something along those lines.

Jason raises his eyebrow. I can tell he is seriously starting to doubt my credibility. "What did he say exactly?"

I scrunch up my forehead, trying to think. *What did he say actually? What made me suspicious? I couldn't very well tell Jason about the sensation of dread I experienced when hearing the man talk, could I?*

And then I remember. "He said something about killing you! To take you out of the way if necessary!" I call out victoriously. *See, I knew I had a reason to be suspicious.*

Jason blanches and I realize my triumphant tone was not necessary.

"Could you have heard wrong?" Jason asks me hopefully.

I think back to the howling wind and wonder, *did I hear the man correctly? Maybe that's not what he said after all.*

But then it hits me. "Wait a minute! I'm sure the guy was up to no good because nobody is supposed to know we're here, right?" And I raised my eyebrow at him suspiciously. "And whoever it was didn't think you were around. I thought you had to go to a meeting?"

"I did, but when I got to the main road, a tree was blocking the road. It fell in last night's storm. They're working on removing it, but for the time being, we are stuck here." Jason swallows hard as the significance of those words occur to him and I know we are in real danger here. "Stick close to me," he says as he grips my arm. I close my eyes as his fingers meet my skin, willing my body not to melt with his touch. The fact that we are in the middle of a life or death situation is not calming my attraction to him at all. If anything, it is intensifying it. I'm pretty sure my blood should not be rushing where it currently is rushing to. It should be going to my vital organs and as horny as Jason makes me, I'm pretty sure that place is not a vital organ right now.

Jason pulls the screen door open with caution. With the tip of his boot, he pushes the slightly ajar door open all the way. The warmth of the cabin comes rushing at us and I shiver, not realizing how damp and chilled I had been outside.

To my relief, we can see that Allie and Sean are in the living room, leaning over the record collection again. They are arguing over the greatest group act of the 1960's. Sean is claiming the Beatles while my daughter is pulling for the Rolling Stones.

Jason's eyes dart around, looking for his fellow agents. Other than Allie and Sean at the record player, the house appears to be deserted. My pulse quickens as I observe Jason's fingers inching towards his gun holster.

"Where's Grampy?" Jason asks Sean. I guess he isn't planning on explaining that Walter isn't his real "Grampy" yet.

Sean looks up and shrugs at his father. "I don't know, but Agent Harding's in the bathroom." He wrinkled up his nose. "I wouldn't go near there if I were you."

Jason grimaces as he takes a step towards the hallway. I notice that Jason has not relaxed his reach on his gun.

At that very moment, Agent Harding steps out of the bathroom, newspaper tucked under his arm. The sound of the bathroom fan is audible and I detect a toxic odor even from thirty feet away.

"Damn, what did you eat?" Jason asks, covering his nose with the crook of his arm. "That smells like something died in your intestines." Men can be so uncouth.

Agent Harding shrugged. If he was insulted by Jason's crass accusation, he didn't show it.

"Where's Walter?" Jason asked, attempting to peer around Agent Harding's wide girth.

Harding shrugged again. "I came in when the kids did and he was sitting outside. Said he wanted to get some fresh air."

Jason and I glanced at each other uneasily. Walter hadn't been outside when we walked in.

"Shit," Jason mutters under his breath. He spins on his heel and dashes off towards the front door. I race after him, taking two steps for each of his one. I grab the door before it slams in my face and chase him out to the porch.

He is standing in the middle of the driveway, eyes darting around nervously, hand inching towards that gun again.

Panting, I join him. "Do you think Jimmy got Walter instead?"

"Get back inside, Amy," Jason growls as he scans the area. "It's not safe out here for you. Go watch the kids."

I place my hands boldly on my hips. "Harding's got them. Let me help you."

What? Who are you and what have you done with Amy Maxwell? The Amy Maxwell I know would be hiding under the bed, dresser pushed up against the door, shaking like a leaf. Who is this ballsy chick, willing to risk life and limb for a little adventure?

Jason opens his mouth to protest again, but there is no need. We hear a rustling coming from the direction of the woods and Walter steps into view, clothes disheveled, a leaf stuck in his hair. There's a scratch on his cheek and he's bleeding.

"Walter!" Jason calls out, rushing towards him, hand still on his gun. "What happened?" he asks when he reaches the older man, who appears visibly shaken.

"I'm okay," Walter pants, obviously out of breath. "I was on the porch and everyone else was inside. I was actually reading the life story of Benedict Arnold…" He gestures towards the Adirondack chair where we can see the pages of a book flapping in the breeze.

"Benedict Arnold?" I ask.

Walter nods. "I found it in the cabin. In the night stand drawer. I was bored so…" he shrugged.

"*Anyway*, back to the story," Jason says, sounding annoyed.

Walter touches his forehead as if he is deep in thought and desperately wracking his brain to remember. "Oh, yeah. Anyway, I heard a noise coming from the woods and I thought it was odd because everyone was in the house. It sounded like someone talking. And if everyone was inside, who was talking? And who were they talking to?" I take Walter's arm and lead him over to the porch where he gingerly sits down on the step. The scratch on his check has stopped bleeding, but I notice he has a rash of scratches on his arms.

"I crept over to where I heard the noise and I saw a dark shadow of a man dash into the woods. So I took off after him but I lost him about a quarter mile in." He shrugs. "I'm not a young man any more, you know."

"Was it our suspect?" Jason asks.

Walter shrugs. "I don't know, Jason. I can't see that well, either."

Jason slaps his forehead. "Why didn't you call Harding for back-up?"

"It all happened so suddenly," Walter explains. "Sorry, Jason. I didn't think."

Jason groans as he shakes his head. He takes a step towards the woods. I drop Walter's arm and creep behind him. Jason swivels around to face me, fury in his eyes.

"Amy, I told you to wait here," he practically growls at me.

I shake my head defiantly. "No way. I'm not letting you go into there alone. There's a madman out there. A madman who wants you *dead*."

Jason sighs and turns to Walter. Pleadingly he asks, "Can you take her inside?"

"I'm not going," I reiterate.

Walter nods as he struggles to his feet. He seems rather unsteady and I realize that chasing a criminal in the woods may be out of his scope of practice.

"Let me help you," I offer as I dash to his side, trying to steady him on his feet. He needs a band-aid for the cut on his cheek and I am wondering if we have any inside the cabin. I glance up to ask Jason if there is a first aid kit and he is gone.

"Son of a bitch," I mutter, realizing that he has outsmarted me.

Walter chuckles. "You might as well help me into the house then," he remarks with a wink.

"You men are in cahoots," I mutter as I help the older man into the house. I can't help but pause and stare longingly out into the woods, my fingers lightly brushing my lips.

~EIGHTEEN~

After sending Harding to follow Jason, I help Walter clean up his cuts. He tries to wave me off, insisting that I was fussing over him, but what else do I really have to do?

After pacing for a good half hour, continually peeking outside, and not being able to see through the night rain, I absentmindedly prepare a dinner of frozen pizza and burn my hand taking it out of the oven. I dash over to the sink to run it under warm water when I notice a figure slinking around by the bushes outside the house.

My heart starts racing and my throat becomes dry as I try to call out to get Walter's attention, but no sound comes. One eye on the suspect, I peek over my shoulder. Walter is sound asleep on the sofa, head hanging off the back, snoring loudly. His gun and holster are on the coffee table despite the fact that the kids are on the floor, playing tic tac toe on the giant sketchpad.

I don't want to alarm the kids, but I need to get Walter's attention. He's the one who knows how to use the gun after all. "Walter," I hiss as I watch the dark figure creep around towards the front of the cabin. *Shit. He's getting close to the front door. Did we lock the front door when we came in?* I can't remember.

"Walter!" I am panicking now, eye on the front door. *Is that locked? Shit. I can't tell.*

I have no choice at this point in time. If that door

really is unlocked, we're dead where we stand. I dash over to the front door, not only locking it, but sliding the deadbolt into place. The clacking noise causes the kids to glance up, but it still does not interrupt Walter's nap. Even over the wind and the now pounding rain, I can hear the sound of boots stepping on to the porch.

"Walter," I am practically shouting, my hand still on the door as if touching it will keep the bad guy away. Walter snorts, but he doesn't wake up.

"What's the matter?" Sean asks, concern on his face. Allie gazes at me wide eyed. I realize they're relying on me to keep them safe. I'm the person they think is going to protect them right now. *Damn, I don't want to let these kids down.*

Realizing that I have no time to wake Walter, I abandon the door and reach over to the coffee table and grab Walter's gun (a .22? .38 special? Colt .45?) Since I never held a gun before, my hand drops; it is much heavier than I thought it would be. I stare at it, trying to figure out where the safety is. *Is the safety supposed to be on? Or off? And how do I know?* Pointing it towards the ground, I turn it over, searching for God knows what. Then I realize, the kids are now staring at me. So much for not attracting their attention.

Allie's big eyes get bigger as I whisper, "Go into one of the bedrooms."

Allie shakes her head as she leaps to her feet and pushes her body against the wall. "No. I'm not going to let you do this by yourself." Sean nods and stands between me and the door.

"Don't be fools," I growl under my breath. "There's no point in you two getting hurt, too." And then I realize. They're just being as stubborn as I was with Jason an hour ago.

Jason! Where is he? Oh no! What if the bad guy got Jason and Harding already?

The sound of the footsteps is getting louder; it sounds like whoever is on the porch is walking its length, which extends the entire front of the cabin. SLOWLY.

"Get behind me," I whisper. "Do *not* get between me and the gun." Both kids nod as they push their backs against the wall. "I'd prefer if you'd get the hell out of the way, though," I add, hoping that they may take my advice. Allie shakes her head resolutely.

Suddenly, there is a crack of thunder, a surge of light, and the entire cabin goes dark. Allie screams in my ear and clutches my arm (the one holding the gun, I might add).

"Relax!" I shout. But even as my mouth shouts the words, my body tells me, *RUN! Oh my God, get the hell out of here!*

Stop, Amy! Keep it together. Allie and Sean are depending on you. And Walter. But I don't care about Walter as much as I care about the kids. They are helpless, looking to me to protect them. And if I was shaking so hard I couldn't even point a gun, what good was I to them?

I steady my hand as Allie continues to whimper in

my ear. The rain is pounding at the windows steadily and the sound of the screen door creaking open reaches my ears. *Shit.* I can hear that the doorknob is jiggling now. Whoever is on the porch is trying to get in. I try to glance around the room. If that thunder bolt didn't wake Walter up, he must be dead. But I still can't see him as my eyes have not adjusted to the dark yet.

"Back up," I whisper to my daughter and Sean as I take a step backwards, ordering my legs to stop feeling like Jell-O. My heart is racing so rapidly that it's sucking the air out of my lungs and my breath is trapped in my throat.

We are almost in the kitchen when a sound, like rapid car backfiring, pierces the night air. We are all alone on a mountain top, no neighbors for miles. That can't be the sound of a car backfiring. That can only mean one thing. *Gunshots.* And Jason is outside.

I have no time to panic because now the front door is being pushed open and is slamming against the chain. I can hear the person on the other side curse under their breath and start banging against the door, trying to force it open.

"Hide in the cabinets," I command the kids under my breath and amazingly, I feel Allie let go of my arm as she follows my orders. Now it is just me and the gun pointed at the door and whoever is trying to open it. I can hear something heavy slamming against it, perhaps the Adirondack chair that had been sitting on the porch.

Steadying my grip on the gun, I pull back what I

believe to be the safety. I've read enough detective novels to figure it out. Or so I hope. My finger anxiously twitches as I feel for the trigger, ready to shoot the intruder as soon as he enters. He may get me first, but at least I can stop him from getting the kids.

Calm, Amy. Relax. Just steady your hand, focus on the target and pull the trigger. What's that saying? Don't shoot till you see the whites of their eyes?

At least that is my plan as the door swings open, slamming into the door jam. Thunder ominously cracks and lightning illuminates the sky. I can see the dark figure crowding the doorway, the silhouette of a gun in his right hand. And that's when I lose it. I don't see the whites of his eyes, but I squeeze my eyes shut tightly and pull the trigger nonetheless.

There is a deafening crack and the recoil of the gun throws my arms towards my head and slams me to the floor. It is hard to breathe; dust is in my throat and I smell the odor of a gun that has been fired. When I open my eyes, I can see that all around me, sheetrock is raining down, creating a cloudy atmosphere in the room. And the figure in the doorway is no longer standing there.

I jump to my feet, clutching the weapon. *Did I shoot him? Did I hit him?* And then, the sickening thought, *did I kill him?* I know it was in self-defense, but the thought of killing another human being makes me want to vomit.

I creep over to the doorway and see that the man is clearly gone. I guess shooting the ceiling scared him off? The rain is blowing in the door as I step out onto the porch, wondering where he has gone. I brace myself against the wind and rain and step further out onto the porch, peering over the railing.

This simple act may or may not be Mistake #8. I'm not sure if the outcome would have been different had I *not* done this, but I'm pretty sure what transpired next would have played out differently.

Without any street lamps or lights from the cabin, all I can see is the vast darkness that spreads in front of me. I shudder and wrap my arms around myself, gun still in hand.

He must have run off. I should go back inside and have Walter call Jason. I'm sure he could not have slept through the sound of a gun going off.

The front door slams, startling me, and I think it is because of the wind. I take a step towards the door to open it and that's when I see it. The wide droplets of blood on the porch and the rain splashing them, causing them to spread over the wood. They snake down the steps and my eyes follow the trail of blood until I can make out a still figure lying face down in front of the bushes. I am certain that it is Jason.

I swear it feels like my heart is in my throat as I take a step closer to the door, rain beating mercilessly at my back. I am now outside, exposed to the killer. The fact that I have a gun in my hand does not cheer me in the least. I obviously have shot at the son of bitch and I can only imagine that he is a bit pissed off. I am thinking that now on top of killing *Jason*, he is looking to finish me off as well.

I grab the doorknob and turn, only to discover that it will not give. *Crap! I'm locked out!*

I barely have any time to process that thought when I feel an arm grab me around my waist and a hand cover my mouth. And that's when I faint.

~

"Amy!" I can hear Jason's voice, but I feel like I'm in a tunnel or underwater or something bizarre like that. My head is pounding and my body is cold and wet…I must be underwater.

And then I recall what happened. I am locked outside in the pouring rain. With a killer.

I am suddenly aware that I am in grave danger and I try to leap to my feet, blinking my eyes open, but it is dark and damp and it is all confusing. *Why does my head hurt so damn much?*

"No, Amy, don't!" I hear Jason call out to me again, but I don't know where his voice is coming from. It sounds faraway, like it's coming from the sky. *Is he dead? Is he calling to me from heaven, trying to warn me about the killer?*

I feel a tight grip around my body and someone sitting me up against a wall. A wet wall, with a waterfall running down the side.

"Amy, come on, wake up," Jason's voice is pleading with me again. *How is he talking if he's dead?*

My eyes are adjusting to the darkness and murky

conditions. I can see a dark figure standing over me. I know I should be frightened, so my heart is speeding up. I can also feel my body trembling; it feels like it did when I was giving birth, I can't stop the shaking.

The dark figure leans towards me and I shrink against the wall until I see his face. *Jason.* I sigh with relief. And then I remember the person at the door. The one who was trying to bang the door down to get in! I start to panic again.

"There was someone at the door! Trying to get in! They were hitting the door with the chair, over and over again! We have to get inside because they could be out here!" I struggle to my feet and Jason puts his hand on my shoulder.

"No, relax, Amy. That was me at the door. I tried to break it down once I realized the deadbolt was across the door. I was afraid you were in danger."

I'm thrilled there is no gun toting killer running around until I realize, *if Jason was the one at the door, he's the person I must have shot.* My eyes inspect his body, looking for where I must have shot him, but I see no bullet holes or blood on him.

"Did I hit you?" I ask with concern, shouting over the wind.

Jason shakes his head. "No, I'm fine. You shot the ceiling. I just ducked out of the way."

I nod and then I remember the gun shots before Jason tried to get into the house. And the blood all over the porch. *If it wasn't his blood, whose was it?*

"Jason! There was blood on the porch! And I heard gun shots before you tried to get into the house! And then I thought you were lying out in front of the bushes!"

Even in the darkness, I can see Jason's expression is grim. "It wasn't my blood. It was Harding's blood."

I feel my stomach lurch. "Agent Harding?" *Oh my God! The killer shot Harding!* I scramble to my feet, Jason not able to subdue me this time. "Is he okay? We've got to help him, Jason! And...oh my God, we've got to get help!"

Jason shakes his head. "It's too late. I checked him already. Shot clean through the head. He died instantly. Or at least quickly enough. It's too late for him."

A sob sticks in my throat, sadness for a man I really didn't even know who met his untimely demise at this desolate cabin, trying to protect me and my daughter.

"There's a crazed gun toting lunatic running around on this mountain top! What if he shoots you next?" I'm practically screaming now, as my head swivels from side to side, nervously scanning my surrounding, half expecting the killer to leap out of the bushes.

Jason clamps his hand over my mouth. "Shhh! Amy, be quiet! He'll hear you!"

"Oh, yeah, right," I say while nodding my head. "He's out here somewhere, right?" I mumble through his hand. "He killed Harding and he's trying to kill you."

Jason pulls me closer to him and whispers in my ear. "Amy, you've got it all wrong. There's no madman out here shooting at me. *I'm* the one who killed Harding."

I think I must have passed out again, because the next thing I remember, Jason and I are walking towards the porch. Well, Jason is walking. I'm kind of being dragged by Jason. *Whom I now realize is the killer.*

If I was scared before, huddling in the house with the kids, trying to keep the killer from knocking the door down, I am now officially *going to pee my pants* kind of scared.

Why ever would you be pee your pants scared*, Amy?* Well, Jason has a tight grip around my waist, a gun in his hand and my legs feel like a Slinky. I have no idea where I dropped Walter's gun and now we are creeping towards the house where the agent who is protecting Allie and Sean (hopefully between the thunder and the gunshots, he is actually awake) is now defenseless from Jason because *I* took his gun.

Good job idiot, I admonish myself, feeling like this would be an *I Love Lucy* episode if it wasn't going to end in massive bloodshed. Tears spring to my eyes as I think about my daughter; the only thing keeping her safe from Jason the lunatic is a splintered wooden door that he can obviously easily kick open.

Probably even with his arm around me he can manage to get into the cabin. He's like Evil Superman with his rippling biceps and chest muscles. I can't believe I found him attractive at some point in time. I should have trusted my gut and steered clear of him. I can't believe I let him kiss me! Ugh, I can't believe I liked it!

All these thoughts are swimming through my head as

I try to resist him by digging my heels into the ground. It's to no avail as the earth is so moist that the only thing that's touching my feet is mud and I'm slipping all over the place. I'm probably making it even easier for him to drag me, I realize so instead I let my body go limp to make myself dead weight.

"Amy, what the hell!" Jason yelps. "Are you hurt?"

I ignore him, satisfied that I am hindering him. Hopefully Walter can get the kids to safety. I wish I could somehow warn him, call him, send a smoke signal, anything. But I guess all I can do is try to buy time. Maybe I'll annoy Jason so much that he'll just kill me and leave them alone.

"Amy, seriously, if you're not hurt, can you walk please? Now is not the time to do this!" Jason is pleading with me and I am pleased that I am managing to outwit my undercover agent/ killer neighbor.

"Nope," I reply with an air of superiority. "You may have me and you will probably kill me, but I'm not letting you get to those kids without a fight. You're going to have to kill me first." I am quivering as I speak. I never thought I would die a hero, but here was my chance. My last chance to do something good. Maybe my mother would actually be proud of me for once. Or, more likely, she would say something along the lines of "Oh, Amy had to go and get herself killed wearing that hideous outfit. How embarrassing!"

"What in God's name are you talking about?" Jason asks, loosening his grip on me considerably. For a moment, I think maybe I can make a run for it. Until I realize, there was no running. Where would I go? I couldn't outrun Jason and I would end up deep in the woods, lost at night and in the rain.

"Amy, what are you talking about?" Jason asks again, this time gripping my shoulders and practically shaking me.

I stick my chin out. "That's right. I'm not going to let you hurt the kids. How can you do that to Sean? I thought you loved him like he was your own son? And Walter? You lived with him and he took care of your mother..." My lip starts quivering and I feel a different moistness on my face. This time, it's warm, salty tears, not freezing raindrops.

"Why would you think I would hurt *anybody*?" Jason asks indignantly.

"What? You admitted to killing Agent Harding!" My finger shook as I pointed towards the dark lump lying near the bushes, not thirty feet from where we stood. "You *killed* him!"

Jason's mouth drops open and then he snaps it shut. "Oh, God. Amy. I didn't kill him because I *wanted* to! I killed him because I *had* to! I thought you understood that!" His hands slide off of my shoulders and he cradles his head in his hands, shaking it.

"Why would you *have* to kill him?" I shout, not believing him.

"Because he was going to kill me! When we were looking for the *guy* in the woods, Harding took a shot at me. I ran as fast as I could to get back to the cabin and he chased me. He caught me here and I had to shoot him!"

I am staring at him in disbelief. "Why would he try to kill you?" None of this makes sense.

Jason hung his head. "We had a feeling someone was tipping off our guy about our plans. He was always one step ahead of us, like he had inside info. We had a feeling it was an agent. When Harding pulled his gun on me in the woods, I was certain it was him."

My brain is trying to process this information and something does not add up. Suddenly, lightening brightens the sky, followed by a deafening crack of thunder. And then, right behind the cabin, we see a tree split in half and come crashing to the ground, narrowly missing the building by mere feet. *The kids!*

Jason's eyes widen as I gasp for air. "Come on! We have to get them out of here!" he shouts to me over the torrential rain. He grabs my hand and pulls me towards the house before I can protest. "Do you still have the gun?"

I shake my head. I have no idea where I dropped the gun. "Maybe it's on the front porch! I had it until I passed out!" The wind whips my hair around my face, the rain plastering it to my cheeks. I stick my tongue out, pulling the wet hair off of it.

Jason nods. "Okay, we're definitely going to need it!" The air swirls around us, the tree rustling ominously like a tornado is approaching.

"But why?" I ask as I trudge after Jason. "If Harding

is dead, then we don't have to worry about it. We just have to get them out of here so that tree doesn't fall on them!" *Duh.* Sometimes I think that *I* should be the agent.

Jason shakes his head as he cranes his neck around. "No, it's still not safe, Amy. Remember the guy on his cell phone in the woods?"

I nod. Of course I remember. That's what set off the whole chase through the woods in the first place... And that's when it hits me. The reason that it wasn't adding up. Harding was in the bathroom. I gasp as I cover my mouth with my hand.

"The guy on the phone wasn't Harding," Jason explains, even though I now know that. "It was Walter."

~NINETEEN~

We inch towards the house, me gripping Jason's waist, holding on for dear life, and Jason trying to maneuver through the mud with me attached to him like a hemorrhoid. We approach the darkened porch and I see the gleam of the pistol in a puddle. (Was it a pistol? Semi-automatic? I have no clue about guns.)

"Thank God," Jason exhales as he reaches for it. He grabs my hand and places the gun in my palm. "Can you try to aim a little better this time?"

"Hey! I've never fired a gun before. I think I did pretty well," I retort indignantly, annoyed that he would bring up my lack of sharpshooter skills right *now*.

"Sure, tell that to the ceiling with a hole in it," Jason replies and then says, "You know what, I changed my mind. Give that back to me." He holds his hand out and I gratefully return the gun to him.

"It doesn't matter anyway," I explain. "Walter doesn't even have a gun. That *is* his gun. I grabbed it off the table when I heard you trying to get in the door. Uh, you know, when I thought you were a bad guy."

"Uh, huh," Jason murmurs as he sticks his key in the keyhole and attempts to open the door. The door doesn't budge. "*Fuck*. He's got something wedged up against the handle," he mutters with extreme frustration.

"Well can't you use the chairs and break the door down again?"

Jason shakes his head and points to the corner of the porch where a pile of wood is laying. "Nope. Those are the chairs."

Oops. Guess he broke them last time.

"Sorry. But in all fairness, if you had just said, *this is Jason*, I would have let you in," I point out.

"But then you wouldn't have Walter's gun," he retorts.

"Oh." *Touché.*

As I am pondering this, Jason cocks his head towards the side of the house. "Come on. We'll climb in through the bathroom window. I noticed that was open when Harding and I went off into the woods chasing after the fictitious *guy on the phone*." Even in the dark I can see the smirk on his face.

Immediately, I recall Harding stepping out of the bathroom, folding the newspaper under his arm. *He probably opened the window after...uh, using the facilities.* It seemed like days had passed since then, even though it had been less than three hours ago. My stomach begins to growl, as if it is reminding me that the dinner hour had passed and it is protesting my neglect.

"Hey, listen, there *was* a guy on the phone. I didn't know it was Walter," I explain with a slight whine in my voice.

"Shhh!" Jason warns as we approach the side of the house. "We have no idea where Walter is."

"He was asleep on the couch before all this went down," I tell him. "Snoring away, without a care in the world."

I can see Jason purse his lips. "I doubt he was sleeping. He was probably biding his time, waiting to ambush you when Harding got back from killing me and dumping my body in the woods."

I can't believe what I am hearing. *Dear sweet Walter? The gentle old man from across the street? It seems impossible.* I am not sure if I should believe Jason. *After all, it's his word against...I glance around nervously. Well, nobody's. There is nobody around to dispute what he is telling me. The only people who could dispute it are Harding and Walter. One is dead and the other is inside the house. What if he's lying to me and it's him who wants to ambush Walter, not the other way around? He seems to be good at lying. He had me convinced he was just a normal, run of the mill neighbor. Well, I was suspicious...*

These thoughts are turning in my head as I trail behind Jason. He is pushing his way through the heavy foliage, branches snapping below his feet as he makes his way towards the open bathroom window.

"What makes you think it was Walter and not Jimmy Donoghue? Don't you suspect Donoghue?" I whisper.

Jason turns and stares at me incredulously. "How did you know that?"

My face flushes, even though I know he can't see it in the near dark conditions. "I overheard you..." I manage to mumble.

Jason sighs. "You're going to get yourself killed

eavesdropping one day, Amy Maxwell. But Jimmy Donoghue is actually in police custody right now." He holds up his phone and shows me an incoming text. "So there's no way it was him."

"Oh," I reply, certainly subdued. *There goes that theory.*

Shaking his head, Jason glances around, looking for something to boost himself up with. The window is a good six feet off the ground. I can tell that he's strong, but I don't know if he can pull himself up at that angle, with the window sill being wet from the rain.

"I'll boost you up," he says to me, indicating the window.

"What?" No way!" I yelp, backing away. I trip over a bush and go sprawling right on my ass.

"Why not?" Jason asks, reaching his hand out to me. "I want you to go in first and there's a step stool in the bathroom that you can send out to me."

I shake my head defiantly.

Jason sighs loudly as he grows irate. "Well the only other option is you push me in the window and honestly, I don't think that's a viable one. I'm twice your size and quite frankly, I don't think you have the upper body strength for it."

I'm not even listening to him. I'm busy thinking. *What if he's pushing me in the window and he shots me in the back? It seems like a cowardly thing to do, but so does killing a fellow DEA agent.*

I want to believe that Jason's telling me the truth; but

at the same time, I don't want to be that gullible fool. This whole thing is just so bizarre, I don't even know what is real and what's imagined. Without warning, I start to cry.

Jason, who was scowling fiercely at me, softens his face and it is then that I know he isn't lying. "Oh, no, Amy! Don't cry! Oh, shit, come on...don't cry." He holds his arms out to me and I fall into them, completely trusting. I don't care if it's naïve, I don't care if it's foolish. I believe Jason is telling me the truth, no matter how wacky the story is. And now, I believe, no, I *know* my child is in danger, trapped in the house with a murder.

I abruptly pull away from Jason. "Come on, I'm ready....what the hell are you waiting for?" I awkwardly brush aside my tears and offer him a lopsided smile. "Let's go save the kids."

He gazes at me skeptically. "Are you sure you're ok?"

I bob my head rapidly. "Yup, never better! Now let's go get that son of a bitch!"

Jason smiles warmly. "You know what Amy Maxwell? For a non agent, you're a pretty awesome woman."

I resist the urge to burst into tears again at his complement and just turn my attention towards the window.

"Step into my palm," Jason instructs me. I step up as I push my palms on the side of the house for support. And proceed to get a giant splinter. Biting my lip so I don't cry (and thus ruin Jason's opinion that I'm *awesome*), I continue to propel my body upwards with Jason's assistance. I grab ahold of the window sill and shove it open all the way. Jason is now heaving my butt through the windows with both hands. I try to focus on the matter at hand and not the fact that despite the life and death situation that we are in, his touch causes a tingling in my groin.

As soon as my body fills the space, I grip the sides of the window frame and sit on the sill, dangling my legs inside the window.

"Try not to make any noise," Jason reminds me from the ground.

I nod, even though he probably can't see me in the dark and I drop down to the floor as quietly as possibly. Fortunately, it is only a drop of a foot or so and I manage to hit the tile noiselessly.

The bathroom is dark and I am walking my hands across the wall to find the light switch when I realize that idea is stupid. If I turn on the light, it will alert Walter to the fact that there is someone in the bathroom.

And besides, all the lights went out, remember, Amy? Instead, I crouch down on all fours, blindly feeling for the step stool that I'm supposed to hand out the window to Jason. I find it just as my head whacks the side of the tub. I suck in my breath, resisting the urge to cry out. It was quite a hallow noise; I wasn't sure if that was the tub or my head.

Damn it. I hope the sound of the storm outside covers

the noise of my head bonking the tub.

My legs still unsteady, I stand and lower the step stool out the window without a word. I feel Jason taking it out of my hands and I back away from the window so that he has plenty of room to climb in. Within seconds, I feel his dripping wet body land softly on the tile next to me.

"I'm going to go first," he whispers in my ear, his warm breath prickling my frozen earlobe. "Stick close behind me, but get out of the way if Walter attacks."

"But he doesn't have a gun-" I start to say. But then my body goes cold as I realize, *he has an entire drawer of kitchen knives at his disposal.* And I told Allie and Sean to hide in the kitchen. He's got them right where he wants them and what's worse, they trust him. They have no idea what has gone on outside the cabin tonight. They don't know that Walter is the bad guy. Heck, Sean thinks of him as "Grampy"; why would he ever think that "Grampy" would hurt him?

Suddenly, I am panicking, my palms sweaty and my mouth cottony. We need to get the kids out of this cabin as soon as possible. I poke Jason in the ribs, trying to get him to move a little faster.

"Could ya stop?" he growls through gritted teeth. "I'm ticklish."

"Jason," I hiss. "The kids *trust* Walter to keep them safe. We gotta get them out of the cabin!" The urgency in my voice is palpable. I am trying my hardest not to cry again.

"No, you don't say?" Jason remarks with sarcasm. *Ok, so maybe it wasn't necessary to mention this fact to the secret agent.* But as the events of the night unfold, I am starting to see myself as a bit of a sleuth, like Nancy Drew. Or maybe more like Colombo.

Jason presses his ear against the bathroom door, trying to get some indication of where Walter and the kids are. "I hear voices," he tells me. If I wasn't so damn nervous and fidgety, I would have made a sarcastic comment. But just like the *Wonder Pets* say, *this is serious*! *Crap, I miss Evan.* I feel a tear trickle down the side of my face.

Dear God, if you get us all out of this alive, I swear I will never complain about watching endless hours of children's programming with my toddler. I will let Colt keep the sling shot in his fort, eat as many cookies as he wants, and not make him wipe the dirt off his face. I won't tune Lexie out when she natters on and on about pens with feathers versus pens with glitter. I won't yell at her for taking her dolls outside. I won't stalk my teenager, I won't check her messages. I will trust her, because it is ME who got us into this mess, simply by not trusting her. I'll be a better mother, I swear.

Jason draws the bathroom door closer to his body, opening it inch by inch, attempting not to make a sound. He jerks his head towards the open door and whispers, "I changed my mind. You go first. I'll cover you."

"What?" I hiss. "No way. Then I'll get shot first."

"He doesn't have his gun, Amy," Jason reminds me.

"He's probably hoping for the element of surprise so he'll attack with a knife or a blunt object." He nudges me slightly. "Trust me, you're safer going first."

I guess he has a point, I think as I cautiously step out in the hall. I glance towards the bedrooms. I don't know what I am expecting, but from where I am standing, both bedroom doors are open and completely dark inside.

On tip toe, I inch down the hall, Jason close on my heels. Even though he is soaked, I can still smell his inebriating scent. I take a deep breath to steel my nerves. *He won't let anything bad happen to you or the kids, Amy.* I am trying to reassure myself that everything is going to work out, but needless to say, it's difficult to be an optimist when your child is potentially being held hostage by an DEA agent who might have killed his "wife" who was an undercover DEA agent and the only one protecting you is another DEA agent who has already killed a DEA agent that tried to kill him that very night. Difficult to keep up? Yeah, I'm dizzy just thinking about it.

We are approaching the kitchenette and living room. The kitchenette is to the left and the living room is directly in front of us. Even though I can barely see anything, I can make out the outline of the couch and I smell the burnt toast that Sean made right before the electricity went out.

Lightening illuminates the sky once again and I catch a shadow darting behind the kitchen nook. I frantically nudge Jason, hoping that he saw it too and I don't have to speak. Because at this juncture, I'm pretty sure my vocal cords have frozen up. A fact that would most likely please my husband to no end.

Oddly enough, thoughts of Roger and our honeymoon in Vegas race through my mind. Roger and I at the Chapel O' Love; he is in a comical green suede leisure suit and I am in a hot pink micro mini skirt that showed off my tanned and sculpted legs. Roger and I at the craps table, me blowing on his dice for good luck; us throwing back our heads and laughing with glee when we won. Roger and I making love on the balcony of our hotel suite, not caring that half of Vegas could see us.

A sob lodges itself unceremoniously in my throat. *What? Why am I thinking of Roger now? And that's not the Roger I know...that guy is long gone.* With deep, unexplained grief I wonder, *what happened to that Roger? And what's more, what happened to that Amy?*

Is this why I'm so hell bent on this dangerous, suicidal adventure? What kind of mother puts their thirteen year old's life *in jeopardy for a little excitement? The thirteen year old that is quite possibly in a ton of danger right now on the eve of her fourteenth birthday and she needs her mother to get her head out of her fantasizing ass and FOCUS.*

With that, I banish all disturbing thoughts of Roger, our former life BK (before kids), and concentrate on the task at hand; finding Sean and Allie and getting them away from Walter.

The lightning strikes again, this time causing me to

involuntarily gasp. It illuminates the room and I see Walter is standing in clear view in the kitchen, butcher's knife gleaming in midair, his arm wrapped around my daughter's waist.

I want to scream; really, I do. I open up my mouth with the intention of doing so, but no sound emerges from my lips. In the split second that the kitchenette is lit up by the light, my eyes lock on Allie's. Her eyes are bulging, desperate and frightened, begging me to help her, save her, be her mother.

But I am powerless as I stand there, my legs and arms feeling floppy, as if no bones hold them up, as if they are just skin with loose adipose tissue flapping around underneath.

"You just couldn't leave well enough alone," I hear Walter's gravelly voice which I once found endearing. Now I now can only think of it as sinister. "You had to come and live with us. You couldn't just stay out of the way and let me take care of Mary on my own. She was a busy body; she got what was coming to her. You, on the other hand, were clueless. I would have just disappeared. You wouldn't have had any idea why. Perhaps you would have thought the mob kidnapped me or some crap like that. You were focusing on that Donoghue idiot. He was just one of my lackeys at the high school. That idiot couldn't run a drug ring! He could barely handle the small tasks I gave him to do. Maybe you would have figured it out, but I would have been long gone. But no…you had to come track me down *for my safety* and drag me to this God forsaken place."

I realize that he's not speaking to me, but to Jason. I feel Jason behind me tightening his grip on my arm. Walter is alluding to Jason's mother as a disposable piece of garbage.

"And *you*," Walter growls. Even in the darkness, I know he is narrowing his eyes and focusing on me. "If you would have just minded your God damned business and cut the crap with all your neighborliness, your kid wouldn't have a knife to her throat right now. I think she's bleeding on me. Would be a crying shame if my hand slipped."

I am tempted to leap forward at this revelation which is coupled with the sound of Allie whimpering. But I don't move; not only because I am still paralyzed with fear, but because I am putting my total faith in Jason. He may not have saved Stacey or his mother, but I felt 100% confidant that he was going to get us out of this mess. Well, 95% confidant anyway.

"Too bad you didn't figure it out before you dragged Harding up here, Jason. You would have had a shot to outwit *me*. But once Harding volunteered to babysit up here, you were outplayed." The sky lights up and I see Walter shaking his head in dismay.

"Pathetic, really. I thought you were a way better agent than that. I mean, hell, I lived under your nose for what, two months and you didn't figure it out? I guess you were too busy with that retarded kid of yours-"

"Shut up!" Jason growls, the first time he has said

anything since Walter began his litany five minutes ago. I can feel the muscles in his forearm tense as he wraps his arm tighter around my chest, pulling me towards him as if that will protect him from Walter's harsh words. "He's *not* retarded."

"Whatever," Walter snorts. "Maybe the apple don't fall from the tree. You're not exactly the picture of brilliance yourself." Then he stops and chuckles with an evil undertone. "But then again, Sean isn't even really your kid, is he, Jason? He's Stacey's kid from another relationship. He he he, that Stacey probably had a ton of relationships over the years, didn't she? Hell, I'd be surprised if she even knew who Sean's real father was. Hot piece of ass like that, she probably had a hard time keeping her panties on."

Jason's arm constricts even more and I feel the cold steel of the gun brush past my other arm as he slowly raises it to aim at Walter. I tense up, thinking, *no! He has Allie! You can't see that well in the dark!*

Walter is still pushing his limits, trying to infuriate Jason even more for some unknown reason. Maybe he's suicidal, but what he says next is the straw that breaks the camel's back. "So how's it feel to raise another man's son, Jason?"

"Shut up," Jason snarls, spitting in my hair in the process. "Sean is my son and you trying to demean our relationship or disparage Stacey, is not going to change that."

"Eh, whatever. It doesn't much matter what you

think. I'm the one with the knife held to the girl's throat, aren't I? And if you don't want to see her blood spilled on the ground, you'll put your gun right up here on the counter like a good boy," Walter instructs, jerking his head towards the nook.

Grumbling, Jason lays his gun on the counter. "Anything else, Walter?" I try not to gasp in shock. *What is he doing? He's giving in?*

Walter nods in my direction. "Tie her up."

What????

"Are you crazy?" Jason asks as I feel myself blush.

Walter presses the blade of the knife against Allie's throat causing her to squeal. "Are you really in the position to be asking that, son?"

I hear Jason sucking in his breath. "What am I supposed to tie her up with exactly?"

"Rope on the chair over there. Walter indicates the wooden chair in the living room. Jason sighs as he stomps off to retrieve the rope. Holding it up, he asks, "What now?"

Walter clicks his tongue. "Am I to really believe this is the first time you've tied up a woman, Jason?"

At this point, I really am frightened, however, the suggestion that Jason is into bondage makes me blush. Not that I'm into bondage. Just the image of Jason tying a woman up seems rather... *never mind.*

"Tie her to that chair. And don't even think about making those knots loose. I'm going to check it," Walter growls.

Jason purses his lips and nods at me even though I am staring at him pleadingly. "Come on, Amy," he tells me. Something in his voice is begging me to trust him.

I sit in the chair obediently, never taking my eyes off of Allie. The gun is still on the counter, but it is too far out of my reach to make a grab for it. "Put your hands out in front of you," Jason commands.

"And her feet!" Walter calls out.

Jason nods at me. I lift my feet obediently. I feel like an absolute jackass. Jason winds the rope around my appendages a little tighter than I feel is necessary.

"Ouch," I wince.

"Sorry," he apologizes.

"That better really be tight, Jason. Or I will slice this girl's throat and her mother will be forced to watch her die right here. And then I will use the same knife to stab her mother to death. Right in front of you. You don't want to be responsible for the death of a young girl AND her mother, do you?"

"You forget one thing, Walter," Jason says calmly, his breathing suddenly controlled and even. "I still have *your* gun." With one swift motion, he raises his arm to shoot. I can't help the blood curdling shriek that escapes from my throat as Jason aims at Walter and pulls the trigger.

I hear Jason curse under his breath, "What the…"

And then, Walter's evil laugh again. "Shit, that's my gun ain't it? Oh, Amy, you dumb blonde…you fell for that trick. I *purposely* left that on the table, hoping you would grab it and shoot Jason as he walked through the door. Your prints would be on it and everything. But I guess I overestimated your close range shooting skills, huh? Only one bullet in the chamber. Hell, I couldn't take the chance that you would figure me out and use my own weapon *against* me, could I?"

At first, I am very affronted by this statement. First off, I am not blonde. My hair is a mix between a dishwater and mousey brown. Secondly, I can't believe he was not only going to let me kill Jason, he was going to frame me for it. Thirdly, I am pissed he has alluded to my lack of shooting skills. For God's sake, it was the first time that I even held a gun! If I had ever gone to a shooting range before, I would have shown that crumidy old codger a thing or two. I can't believe that I thought he was a sweet old man just ten minutes ago.

Suddenly my mind catches up with my body and it feels like it is crawling with spiders. *We are dead where we stand.*

I start to envision worst case scenarios, starting with Walter slicing Allie's throat and then offing us one by one. I didn't think I could be more panicked than I had been just a few moment ago, but my body's reaction proves me wrong. I'm cold and shaking, but sweating in places I didn't know exist. I feel hot and clammy, yet my teeth are now chattering. Through my mind runs all the things that Allie will never get to do; have a sweet sixteen party, a college graduation, a wedding... I am also thinking, *shit, I really wanted to finally get to Europe...I knew we shouldn't have waited till the kids were grown. I should have been like Joey and said fuck it and went years ago.* I want to say a prayer, offer my daughter some sage wisdom in our final moments, but nothing comes to mind. My brain is like cotton candy.

This is the point where my life starts flashing before my eyes and I realize that my 8 mistakes led us to this point in time. I can just see the obituary now.

The 8 Mistakes of Amy Maxwell: "Amy Maxwell, 35 year old wife of Roger, mother of 4, died on a mountaintop in a remote location all because of 8 mistakes. Basically, she couldn't mind her own business. Her first mistake some may consider just being born…"

My depressing death rant is interrupted by the thunking noise that is similar to a gong. There is a scream and the lights come back on.

"What the…" Jason yelps. As our eyes adjust to the sudden flood of lights in the cozy little kitchenette, we see standing over Walter, who is slumped on the floor at the moment, Sean with hard ionized skillet in his hand, raised above his head, poised to strike again at a moment's notice.

Allie is the first one to move. She shrieks and wraps her arms tightly around Sean's neck, planting one hell of a kiss on his cheek which is now the color of an eggplant. Jason nearly knocks me and the chair over as he rushes towards the unconscious Walter, quickly whipping handcuffs out of the inner pocket of his jacket.

Where did those come from? He had those all along?

Allie rushes at me. And I can tell she is frightened; she's trembling like a leaf on a tree in December and her face has soaked my shirt from tears. I haven't seen her this upset since our cat Mittens was run over by our next door neighbor's motorcycle. I want to hold her closely to my body, but I am currently tied up.

Instead, I relish her warmth and the smell of the coconut shampoo in her hair which reminds me of a day on the beach. She pulls back after a few minutes, and I expect she is going to be embarrassed by the uncharacteristic display of affection, but instead she says, "Thank you for looking out for me, Mommy. I was so scared."

I can't help but smile as I plant a kiss on top of her head, just like I used to do when she was little and fell off her bike and scraped her knees.

Walter is not unconscious for long, but it is enough time for Jason to render him as a non-threat to us any longer. He slaps the cuffs on him and as further insurance, handcuffs him to the stove. With a satisfied nod, he tells me that help is not far away. He texted for help when he and Harding dashed into the woods. His fellow (trustworthy) agents will be coming to haul Walter away and take the body of Agent Harding to the morgue.

When Walter starts to stir, he is confused and groggy and tries to sit up, but Jason prevents him from moving by straddling his legs and pressing them together with his ankles. Between the "attack" in the woods which Walter had staged earlier and his run in with the frying pan,

Walter looks like an escaped mental patient.

Within ten minutes, the back-up has arrived and Jason has *finally* untied me after mentioning that the ropes were not that tight after all. I have thanked Sean profusely, much to his chagrin. He has turned several shades of scarlet from the tips of his ears all the way down his neck. I'm quite certain his flushing extended well down his torso. He just shuffles his feet on the floor and mutters something about it not being a big deal. Just then, a thin, bearded and bespectacled man taps me on the shoulder.

"Mrs. Maxwell?" he asks, his voice sounding much deeper than I would expect from such a timid looking man.

I shrink back, suddenly wary of strangers.

His face flushes and he stammers, "Um, I'm sorry to startle you. I'm Agent Doug North." He offers me his birdlike hand and I shake it, still skeptical.

"He's okay," Jason confirms, coming up from behind me and placing a protective hand on my shoulder.

I cock my head to the side and offer him a smirk. "Are you sure? Because you told us Walter and Harding were okay, too."

And I am three for three on making the men blush because now Jason's cheeks are pink. "Glad to see the last three days hasn't affected your sarcastic sense of humor," Jason mumbles.

Three days? That's all it was? I feel as if finding Mary's body had happened three months ago, not days.

I start to reply to Jason and then realize that he is deep in conversation with Agent North, periodically gesturing towards me and my daughter. Then, he offers me a hasty wave and a melancholy smile before he heads out the front door to show another agent where Harding's body is.

I stare at him, every part of my being wanting to chase after him. I don't know why I feel like that and what's more, I don't know why I can't move. My limbs are heavy and everything is hazy around me.

Before we know it, Allie and I are in the back of a warm and dry Crown Vic, pulling away from the cabin. I must be in shock because I don't remember changing into the dry clothes that I am now wearing or climbing into the back of the vehicle. I crane my neck as the car pulls down the driveway, hoping to catch a glimpse of Jason. But all I can see is the darkness. I press my fingers against my lips, desperately wishing I could feel the warmth of his lips from just a few short hours ago. *I can't believe that was today. Today has to be one of the most shocking days of my life.*

"I'm so glad I'm going to be home for my birthday," Allie tells me. "Especially since it's Friday the thirteenth. It would be crazy to be in the woods for Friday the thirteenth."

I kiss the top of my daughter's head and murmur, "I'm glad, too."

Swallowing my tears, I lean back against the seat, Allie's head on my shoulder as I finally drift off to sleep.

~TWENTY~

"Mommmmmmmmmyyyyyyyy!" I try not to cringe as I hear Lexie squealing from the living room.

Deep cleansing breaths, Amy. Remember what the shrink told you. Ignore the high pitched voice and just know it's your daughter excited to share a discovery with you. Relish in her eagerness.

"What's the matter, Lex?" I ask as I finish folding the bath towel in my hand, resisting the urge to bite my fist. I've been working on not letting Lexie's ramblings and high pitched squawks affect me, but damn, it's difficult. But, hey, Rome wasn't built in a day.

"The new neighbors are moving in right nowww! They have a moving van and everything!"

Lexie's words hit me right in the solar plexus. *Is that a real place? I don't even know.*

The new neighbors.

I haven't even laid eyes on the Monroe family and I hate them already. Cammi Donoghue (who had the absolute audacity to remain in town after big Jimmy's trial and conviction) was sure to give me a detailed report on the family that was moving in.

The father was a psychology professor at the county college and the mother ran a quaint little tea room in the next town. They had two perfectly groomed tow-headed boys, who Cammi pointed out were well mannered and she would not hesitate to let her precious Jimmy play with them. When she had relayed this information to me over coffee that she had invited herself over for, I secretly hoped the Monroe boys would turn out to be evil demons and duct tape Jimmy to a tree outside. In the rain.

From Cammi's description of the Monroes, they sounded like people my sister Beth would love, but that was not even the reason I had gotten it in my head to despise them.

The reason I hated them was because they were moving into the Sanders' old house. Or rather, Mary Collins' old house. And Jason and Sean had moved out.

I part the bedroom curtains, just in time to see the moving van back into the driveway across the street. A car, very similar to the one that brought Allie and me back from the cabin, pulls up to the curb. Before the occupants climb out, I find myself reminiscing about the day Allie and I came home after our three day long ordeal.

After our horrendous three days on the mountain, Allie and I arrived home to complete and utter chaos. I don't just mean that the house was in shambles (it was), or that the kids looked like they belonged in a Dickens novel (they did…in fact it took me two days to scrape the dried macaroni and cheese off of the baby's face). Roger and the kids were emotional wrecks.

When Allie and I pulled up to our house in the wee hours of the morning that day, the house appeared quiet and peaceful. As we stepped out of the car, the front door flew open and like a dam bursting forth, five people rushed from the house. Completely blindsided and overwhelmed, I felt myself enveloped by ten arms and grabby hands, wet faces and sticky lips.

There were tears and laughs and sighs of relief. My family pulled Allie and me into the house, my mother holding Allie out at arm's length and telling her how much she grew, much to Allie's dismay. Roger pulling me aside and squeezing me tightly, telling me I can never ever leave him again. Evan and Colt and Lexie, hugging their sister, telling her how much they missed her. And the coup de grace, my sister telling me she was exhausted from being me for three days.

Evan had cried for "Mama" the first few hours and then he just wandered around sucking his thumb, with a dejected look on his face, according to Roger's report. Colt was upset and hid himself away in his fort, much to his grandmother and Aunt Beth's dismay. They couldn't find him for nearly an hour, leading my mother to fear that he had been kidnapped. When they finally found him, curled up in a ball in the corner of his fort, they didn't have the heart to wake him and scold him so they just left him there...overnight. (They claimed they put the monitor out there and there was an agent watching him in the fort, but I think they just forgot about him). Lexie followed her grandmother around like a lost puppy, bemoaning her situation and asking my mother questions about our disappearance that she had no answer for.

By day three, my sister, the epitome of grace under

pressure, was shaking and drinking wine by the gallon while sobbing continuously. My mother was mainlining coffee and chasing the kids around until she gave up and flopped onto the couch, letting the boys roam free and Lexie just prattle on in her ear.

Across the street, the car doors are slamming, jolting me out of my reverie. I startle and find myself staring at a very scholarly looking man in a tweed suit. The kind with the pads at the elbows. His hair is swirling around his head, his obvious comb-over completely disheveled. He is wearing coke bottle glasses and even from my perch at the window, I can tell that his face is pockmarked from acne scars and he is slightly overweight. I sigh with relief.

No more Jason Collins living across the street, I think to myself. No one to drool over and watch with my mouth open. That's a relief.

And then, my relief turns to dismay as I repeat, *No more Jason Collins living across the street.*

I hadn't seen him since the night at the cabin. Which was good. And depressing. We never got to talk about that kiss in the woods or what it meant. Which was also good, of course, but I couldn't help feeling like an unresolved issue was swirling around me.

There had been an inquest; Walter was being brought up on murder and attempted murder charges. Allie and I had been subpoenaed and my heart had skipped a beat. I thought maybe we would have run into Jason in court, so I carefully chose my outfit, changing my clothes about fifty-two times before leaving for the courthouse. But it was just me and Allie, our lawyer and a judge. We didn't even see Walter that day, not that I wanted to. The judge took our statement and we were dismissed. He said we most likely would not have to go through the pain of testifying because Walter admitted to everything. In fact, he proudly confessed to his crime spree and his fifteen years as a member of the mafia.

The doors slam again and I glance up to see a breathtakingly beautiful blonde bimbo, er, I mean woman, standing next to the car. Two perfectly coifed little boys wearing khakis and zipper down fleece jackets hop anxiously up and down on one foot on the sidewalk next to the woman as she offers them a plastic smile.

I groan as I slap my forehead with my palm. *Great, Cammi Donoghue on one side and this one across the street...there goes the neighborhood.* I can just see Jason's tongue hanging out of his mouth when he caught a glimpse of the bimbo.

Wait. Did I just say Jason? Oh crap. I meant Roger. Damn it, damn it, damn it. There's no more Jason, Amy.

The "incident" had been nearly six months ago. A lot has happened in those six months. Allie has been less distant. Of course, she is still the same old bitchy, snarky teenager from before, but every once in a while, that tough exterior cracks and I get a glimpse of my sweet, thoughtful and loving baby girl underneath. Don't tell anyone, but she started sending me texts every night that say, "Night night, Mommy XOXO". No matter if we scream or shout or curse at each other that day, I still get the text. I always send her one back that says "Sweet dreams, baby girl XOXO", and I leave it at that. I have not shown them to anyone or even mentioned it to Allie; I would hate for her to stop because she's embarrassed.

Laura and Kaitlyn came over for a long overdue chat and we all shared a group hug (after some screaming) and promised not to let Victoria come in between our friendships again.

Roger agreed to accompany me to counseling after I got home; he thought it was just for me to adjust to the traumatic incident that I had just undergone, but it was really marriage counseling. We have been doing surprisingly well, taking one night every single week to have a "date" night. The kids stay with my mother or my sister, who have both volunteered to get more involved and help me out once in a blue moon. My sister even gave me a gift certificate for her posh salon for Christmas and watched the kids for me when I went to have my hair done.

Colt has not had any more problems in school. He and Jimmy Donoghue are now in separate classes after their fight. Colt made a new best friend, Charlie. Charlie is a girl, but she gives Colt a run for his money. He was thrilled to find out that she has a fort and also loves to eat worms, too. I'm pretty sure she could beat the crap out of him if necessary. I see a romance blossoming in the future; she's definitely wife material.

Sean and Jason have not been back to the house. I

saw a moving van and a few guys carrying out boxes and some furniture a few weeks ago. Right after the For Sale sign had gone up. I guess Jason had someone pack up the house for them, whatever belongings they wanted to bring with them to wherever they were going next.

Sean has called Colt a few times, but Colt isn't exactly a phone kind of kid. Surprisingly, Allie ended up talking to him for over an hour the last time he called. I think I overheard something about them going to a movie together. A horror movie about kids trapped in a cabin in the woods.

"Mommy!" Lexie is shrieking, her cries coming closer by the second. I can tell she is taking the steps two at a time.

"In here, Lex!" I call out to her, cringing because I can tell she is dangerously close to Evan's room and I've just managed to get him down for a nap.

The door is flung open and my gregarious child pounces into the room. "Can I go say hi to the new kids across the street? Mrs. Donoghue said that they are eight and ten. I'm ten, too," she informs me in case I missed that fact, like I have been hiding under a rock for the past ten years or something.

"I guess so…" I start to say as she bounds out of the room without letting me finish.

"Thanks, Mom!" she calls over her shoulder.

"Lexie! Wait!" I call after her just as I hear Evan start to stir in his room.

Damn it! I can't let her dash across the street by

herself! The street isn't busy, but Lexie has no idea how to look both ways...

I hear the front door slam and I shout to Allie who is barricaded in her room as usual, "Allie, watch your brothers! I have to walk Lexie across the street." I leap down the steps, seriously considering that I have possibly dislocated my ankle, and dash out the front door just in time to see Lexie reach the other side of the street.

I sigh with relief as I realize, *well, she is ten. I guess it's not unreasonable to think a ten year old can cross a quiet side street without assistance.*

I stare at my daughter as she bounds up the steps and happily knocks on the front door, not a care in the world. The blonde woman answers the door and peers down at Lexie, offering her a fake smile. I can see Lexie gesturing wildly in the air and then turning to point at me, hovering on our front steps.

Oh crap, don't call attention to me, Lexie! It is 1:00 in the afternoon, but the kids are on spring break and Roger is golfing with fellow principal buddies. I've been doing some spring cleaning all morning because I have the extra kids at home to help out with the baby, so I haven't bothered to clean myself up or run a brush through my hair. Hell, I think I slept in these sweats last night, now that I think about it.

I wave half-heartedly and the woman waves back...enthusiastically, I might add. I cringe that she's seen me in this attire, but I can't help thinking that maybe she isn't as bad as I thought she'd be. I step toward the

Heather Balog

curb to speak to her, wishing I had made cookies or something to bring over as a house warming gift.

I wave to the new neighbor as I rock my feet on the edge of the curb, not daring to step off and cross the street in the state I'm in. Maybe she has vision problems and can't tell I'm a hot mess from thirty feet away. It reminds me of how I used to speak with Mary every morning. *Poor Mary.* She never even had funeral services. Jason had her cremated in a private service. We found out about it a few weeks later while perusing the obituaries in the Sunday paper. Roger always reads the obits to make sure he's not in them. Yes, I know, I married a very strange man.

"Hi!" I call out. "Amy Maxwell! That was my daughter, Lexie. Sorry about her," I remark as I indicate Lexie who has dashed into the backyard and out of sight. "She saw the moving van and she wanted to meet the kids-"

The woman dismissed my apology with a wave. "Oh, it's perfectly fine! They're chasing the dog around the backyard right now. Tormenting her, in fact."

"Are you sure you don't mind?" I inquire again after a pick-up truck chugs down the road at twelve miles an hour. "I'm sure you have so much to do."

"Not at all," she answers with a smile that seems genuine. "Besides, the boys will stay out of my hair if there's another kid to entertain them, if you know what I mean."

I nod with understanding. I certainly do know what

she means.

"Ok, well, be sure to kick her out when she becomes a pest," I reply as I start to turn around. Then I suddenly remember my manners that my mother had always drilled into my head. "Oh, and maybe tomorrow the boys can come play over our house. The kids are off all week."

"Sounds like a plan," the woman shouts over the sound of a motorcycle whizzing down the block. "Oh, and I forgot! My name's Mary! Mary Monroe!"

I stand rooted to the sidewalk, not sure how I feel about the new owner of the house having the same name as the woman I had found viciously murdered in the very same living room six months before. But I manage my hand and offer a parting wave, "It's nice to meet you, Mary." And I think I meant it.

I hear the neighbor's front door closing as I head back towards my own house, hoping that Allie is indeed watching Evan while simultaneously wondering what to order out for dinner. Hey, I've been busting my butt cleaning all day, I certainly wasn't going to mess up the sparkling clean kitchen, was I?

I notice a weed growing out of the sidewalk as I approach the front walk, so I bend down to rip it out. *I really need to get on Roger about weeding more or at least hiring a landscaper,* I am thinking as I discover many more tiny pesky weeds creeping out of the cracks. It's almost cathartic, ripping those unwanted suckers out by their roots. Soon I find that I've been weeding for quite some time. My ADD has gotten the best of me.

Allie has been outside to tell me that Evan was sleeping but now he's awake and Lexie has even raced past me a while ago, done playing with the neighbors.

I stand up to stretch my back when I hear a car door slam behind me and thinking that it is Roger, home from golfing, I brush the dirt off my knees and whirl around to greet my husband. I almost fall back onto the ground from shock. It is like I have seen a real life, living, breathing ghost.

Ambling up my front walk is none other than Jason Collins.

His hair is a little grayer and rumpled than I recall it, his face seems older and more drawn. He's wearing a suit, so I can only imagine the biceps and pecs underneath. He has the gait of someone who is tired and worn out. I can tell that he has aged significantly in the past six months.

Yet, my heart still flutters in my chest, my breath catching somewhere in my windpipe, unable to escape.

He stops about four feet from where I stand, stooping almost. We stare at each other for several moments, neither one of us wanting to break the charged air around us. The electricity is still as thick, if not more so, than it was even the day we stood in the woods and he lowered his lips to mine.

Finally, Jason speaks. "Hi, Amy."

I nod and manage to croak, "Hello, Jason."

He smiles, his mouth almost crooked, drooping on one side, like a shy boy at the school dance. "It's good to see you again."

"You, too," I reply, nervously rocking on the balls of my feet. *Stop it, Amy*, I try to command myself. *You look like a mental patient!* But I can't help it. The sight of Jason reduces me to a blubbering puddle of gelatin. My brain doesn't work, my body doesn't work, my mind doesn't work.

"I guess you're wondering why I'm here," Jason remarks casually.

Why he's here? Oh yeah…why are you here Jason? Are you going to try to sweep me off my feet, tell me our kiss in the woods was the best you ever had and you can't live without me? Well I can't go Jason. I have a life here, you know. A husband that I discovered I really love, kids I adore…but you could certainly try, you know.

Jason waves a sheet of paper in the air. "The new owners forgot this at the lawyers."

Oh.

Jason stares down at my sidewalk with the weeds poking out of the crack and sweeps over them with the tip of his dark brown dress shoe. "The lawyer said she could mail it to them and I haven't wanted to come back to the house after…my mother died and all. But…" He suddenly lifts his head and catches my eye. He holds my gaze as he says, "I think I need some closure, you know."

I am uncomfortably aware that my face is moist, a lone tear trickling down my face. *Don't cry about this, Amy! Don't be a weenie! This isn't about you! He's talking about his mother!*

But in my heart, I know he's not only talking about his mother. His eyes are telling me the whole story without his mouth speaking the words. He's talking about that moment we shared in the woods; that kiss that we can never take back nor would we want to. It wasn't a kiss of true love, he and I both know that. It was a kiss of desperation; he was desperate to save someone and I was desperate to be saved. Maybe we felt affection for each other, connection on a deeper level that was never expressed with words; but ours was never a relationship that would ever or *could* ever work. We were both searching for something those three days at the cabin, and we found it in the end. For that fleeting moment in the woods, with that single kiss, we found what we needed. And now, we had to go back to our regularly scheduled lives. Forever, that would be all we would have together and it would be enough.

"I know," is all I can manage to squeak out as I swipe the lone tear from my face.

"I'll see you around," Jason replies as he smiles weakly and offers me a consolatory wave, one that lets me know that he probably won't be seeing me around at all. This is it, he's leaving and this is our last moment.

My heart starts to sink as he turns back towards his mother's old house and then, it is suddenly buoyed with the realization that I can say something profound about our situation, because after six months of replaying that kiss in my mind, I finally get it. "Hey, Jason?"

He turns back towards me and I can actually see his

eyes shining with would be tears. "Yeah?"

"Don't cry because it's over, smile because it happened," I tell him. *Good old Dr. Seuss; that guy really got it.*

Jason is confused for a second and then his face breaks out into a wide grin. "You know what, Amy? I will. Thanks." He pauses and then says, "And Amy? I still think you'd make a damn good agent." He winks, causing me to blush. And with that, he turns on his heel and dashes towards the house across the street.

Instead of staring after him like a needy, lovesick teenager, I turn and open the door to my own house. I am immediately greeted with screams and whines.

"Mom! Colt isn't listening to me! I told him not to slide down the steps with the refrigerator box! He's going to hit his head on the bottom of the steps and fall out and then he'll be in a comma!" Lexie was wailing in desperation. She is actually wringing her hands like a little old wash woman.

"It's coma, you idiot, not comma," Allie retorts as she chases after Evan to get the TV remote out of his mouth.

"Don't call me an idiot, you moron!" Lexie retorts back.

Normally, I would throw my hands up in the air and shriek at the top of my lungs until nobody is even listening to me anymore. But not today. Today, Jason's smile has rejuvenated me. Today, I am going to live by the words of wise old Dr. Seuss.

"Don't call each other names," I say evenly. "And Colt, get the couch cushions and put them at the bottom of the steps before you slide down. That way you won't end up in a coma."

I wink at my kids, three out of four who are staring at me with their mouths wide open.

I turn my back on them to close the front door, a sly smile playing on the corner of my lips. *You know what, Amy Maxwell?* I thought. *You just might be a good mom after all.*

Other novels by Heather Balog:

All She Ever Wanted
Letters to My Sister's Shrink
Note to Self: Change the Locks
Falling When the Bough Breaks

Connecting with Heather Balog:

Heather blogs at:
www.thebadmommydiaries.com
Like her Facebook page:
https://www.facebook.com/HeatherBalogsBooksBlog
Backtalk
Follow her on Twitter:
@Badmommydiaries

Made in United States
Orlando, FL
27 February 2022

15192779R00187